and she was

Also by Jessica Verdi

What You Left Behind
The Summer I Wasn't Me
My Life After Now

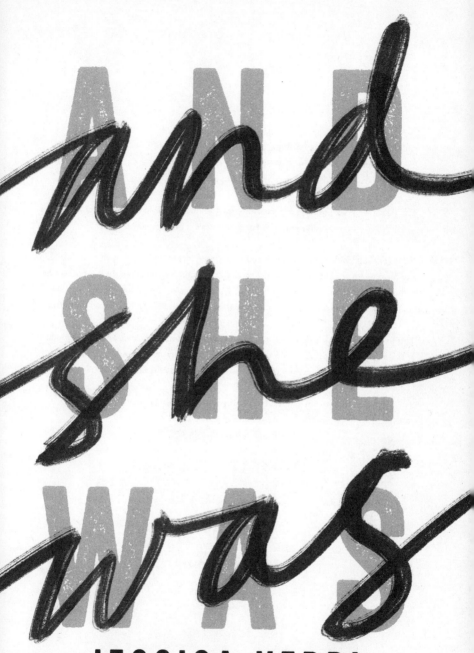

and she was

JESSICA VERDI

Point

Library of Congress Cataloging-in-Publication Data available

ISBN 978-1-338-15053-7

10 9 8 7 6 5 4 3 2 1   18 19 20 21 22

Printed in the U.S.A. 23

First edition, April 2018

Book design by Nina Goffi

FOR YOU, WHOEVER YOU ARE

CHAPTER ONE

Time slows. I sense everything. My breath is fast but steady, my callused palm in its familiar curve around the racquet's handle. I stare the ball down—unblinking, undeterred—and count the nanoseconds. Ready. Eager. Calculating. Finally, with a ferocious forehand stroke, I let out a grunt and connect strings to ball. I can almost hear the poor thing wailing in frustration as it sails away from me. Mary Shea, my training partner across the net, darts into position to volley it back.

In moments like these, when I'm in the zone, my hair slick with sweat and my muscles thrumming, the only things that exist are the ball, the net, and the court, and the symbiotic relationship my body has with each. It doesn't matter if I'm playing against Mary, or our coach, Bob, or no one at all except a steadfast, bruised wall. The rest of the planet tunes out to a distant static; my own thoughts dim to the lowest volume on the dial. On the court, there is no problem that isn't solved by hard work and determination.

Mary and I keep the volley going. It's our third set, match point; advantage, me. If I score the next point, I win. I imagine I'm on the hard court at Arthur Ashe Stadium, going head-to-head with Serena Williams in the finals of the US Open, the audience half cheering, half holding their breaths in suspense.

Someday, I vow, *I'll be there.*

Mary returns the ball close to the net, but I meet it easily and smash it—hard—back to her side. She shrieks as she dives for it, but she's too far away. The little yellow sphere bounces to the ground, unobstructed.

"Yes!" I shout on the last of my air, lifting my racquet high in triumph.

"Very nice, both of you," Bob calls from his trusty portable camping chair by the net post, where he's jotting in his notebook.

"Damn, girl," Mary says, holding her hand out to me. Even though it's just a practice match, we always shake before and after.

"You too," I say, gripping her sweaty palm across the net. "That might have been one of our best matches ever."

She shrugs. "Would've been better if I'd won."

I roll my eyes, out of routine more than irritation. Typical Mary. She likes to work hard and stretch her limits, which you'd think would mean she accepts that losing sometimes is part of the game. No point in practicing with an evenly matched opponent if you care only about winning. But no. She wants it all, every time.

It can be hard watching Mary, the girl who has all the money and resources and support in the world, go off and play in pro tournaments, earning ranking points and making a name for herself on the circuit. Meanwhile, most days, I'm at the local rec center in my middle-of-nowhere town in western New York State, hitting balls against a racquetball wall, my shoes squeaking against the wood floor, my teeth clenched in determination.

Mary and I head over to the bench where our stuff is. Her chestnut hair is still pinned into its usual severe bun on the top of her head, with only the tiniest flyaways at her temples to hint at physical exertion. I don't know how she does it. By the end of a killer match, my wavy, shoulder-length blond hair is always spilling out of its ponytail—more a stinky, tangled rat's nest than anything else. My pale skin is blotchy and absolutely dripping with sweat; Mary's tan skin is smooth and glistening like a lake on a sunny morning.

I wipe my forehead and neck with my towel and take a long chug of water. I'm packing up my gear when Bob comes over. His apple cheeks are red and shiny, matching his bald head. Everything about Bob Nelson is round and glowing. He was a pro player from 1979 to 1985 and doesn't let me get away with not giving my best every single day.

"For the winner." He holds out a small, individually wrapped square of dark chocolate. I laugh and pop it in my mouth. Food is fuel and strength and brainpower, so I try to be very careful about what I put in my body. I actually prefer lean proteins, dark, leafy greens, and whole grains to junk food—one reason of many why the kids at school and I seem to be from different planets. But I can never pass up one of Bob's little prizes. I figure if I bust my butt for a couple hours first, the few extra grams of refined sugar are acceptable. "You've made quite a bit of progress on your two-handed backhand, Dara. I'm impressed."

"Thanks!" I say, relieved. I've been working on that stroke a lot lately on the racquetball court.

He claps me on the shoulder. "Listen. You took lots of risks today, kept up great momentum. I've never seen you this confident on the court. It's time to get out there."

"Really?" Suddenly, I seem to have gotten a second wind. I could dance around the court right now. I know what he means by "out there." Bob wants me to go *pro*. And so do I. High school ended a week ago. It's time to start making my dreams a reality.

Since the moment I could walk, maybe even before that, tennis has been my sole focus. I'll never forget sitting in the little seat compartment of a shopping cart at Target, pointing to a child-sized red plastic racquet and wailing at the top of my lungs until my mom grudgingly agreed to buy it. Since then, everything else—schoolwork, social life, *everything*—has taken a back seat to my training. It's part of me.

Because of tennis, I've never been to a pizza party or kissed a boy. Because of tennis, my relationship with my mother has been stretched, taxed, strained.

Because of tennis, I know what it feels like to be proud. Because of tennis, I have an answer when people ask me who I am, despite all the other blank spaces in my life.

It was all my choice, every time, the good and the bad. And now I can finally go after a professional tennis career.

Almost.

The one thing I don't have is money. And this sport requires a lot of it. Tennis club memberships are expensive, and so are training sessions. As it is, I have to drive an hour and a half each way, every Tuesday and Friday, to Rochester, because that's where the nearest tennis center is located—and where Bob and Mary live. I've won a little money in the few regional junior circuit tournaments I've been able to play in, and earned some more at my part-time job at the juice stand at the mall. But I've spent every dime on coaching and equipment. Bob cuts me a break on his fee because I always double up my sessions with Mary. She trains with him six days a week—four one-on-one sessions, and two with me. This has been our system for the past few years, and I'm equal parts grateful and jealous.

Going pro is even pricier. When you're starting out, the tournaments don't pay much. The prize pools usually total around $10,000—and that's split among the top few finishers. So even if you win, you're not earning a real living. Plus you have to pay for travel, accommodations, equipment, your trainer, and so on. It adds up fast. A lot of players, like Mary, are bankrolled by family money. That's not an option for me. My mom is a nurse. She works hard, taking overtime shifts at all hours of the day and night to ensure we make ends meet, but her paycheck isn't huge. And I have no dad to speak of, no extended family, no one else to ask.

"There's an upcoming ITF women's tournament in Toronto," Bob continues. "Mary's playing in it."

"I know," I say. The International Tennis Federation circuit is where a professional tennis career begins. Ideally, I'd travel to as many tournaments as possible—in the US and beyond—put my nose to the grindstone, and start earning ranking points. I'll work my way up to the Women's Tennis Association 125K Series, continue earning points, and then, if all goes according to plan, eventually advance to the WTA Tour. That's the big one, the one where I could someday see Serena's face staring back at me from across the net. "There's also one before that in Buffalo, a few in Florida, and one in Charlottesville, Virginia." I can recite the ITF schedule by heart. I should be signing up for as many as possible.

Bob nods. "I understand finances are a concern . . ." He lowers his voice. I don't know why; Mary is perfectly aware of my situation. She's even alluded to being happy about it, on occasion. Because she knows if she had to play me—really play me, in a real match—she'd lose there too. "But starting slow is better than not starting at all. If there's any way you could make it happen, I think you should begin with the Toronto one in August. It's got a bigger prize pool than the others, so if you did well—which I'm confident you would—it could get you off to a great start."

"That would be amazing."

He levels me with his gaze. "Otherwise, Dara, what's the point of all this?" He waves a hand around us.

His words punch the air out of me far more effectively than two hours of running around the court did. It was easier to pretend I had plenty of time to figure things out when school was still in session. But I need to make a move. Now. Or the Marys of the world are going to pass me by and Bob will have to move on to more serious players.

Toronto, Canada. It's only a three-hour drive from home, but it might as well be the moon. I've never been out of the country; I've barely even left this little pocket of upstate New York. Seeing what else is out there has always been on my to-do list, but so far it hasn't been an option.

Mary's dad arrives then, and Bob excuses himself to give Mr. Shea the rundown on today's session.

I take a quick shower in the tennis center's swanky locker room, run a comb through my hair, and throw on a clean pair of leggings and a tank top. My body feels good—clean, and tired in the best way—but as I leave the building, my head is murky with half plans.

"Hey," a familiar voice says, and I look up to see my friend Sam jogging down the sidewalk toward me. His camera bounces against his chest.

My face muscles relax instantly. Sam Alapati and I have been best friends since Mom and I moved into the house next to his in Francis, New York, when I was three. Apart from my mom, he's the most important person in my life. It didn't take long for the kids at school to grow impatient with my training schedule and stop inviting me to things. And I'm not sure if Mary would be my friend if not for tennis. But Sam's different. He exists in his own realm.

"What are you doing here?" I ask him.

"I spent the morning at the Eastman Museum, and then I remembered that you're in the city on Tuesdays too. But I guess I'm too late to get to watch you play."

"You watch me hit balls in the backyard all the time," I say.

"That's not the same."

"True."

Mary comes out of the building then with her dad.

"See you next time, Dara," Mr. Shea says. He's a really nice guy. Genuinely proud of his daughter, and willing to give her whatever she needs to achieve her goals—and I don't just mean financially. He and Ms. Shea are always at Mary's tournaments, cheering her on from the stands.

"Yup, see ya," I say.

Mary lays eyes on Sam and automatically smoothes the two stray hairs back into her bun. "Oh, *hi*, Sam! I didn't know you were here!"

I resist the urge to make barf sounds. Sam is cute, I guess, with his dark-brown skin, messy brown hair, and easy smile, but I don't see him that way. He and Mary met a couple months ago at a junior tournament—the last time Sam saw me play. I never knew Mary was the gushing type until I saw her fall all over herself to meet him. She didn't seem to care that he'd brought his then-girlfriend, Sarah Quick.

Sam broke up with Sarah just before graduation, because, he said, it was pointless for them to keep pretending like everything was normal when they were about to go to college in different states. Secretly, I was happy. Because now he and I get to spend the summer together, Sarah-free.

But I wonder if Sam will pick up what Mary's offering, now that he's single.

"Hi, Mary, how are you?" he says politely, and I know immediately that I'm safe from having to spend the last summer before he goes away to school watching him make out with my best frenemy.

"I'm doing well! I have five tournaments lined up for the summer already."

Sam's eyes dart to me in sympathy and then back to her. "That's really cool. I'm sure you'll do great."

She beams. "Are you headed to college in the fall?"

He nods. "Massachusetts College of Art and Design." His dream photography school. They chat about that for a minute, and as I watch them talk, these two people who are about to get everything they've ever wanted, the sudden need to get out of here takes hold of me.

"Did you drive in, Sam?" I interrupt.

He shakes his head. "Bus."

I make a "follow me" gesture with my head. "Car's parked around the corner. We should get going if we want to beat rush-hour traffic."

"Okay," he says. "Bye, Mary. Bye, Mary's dad."

We get in the car, and as I drive, Sam scrolls through the photos he took at the museum.

"What do you think about me signing up for a pro tournament in Canada?" I ask after a few miles, cutting into the silence and mundaneness of this well-traveled road.

He looks up from his camera. "Really?"

"Yeah, Bob brought it up today. He thinks I'm ready."

"Dara! That's awesome!" Sam knows how important Bob's opinion is to me. But it only takes half a beat for him to catch on to my lack of enthusiasm. "Aren't you excited?"

I glance at him. "Of *course* I'm excited. You know how long I've been working toward this."

"I do."

"But . . ."

He knows. "Yeah." He clicks off his camera, then asks quietly, "Have you mentioned it to Mellie?"

"Not yet." What his question really means: *How are you going to get your mom to agree to it?* Because it's not just the money issue that makes this a touchy subject for her. Mom's never been excited or invested in my career. When I try to share news about progress I've made in a training session, she says minimally encouraging things with no real emphasis behind them, or just changes the subject completely. It's not a good feeling, knowing the person closest to you doesn't support the thing most important to you.

"Any suggestions on how to bring it up?" I ask Sam. This conversation about Toronto is going to be crucial—I have to figure out how to get her on my side, not drive the wedge in further. And Sam knows my mom almost as well as I do. *His* mom, Niya, is best friends with my mom.

"Ease into the subject casually, you know?" Sam suggests. "Don't give her a chance to put up her defenses . . ."

While Sam thinks, sometimes out loud, sometimes not, I exit the highway and drive past all the totally thrilling, all-too-familiar Francis landmarks. Two churches and a temple. The few vegetable-covered tables in the parking lot of Dr. Fred's dentist office—our version of a farmer's market. The two-pump gas station. The McDonald's.

"What if you ask her about getting a passport?" Sam asks finally. "You'll need one if you're going to Canada. And it won't be like, 'Oh hey, Mom, let's talk about *tennis.*'"

"A passport," I repeat, mulling it over. It's not a bad idea. I *will* need one—for this tournament and hopefully other international ones in the future. "She won't be able to disagree that I should have one in case of emergencies or whatever, right?"

He nods.

"How do you even get a passport? Do you need to go into city hall or something?" I ask.

"I think you can do it at the post office. I remember I had to bring my birth certificate."

Which means I'll need to track down my birth certificate. When I went to apply for my learner's permit, the DMV lady asked for it, but we hadn't brought it with us, so Mom signed some sort of "statement of identity" thing for me instead. Still, she must have my birth certificate somewhere.

"Okay, so I start with telling her I need a passport, and then, once the discussion is going well, I'll veer into the specifics of the Toronto tournament." I elbow Sam. "You're so smart."

He smiles. "Aren't you glad I mooched a ride off you now?"

I laugh.

When I pull into my driveway, Sam unclicks his seat belt and opens the door. "Good luck."

"Thanks," I say, but make no move to get out of the car. I watch as he crosses the lawn to his house, scanning through his photos once more. He doesn't watch where he's going, but there's no need— we could both do the path between our houses blindfolded.

I bat my fingertips against the steering wheel a few quick times in an attempt to get fired up. Then I get out of the car and jog up to our little yellow house.

"Heya," Mom calls from the kitchen when I swing open the squeaky screen door. "How was practice?"

I drop my bag in the foyer and round the corner. She's in her light-pink scrubs, her brown hair in a swingy ponytail, sitting at the kitchen table clipping coupons from the grocery store circular. I can't believe paper coupons are still a thing—you'd think they'd have moved to apps with scannable bar codes or something by now. But Mom loves searching through the papers, finding good sales, and organizing her coupons in her Velcro coupon pouch.

"It was really good," I say. Normally, I'm happy when she asks about practice, but today I kind of wish she hadn't, so I could have started with the passport stuff like Sam and I planned.

"Glad to hear it." She doesn't pause in her task.

A sealed package rests on the counter. I recognize the box immediately, and it's like a railroad switch—the only thing that could get me to veer onto a different track right now.

"Hot Sauce King!" I cry. I grab the box and bring it to the table. That gets Mom to put her scissors down. Her eyes light up. "I was waiting for you to open it. What do you think—wait until fajita night tomorrow, or taste test now?"

"Taste test now!" I grab the scissors and slice through the packing tape. Mom gets up and grabs six teaspoons from the silverware drawer. A deep respect and admiration for spicy food is one quality Mom and I share unreservedly. A few times a year we order new hot sauces online and have a tasting party.

There are three bottles inside: Knock-You-on-Your-Butt Spicy Sauce, Fire Mouth Habanero, and Chef José's What Doesn't Kill

You Makes You Stronger. I've been wanting to try that last one for a long time. Mom and I make quick work of opening the bottles and pouring a small amount of each into the teaspoons. When they've all been doled out, we each pick up the Knock-You-on-Your-Butt and face off like we're going to thumb wrestle.

"Ready?" she asks.

"I was born ready."

"One, two, three!"

We spoon the sauce into our mouths. My eyes immediately water, and Mom forces herself to swallow before breaking into a surprised cough.

"Holy crap," I croak.

"That's a nine at least," she says, taking a giant gulp of water. Rookie move—water doesn't do much to cool your mouth in times like these. Laughing, I go to the fridge and pour us each a big glass of almond milk.

I take a sip, smack my lips, and say, "Eight." We always rank the sauces on a scale of one to ten.

When our palates have sufficiently recovered, we move on to the Fire Mouth Habanero. We both agree this one is probably about a five, though someone with a weaker constitution would probably give these all a ten. The What Doesn't Kill You Makes You Stronger is way more up my alley—I give it a nine; Mom a ten. I don't know why I love the sensation that my taste buds are burning a fiery death, but I do.

"We're ordering more of that one next time," I say, tossing the spoons in the dishwasher.

"Definitely." She slips her coupon pouch into her purse, grabs her insulated lunch bag from its hook on the pantry door, and starts pulling sandwich fixings from the fridge—a telltale sign she's about to start a shift. She works in the ER and doesn't always get to take an official dinner break. "So, Niya was telling me about this new movie she and Ramesh just watched. It's a documentary about a guy who had to get his leg amputated, but kept it—in a grill, of all places. And then the grill was sold, and the new owner found the leg and refused to give it back." She grins over her shoulder. "We should watch that one night next week if you're free."

"Sure," I say. "Maybe Monday after I get home from the juice stand?"

"Works for me."

It's easy, hanging out with her like this. Our relationship is like a coin, and these are what I call "heads-side" moments. Both our schedules are nuts and we don't always spend as much time together as we'd like, but we do make sure to set aside time for our traditions. Puzzles together on the front porch when the weather is nice, Netflix on lazy nights, going out to restaurants for special occasions and ordering the spiciest things on the menu, occasional homemade dinners with Sam and his family. I know if I'm ever in trouble, Mom will be there for me. We're a team. Not quite a doubles team, where everything one of us does depends on the other, but more like singles players representing the same country in the Olympics. A team in which the members operate independently, but with a shared goal.

But I know the second I broach the topic of the passport and Toronto, the coin is going to flip. And the tails side is a completely different story. A wall goes up between me and Mom, and we might both still be competing in the Olympics, but we're bitter rivals. Sometimes this happens when the subject of the past comes up—she doesn't like talking about her family or where she came from, and she always shuts down in those moments. But the main thing that sends the wall up is tennis.

Mom has absolutely no faith that my tennis career is going to happen. For a long time, she humored me, and drove me to practice as if it were just another mom job like doctor's office visits and parent-teacher conferences. But lately, any time the subject of my going pro comes up, she goes on the offensive, saying it's too expensive or unrealistic. I actually think she's *hoping* I'll fail so she'll be able to insist I go to college in a year. She had to go to work right after high school, and she wants me to have the education, the opportunities, she never had. And yes, in lots of ways, it makes sense to play tennis at the collegiate level. Mom would be happy I was "continuing my academic career," and I'd be happy to have regular sessions on the court. The school could finance a lot of my tennis expenses. Plenty of pros played in college. It's a viable path to the majors for sure.

Except for the tiny fact that it doesn't feel right. I've never been a very dedicated student—I don't think I ever got higher than a B– in anything except phys ed. The court was always my classroom; training was my brand of studying. Commencement never meant a beginning—it meant the end of my biggest distraction. While Sam and most of the other kids in our year were obsessing over transcripts and portfolios and letters of recommendation this past fall, I didn't apply to a single college. I'm done with school and can finally focus on the important stuff. So why on earth would I go back?

I grab an apple from the basket on the windowsill, spin it around to remove the stem, and watch Mom as she drops a handful of baby carrots into a baggie. I don't want to flip the coin; I don't want this good moment to come to an end. But I have to. It's too important. I take a deep breath and segue into the line I'd practiced in the car with Sam: "I'm going to apply for a passport next week. Would you mind digging up my birth certificate when you get a chance? I'll need it for the application."

Like a sponge being zapped of its moisture, Mom's entire body goes rigid. The baggie of baby carrots slips from her fingers to the counter. One of the little orange nubs rolls into the sink.

Really? Already? I didn't even *mention* the word *tennis*. "What's wrong?" I ask, the lingering hot sauce on my tongue turning sour.

"Nothing." She turns to face me. Her expression is hard to read—unlined, but oddly tense. If I didn't have so much practice spotting and analyzing abrupt actions in short bursts of time, I'd miss the swift lick of her lips, the extra beat she takes to make sure there's no emotion in her voice. "What do you need a passport for?"

"Well . . ." I take a realigning moment of my own. *Forget the ease-her-into-it strategy. Just say it.* "Now that school's over, Bob and I agree it's time to start entering pro tournaments. I know we've talked about how it's not possible, but I think I need to *make* it possible. The only way I'm ever going to reach the majors is if I start earning ranking points now. I can't stay in Francis forever."

"Most eighteen-year-olds go off to *college* when they want to get away from their hometown," Mom says under her breath. I ignore it.

"I know money is tight. But I'll take more shifts at work, and then use that money for travel. I'll subsidize it with credit cards if I have to. The most important thing is playing, getting the experience, getting my name out there, and getting ranked."

The corners of her mouth have turned down.

I keep going. "There are some tournaments in the States coming up, but Bob said it would be smart to begin with the one in Toronto in August." I pause briefly. "That's where the passport comes in."

She takes the apple from where I abandoned it on the table and carefully puts it back in its basket. *Everything in its place.*

"What do you think?" I ask finally.

She looks at me. A flash of sadness floods her eyes, but then it quickly subsides, like the changes of a tide sped up on a time-lapse video. "I don't see how it can work, Dara."

My heart drops. This is so unfair. Why can't she even try to see it from my point of view? "Why not?" I ask flatly.

"First of all, how are you going to both take on more shifts at the juice stand *and* travel so much? There are only so many hours in the day. Believe me, I know."

"Well, I won't be traveling *all* the time. Each tournament is only six days. I could—"

"Secondly, please don't put any of this on your credit card. Those bills accumulate faster than you can imagine. And the interest rates are outrageous. I've worked very hard to keep us out of debt. Credit cards are for—"

"Emergencies only," I mumble. "Yeah, I know." This is not the first time I've heard this speech. But doesn't she understand that this feels like an emergency to me?

She checks the clock on the microwave. "I have to go." She grabs her lunch bag, but stops before leaving the kitchen and pulls me into a hug. I don't back away, but I don't relax into it, either. "I'm proud of you, Dara. We just need to be more . . . realistic." She ruffles my hair and leaves the room.

No. She doesn't get to just shut me down like this. She doesn't get to pretend like she cares and then walk out the door, leaving me stuck and alone. Not again.

I run after her. "Can I at least have my birth certificate so I can get my passport? Maybe I do have to come up with a better plan, but when I do, I want to be ready to go."

Her hand is on the screen door latch, and she only turns halfway back. She doesn't look me in the eye. "I'm sorry, I don't know where it is." With that, she leaves.

CHAPTER TWO

I stare at the screen door as it groans shut.

She *lost* my birth certificate?

Or does she just not want to give it to me? Fury burns hot through my veins. I'm eighteen. I don't have to listen to her. I can do what I want. If I want to rack up *a million dollars* in credit card debt, that's my own damn prerogative.

Once Mom's car disappears down the road, I spin on my heel and march straight to her desk in the dining room.

Pay stubs, old report cards, checkbook, tax documents.

No birth certificate.

I go to the living room and pull my baby book off the bookshelf. A few photos of me as a baby, an inked footprint, a lock of hair from my first haircut. No birth certificate.

Where else could it be? I worry my bottom lip with my teeth, a bad habit that tends to show up when I'm unsure about something.

There's no clutter in this house. No secret places it could be hiding. For someone who doesn't spend much time at home, Mom sure loves cleaning the place. From the hints I've managed to eke out about her past, I know her parents were abusive, and she moved out after high school and never spoke to them again. And as for my father . . . Turns out knowing someone's last name isn't a prerequisite for him to get you pregnant. I think it brings Mom a feeling of peace, of control, to keep the house in perfect order. But that just makes it even more unbelievable that she really "doesn't know" where my birth certificate is.

My legs start moving again, this time toward Mom's room. Her nightstand contains books, a book light, an economy-sized bottle of moisturizer, and some lip balm. No documents of any kind. I swipe the lip balm and glide a healthy coat on my chewed, cracked lips, then put it back. Her dresser drawers are filled with folded squares of underwear, T-shirts, jeans, and scrubs. Her closet is neatly arranged with shoes in cubbies, coats and dresses on hangers. I drop to my stomach and use the flashlight on my phone to check under the bed. Orderly boxes of winter clothes. I'm about to stand back up when the flashlight beam glints off something small and shiny at the back next to the wall. I shimmy closer, my hair clinging to the staticky underside of the bed's box spring, and stretch to reach the object.

When my fingertips graze the surface, my pulse beats a triumphant little staccato. *Jackpot.* The light had caught on the metal of a small lock. And the lock is latched onto a safe deposit box–looking thing. There's no way my birth certificate isn't in there.

I slide out from under the bed, bringing the box with me, and push my hair away from my face. I sit back on my heels and try to pull the lid open. The lock is secure. The empty keyhole yawns at me like a bored kid in church.

The first question that comes to mind: Where is the key?

And then the second: Why would Mom have a locked box under her bed at all? God knows we don't have any valuables that would need to be kept safe from potential robbers. I don't think I've ever even heard of there being a burglary in this town anyway. What could she possibly be hiding? My mother isn't the most open person in the world, but she's also pretty basic: work, sleep, *Once Upon a Time* on Sunday nights. Repeat.

I do another search through the house, this time for a key, a small one that might fit in the lock of a mysterious secret box.

I check all the logical places first: desk and kitchen drawers, the tops of bookshelves, the "miscellaneous" basket near the refrigerator. Then I look in the illogical places: the toes of boots, the zippered opening in throw pillows, the ice bin in the freezer.

I'm beginning to think either the key doesn't exist or Mom has it with her at the hospital when, on my third sweep through her room, I find it. I blink a few times to make sure it's really there and not just a trick of my tired eyes. It's small and silver and nestled comfortably under the bottle of moisturizer on her nightstand. Smiling pleasantly up at me like I'm an idiot.

I'd laugh if this whole day wasn't so frustrating.

Sitting on the floor of my mom's bedroom—this has to be the most time I've ever spent in here—I slip the key into the lock and turn.

It clicks, and I lift the lid. The box is very full.

On the top of the pile are two small prescription bottles. I don't recognize the names of the meds, but they're both in Mom's name, and the filled date is only a few weeks ago. She didn't tell me she was sick. And why wouldn't she just put the medicine in the kitchen where we keep the rest of our pharmacy stuff? Why would she lock it away . . . ?

Oh God, she isn't *sick* sick, is she? What if she has cancer? What if she's been dealing with this all alone because she didn't want to scare me, and was waiting to tell me the truth until she got her official prognosis? What if *that's* the reason she doesn't want me to go pro—because she might need someone to take care of her?

My skin prickles as the image of Mom not being here anymore invades my mind. She's all I have. I grab my phone and begin to dial her cell. *Whatever happens, I'm here for you*, I want to say to her. *Nothing's more important than this.*

But a dose of rationale trickles in and, before I hit the green "call" button, I switch over to the internet browser and look up the names of the medications. Huh. One is an estrogen replacement. The other is a testosterone blocker. So . . . not cancer? Looks like she has some sort of hormonal imbalance I didn't know about. Maybe she's gone into early menopause. That could explain why she's been so cranky lately.

My breathing returns to normal as the panic seeps from my body. She's fine. Everyone's fine. I wish she didn't feel like she has to shelter me from this stuff. I'm not a little kid anymore. I can handle it.

I place the bottles on the carpet and return to the box's contents. It's mostly papers. I shuffle through, looking for something that might be a birth certificate. It feels kind of wrong to be snooping in here, going through all of Mom's personal stuff. I already know about one thing she didn't want me to; at this point I just want to find what I came for and be done with it.

Toward the bottom of the pile of documents, I find it. *New York State Certification of Birth*. Yes! First step toward getting my passport—and my freedom—complete.

But as I skim the information on the document, my celebration drifts into confusion.

My first name, middle name, and birth date are correct. But nothing else makes sense. The child's name is listed as Dara Ruth Hogan. That's not my name. My name is Dara Ruth *Baker*.

And the parents' names. Not only are there *two* of them, when Mom always swore she didn't know my father's name, but . . . neither of them is Mom.

Father's name: Marcus Hogan.

Mother's maiden name: Celeste Margaret Pembroke.

Where is Mellie Baker?

I stare at the paper. It shivers in my wavering grasp. But no matter how many times I read the words on the page, no logical explanation comes. I don't understand what I'm looking at. The only thing I know for sure is that she never planned on me seeing this.

I take every last item from the box, spread them out on the carpet, and begin to read. With each photo and document, the disquiet in my stomach becomes sharper, jagged.

A wedding announcement for Marcus Hogan and Celeste Pembroke from just months before I was born.

An old, worn issue of *Sports Illustrated* that falls open to a half-page feature on men's tennis up-and-comers. The names mentioned include Marcus Hogan.

And dozens of pictures I've never seen before of two people and a chubby-armed baby. There's no question: The baby is me. I recognize myself from the pictures in the baby book, and I still have that dimple under my left eye when I smile. Mom's not in a single photo.

I sit back a little. Force myself to take five breaths. Then, carefully, I reach for the photos. Study them.

They span at least six months—mushy newborn up through the start of the cute drooling phase. They were taken in different locations at different times of year. And I'm always with the same two people. A man and a woman. No one else. No Mom.

The man is clean-shaven, with shaggy, light-brown hair and blue eyes. There's something about his smile that is familiar, but I don't think I've seen him before. The woman has long, wavy blond hair, pink lips and cheeks. She looks so much like me, right down to the dimple, that it takes my breath away.

She's only in the earliest photos. In the ones where I'm a little older, it's just me and the man, always grinning and happy. Opening gifts in front of the Christmas tree, on the swings at a park, petting puppies at some sort of rescue-dog adoption event.

And bouncing balls at a tennis court.

Marcus Hogan was listed as the father on my birth certificate. Marcus Hogan was, according to the magazine article, a tennis player. These pictures have to be of him. And the woman must be Celeste Pembroke.

But *who are they*?

I throw everything back into the box, not bothering to be neat or careful about it. The lid makes an almost-satisfying clunk when I slam it down. I don't lock it. Instead, I carry the box, the lock, and the key to the living room, place them on the coffee table, and glower at them from my seat on the sofa a few feet away.

The clock on the mantle ticks steadily.

One by one, possibilities—crazy, impossible possibilities—bleed into me. There are only two explanations I can think of right now. Both bad; one worse than the other.

The two options continue to take shape, but to do so they have to borrow and steal from everything I previously knew to be true. It's not possible for the old and the new to coexist and remain intact. A bend here, an erasure there. As I sit, trying to keep calm, my entire past, my entire *life*, is crumbling apart.

I get up. Begin to move. Slowly at first, then as fast as my bare feet will carry me. Through the room, out the front door, across the lawn.

I don't want to be alone right now.

CHAPTER THREE

I don't need to knock. Being welcome at this blue house any day, any time, has been a constant, something that was decided long before I can remember.

What else was decided before your memories begin?

"Hey, Dara!" Niya calls out cheerfully from the dining room. She's setting the table for dinner, complete with the colorful little chutney bowls I love so much. A gardening podcast is piping through the stereo, and the house is rich with the scent of Ramesh's famous masala sauce. Sam's dad was born in India and brought all his mother's recipes with him when he moved to the US to go to college. Niya's of Indian descent too, but she's lived here her whole life.

I lift a hand in greeting as I make my way downstairs to Sam's room, but I don't say anything. I don't trust myself to; there's too much going on in my head, and I don't know what will come out. Niya is Mom's best friend. What if she knows Mom's been lying to me? What if all those times we sat around that dining room table, eating malai kofta or tandoori chicken or mushroom pizza from the one pizza place in town, she and Mom were holding a silent exchange about how pitifully clueless I was? Or what if she *doesn't* know and I arouse suspicion in her too, without even having a foothold on what's going on myself? I just need to get to Sam.

He's focusing so intently on his computer screen that he doesn't notice when I appear in the entrance to his bedroom. His a-little-too-long-to-be-called-short hair has fallen in his face, and his fingers move skillfully over the trackpad.

Sam works with photographs, but he's more than a photographer. He takes pictures, uploads them onto his computer, and then Photoshops them. Not the lame kind of Photoshop where stick-figure models are made even skinnier, or a zit on the chin of some movie star is erased. Sam uses Photoshop to make art. He plays with our expectations, our preconceived notions of what's "normal," and turns them on their head, so something in the photo is off, but at first glance it looks like nothing's amiss. You have to stare a minute to figure out why you feel so unsettled. And then you see it—the apples on a tree are actually mini pumpkins. A person's smiling mouth has been flipped upside down. It's really cool.

I've asked him to make a piece for me a million times, but he's always said it doesn't work that way. He needs to wait to be inspired; he can't force it. Still, he's given his art to his parents, his sister, Annita, and Sarah Quick. I never understood why he could be "inspired" for them, but not for me.

Especially Sarah. Sam admitted once that Sarah was jealous of me, though I can't for the life of me figure out why. *I* should have been the one who was jealous of *her*, the way she got to take up all his time, and inspired a Sam Alapati original (a seascape with light-pink seagulls that I only got to see once before it was relegated to Sarah's bedroom wall). Jealous of how easy school was for her, and how she made friends everywhere she went. She was the valedictorian *and* the homecoming queen. Sam's had a few girlfriends, but the Sarah relationship was the longest so far—about a year. She had zero reason to be jealous of me.

"Hey," I say. My voice sounds strained. The unthinkable thoughts are fighting their way to my mouth. It won't be long before I lose the battle. I close the door.

He looks up and quickly snaps his laptop closed. "Hey! How did the talk with—" Once he gets a good look at me, his face falls. "What's wrong?"

I sit on his bed and hug my knees.

"Dara?"

The crazy is dancing around on my tongue now. I'll let the more reasonable possibility out first. If Sam agrees it's feasible, or even likely, I won't ever have to voice the other one. "You haven't heard our moms talking about me being adopted, have you?"

"Adopted?" he says.

I nod.

"Like, Mellie's not your birth mom?"

I nod again.

"No chance," he says right away. "If you were adopted she would have told you. Why would she hide it?"

What he's saying makes sense, I know. Adoption is normal. If I were adopted, Mom would have shown me the pictures long ago and explained about my birth parents and wouldn't have had to make up a lie about a one-night stand. It doesn't add up.

The scarier option finds its way to my throat. I swallow it back.

"Dara, what happened? Where is this coming from?"

I clear my throat. "You were right."

He's confused. "About what?"

"Remember how the yearbook staff asked everyone in the senior class to contribute a baby picture, and I only had the few from my baby book to choose from, and you said that was weird, considering how many photos of me as an older kid Mom keeps around the house?"

I'd never realized this until Sam pointed it out. But when I asked Mom about it, she told me that when we moved to the house in Francis, the movers lost a few boxes and the photo albums and scrapbooks were in one of them. Most of the pictures from my early childhood and the pictures from Mom's life before me . . . all gone. And it wasn't like she could ask her estranged parents for copies. Sam told me there should be digital backups of them somewhere, but Mom seemed so sad about the pictures being lost that I didn't press her on it. Now, though, as a parade of red flags marches before my eyes, I know I should have asked.

"You were right," I say again. "Those weren't the only baby pictures she had of me." I take another breath. "I found something today."

He uses his heels to wheel his chair closer to me. When he reaches the edge of the bed, he leans forward, forearms on his thighs, and says, softly, "Tell me."

I chew on my lip. I'm actually glad, in a twisted way, for the opportunity to recount the inexplicable insanity of what I found and how I found it. Because if my mouth is filled with all those words, then the scariest possibility of all can't find a way out. Yet.

I go through the whole story, describing every picture, the people, the birth certificate, everything. It's not hard; each item from that box is emblazoned on my memory.

"Huh," he says when I'm finished.

I stare at him. Wait for more. It doesn't come. "That's *it*? 'Huh'?"

"Sorry. I just . . . I don't really know what to say."

"Doesn't it seem like adoption could be a possibility?"

"Mellie wouldn't have kept that secret from you," he insists.

"Well, clearly, she was keeping *something* secret from me!" I snap. He looks at me warily. I let out a harsh sigh. "Fine. What do you think it is, then?"

"I have no idea."

There's silence for a minute. I'd hoped he would be able to help. See something I didn't—an explanation so obvious, so boring, it passed me by unnoticed. But now he's going to make me say it. The scarier thought. I can't keep it in anymore. "Sam, do you think I was *kidnapped*?"

It's absurd. Utterly impossible. Mom isn't capable of something like that. But the pictures, the name change, Marcus and Celeste . . . they have to mean *something*, and it's the only other thing I can think of that fits.

My heart is pounding as I wait for his answer. Then he does the last thing I expect: He starts to laugh. A *lot*. Loud, rolling laughter.

"Sam!" I hit his arm. "This is serious!"

"Kidnapped? This isn't *Dateline*."

"The only reason *Dateline* is even a thing is because this kind of stuff happens," I counter. "And no one on that show ever thought it would happen to them."

Sam is still laughing. "No way. You're not adopted, and you were not kidnapped. You're definitely Mellie's daughter."

"How can you be so sure?"

"You have a lot in common. You're both independent and driven. You both really like spicy food, more than anyone else I've met."

"That proves nothing."

"Okay, then, your eyes. They're the same as Mellie's."

"Lots of people have blue eyes. We don't really look alike in any other way."

"You make similar expressions sometimes."

"Learned behavior," I shoot back. "And what about the woman in the pictures? She looked just like me, Sam."

"Maybe she's a relative? Maybe your mom has a sister."

"She does," I say slowly, considering it. "She's older." I asked my mom once why she decided to become a nurse, and she said it was because she and her sister used to play hospital with their dolls when they were little, and it was one of her only good memories from her childhood. "Her name is . . . Josie? Joanne? Something like that."

"There you go. Maybe they kept in touch back then."

I shake my head. "I'm pretty sure the woman in the photos is Celeste Pembroke."

"Why?" Sam asks. "Is she wearing a name tag in any of them?"

"Of course not. But Celeste Pembroke is the name of my 'mother' on my birth certificate. And those pictures are pretty clearly of parents with their daughter. Plus, Marcus Hogan was a tennis player, and there are pictures of the man and me on a tennis court. So if he's Marcus, she's got to be Celeste. *And*, all that aside, if Mom knew these people, if it really was her sister or whatever, Mom would have been in the pictures too."

"She could have been taking the photos . . ." He doesn't sound convinced, though.

"All of them? She didn't want to be in a single picture with her own baby? I don't buy it."

Sam's lack of response is proof of his agreement. The room goes quiet again. The sounds of Niya's gardening podcast travel through the ceiling. A chill, defiant of the summer heat and the lack of AC in Sam's room, passes over my skin.

"Okay, there is one other possibility," he finally says.

Hopefully, it's one that trumps kidnapping. "What?"

"Maybe you lived with other people when you were a baby. Maybe Mellie had you but then gave you to those people for a little while. And she was too ashamed about it to tell you."

"No. The birth certificate, Sam. She wasn't listed as my parent."

"Oh yeah."

"I really don't think she gave birth to me," I say quietly.

The need for answers tightens its chokehold on me. I have to confront Mom. And to think that just this afternoon I was nervous to start a conversation about *tennis*.

I stand up. My limbs feel heavy. "I have to go."

"Where?"

"Home." She won't be home for hours yet, but I need to be there when she arrives. I need to think about what I'm going to say.

He nods, understanding. "Call me?"

"Yeah."

....

I wait for Mom in the living room with my phone in my hands.

I text her. *Are you working a double tonight?*

No, she texts back a few minutes later. *Be home by nine.*

I don't know whether to be relieved or even more anxious.

When I close my eyes, I'm on the court of a tennis stadium. But instead of fans in the stands, each blue plastic seat holds another question or disturbing possibility or smiling stranger from the photos. And the rows of seats are endless, climbing toward the sky, with no exits anywhere.

Reaching past Mom's box, still on the coffee table, I grab the TV remote. I scroll by rote through the saved programs on the DVR and select one of the old broadcasts of the US Open. I save all the women's matches from the quarterfinals through the finals and rewatch whenever I'm stressed or feeling down or need a distraction. The sounds and rhythm of the matches are soothing, like a lullaby, and watching the players in all their glory always lifts my spirits and gets my head back on straight. *Watch. Learn. And then go practice some more.* The DVR is nearly full with the record-ings, so each week Mom has to watch her own shows immediately and then delete them in order to make room for whatever is scheduled to record in the coming days. She wanted to change cable companies last year and I wouldn't let her because I couldn't bear to return the box and give up these files.

But right now, even the thrill of the edge-of-your-seat 2015 semifinals match between Serena Williams and Roberta Vinci can't take my mind off reality. I love this match because I never know how to feel watching it—Serena is my hero and I always want her to be number one, but there's also something so infectious about underdog Roberta's excitement and awe that she's winning the match. You can't help but root for her too. It's the perfect example of how tennis can get inside your bones and make you feel a million feelings at once. How—despite the odds or the public's expectations—anyone, with hard work, skill, and desire, can make it to the top.

Today, though, the shapes and colors flicker across the screen, but I don't really see them. The what-ifs and scenarios in my mind are too loud, too overbearing.

Three hours later, Mom gets home.

"Hi, honey. Did you eat dinner?" she says, starting to head to her room to change out of her scrubs like always. But then she notices that I'm just sitting there, unmoving, the match long over, the "Delete Program?" message on the TV screen. Her gaze lands on my face, and I have no idea what she sees, but her smile fades and her eyes crease. "Is everything all right?"

Then she notices the box. It takes a second, but it happens: Her features rearrange into what can only be described as alarm. She knows she's been caught. Her eyes begin to dart around, minimally but rapidly, the evidence of her thoughts going a million miles an hour: *What does Dara know? How did she find out? Can I lie my way out of this one too? Or will I finally have to come clean?*

Might as well get right to it.

"Was I kidnapped?" My tone is calmer now. Over the past few hours, the idea has somehow become less shocking.

She jolts in disbelief. "Were you *what*?" she says. She's not full-out laughing like Sam, but there is a bewildered chuckle in her voice.

"Kidnapped," I say again. "Did you take me from my real parents?"

She lowers herself into the big purple chair across from the couch. "Of *course* not."

"Okay, was I adopted, then? Or did I live with people other than you when I was a baby?"

"No," she whispers. "Dara . . ."

I toss open the box's lid and grab a fistful of photographs. Mom's face goes white. "Who are Marcus Hogan and Celeste Pembroke? Why is my name different on my birth certificate? Tell me what's going on!" There it is—the break in my voice that was bound to appear. But I will not cry. Not yet.

She looks up. "It's not obvious?"

The genuine surprise in her expression takes me off guard. "*What's* not obvious?"

Mom doesn't say anything right away. She just studies me, and the room, and her own hands, as if she's trying to memorize everything before it changes. She looks sad. And scared. Something tells me that whatever comes out of my mother's mouth next is going to alter my life forever.

She gets up, crosses to the coffee table, and reaches for the last thing I'd expect—the bottles of medication. What does that have to do with anything?

She sits on the couch beside me, and takes a wavering breath. One pill bottle is cradled in each of her palms. "Dara, you were not kidnapped and you were not adopted. You are my biological daughter."

"But then who is the woman in the pictures? The one who looks like me? Is she your sister?"

Mom shakes her head weakly. "That is Celeste Pembroke. She was . . . your mother."

The words themselves make perfect sense—that's what I suspected, from the moment I laid eyes on the blonde in the photos. But in order for words to have real meaning, you need context. And here there is none. "You just said *you* are my mother."

"No, I said you are my biological daughter."

"Stop talking in riddles, for God's sake!" I nearly shout. "Just tell me the truth!"

Mom opens the box and selects a photograph. Then she takes in another breath and speaks on the exhale, the most fragile of whispers. "Celeste was your biological mother." She points to the blonde woman. "I am your biological . . . father." Her trembling finger shifts to the man. "This is me."

CHAPTER FOUR

This is . . .

She's . . .

What?

"That's not funny," I say, even though it's clear from the way Mom spoke the word *father*, like it physically pained her, that she's deadly serious.

"I would never joke about this."

I let out a one-note laugh, but it dies and thuds to the ground the moment it's out of my mouth.

Oh my God.

The bottles in her hands. The hormone medications. *That's* what they're for.

I back up a few inches, to put more space between us on the couch. "Explain," I whisper.

"I don't know where to begin . . ."

I stare at her, trying to find a clue, something I've overlooked all these years. She looks like . . . my mom. She's taller than I am, but not much. I guess her shoulders are sort of broad, but so are mine—upper body strength doesn't have to equal masculine. She doesn't have an Adam's apple or stubble on her face. Her hands and feet are big, I guess, but I wouldn't consider them mannish.

Her voice, though . . . it's a bit lower than the average woman's. I never questioned it—plenty of women have deep voices—but there have been a few times when she was mistaken for a man over the phone.

And her mouth is the same mouth as the man in the picture's. Now I know where I recognized his smile from—I've seen it on my mother's face nearly every day of my life.

"I don't understand." It's a puny phrase for such an overwhelming feeling.

"I was assigned male at birth," she says quietly. "Marcus." The name comes out scratchy, as if it's grown weak with disuse. "I had all the anatomical boy parts, and everyone assumed I was a boy. But even before I fully understood the differences between boys and girls, I knew I wasn't what everyone wanted me to be. I couldn't tell anybody what I was feeling, though."

"Which was what?" I press. I need to hear her say the words.

"That God had made a mistake. My body wasn't right. People didn't understand trans issues then the way they're starting to now. There was no Jazz Jennings or Laverne Cox or Chaz Bono or *Transparent*. I never even heard the words *transgender* or *transsexual* until I was out of high school."

There they are. Those are the words.

I've heard about transgender people, of course. I've watched the reality shows and followed the political campaigns to restrict public bathroom access—when two of your childhood idols are Billie Jean King and Martina Navratilova, it's pretty much ingrained in you to care deeply about LGBTQ issues.

If it were anyone else, I'd hug them and say, "As long as you're happy. I support you." Truly. But how am I supposed to do that now, when I'm finding out my own mother has lied to me—intensely—all these years? Lied about my origin and her past and the baby pictures and who knows what else. She didn't trust me—*respect* me—enough to tell me the truth. I'm feeling even more lost now than I did before. Mom's confession is not an answer; it's a domino that's tipped over a thousand other questions.

At least she's making eye contact with me, not brushing me off. That's more than I can say for some of our past arguments.

Please, Mom, I beg her silently. *Make me understand.*

"My parents started to pick up on the fact that I was different early on," she continues. The circles beneath her eyes seem to darken as I watch. "They assumed I was gay, that I was a boy who liked boys, which was not acceptable to them, either. My father was . . . not kind."

"Is *that* why we don't speak to them?" I knew her parents weren't nice people, but she'd always kept the story vague. More lies.

"Yes. I can't imagine what they would think if they saw me now."

Because they'd be expecting the man in the picture. And the woman in front of me is most certainly not that man.

It feels like there's someone screaming in another language inside my brain. I'm able to pick up the tone, the emotion of what's happening, but no matter how hard I try, I can't piece out a single identifiable word or phrase. But I keep grasping, listening.

Mom fiddles with the gold ring on her right hand. "I put all my energy into . . ." She pauses, steeling herself, as if what she's about to say next is even worse than what she's already said. "Into . . . playing tennis to distract myself."

She looks up at me, waiting.

I meet her eyes. A beat goes by. Then another. Two pieces of the jigsaw puzzle snap into place. The *Sports Illustrated* article about Marcus Hogan. My mother.

Hot, fat tears spring to my eyes. This is a betrayal of an entirely different kind. Mom knows it.

"You played tennis," I say feebly.

Her lips bend; her chin tightens in apology. "I did."

"Professionally."

"Yes."

"But . . ." I squeeze my eyes shut, forcing the tears to spill over, and pinch the bridge of my nose. Nothing makes sense. *Nothing.* "But you *hate* tennis! You've never shown *any* interest. All this time you've stood there with a straight face and told me going pro isn't an option and that I shouldn't try—and you've actually *done* it? I can't fucking *believe* this!"

Mom flinches, and I fleetingly wonder if it's in reaction to my use of the *F*-word. I don't swear a lot, and never in front of her.

"I don't hate tennis. I love it." The sigh that escapes her is a sound of regret. "That's why I haven't always been able to—" She stops, tries again. This is hard for her. *Good.* "It's been painful: to watch you achieving so much and finding so much joy in it. It made me miss it that much more."

It's a hundred-mile-an-hour serve, right to the chest. "That is so messed up," I say, with zero sympathy. "That's why you've never supported me? Because it made you feel bad? Guess how that made *me* feel, Mom."

"I'm so sorry." She does sound remorseful, but I don't know what to believe. "I should have done a better job keeping my own feelings out of it. But . . . nostalgia wasn't the only reason I didn't want you going down this path. It's a hard life, Dara. It's a lot of pressure and disappointment. I lived it. I didn't want that for you."

"That's not your choice to make."

"And I feared that if you did well and became famous . . . Well, I worried that people would find out—" She stops. Regroups. "That everything we've built together would fall apart." She looks up at me. "I am sorry. I've made so many mistakes."

"Yeah, like not *telling* me."

"If I told you, you would have wanted to know more. You would have Googled me, looked for pictures."

Right. If she told me about her tennis career, she would have had to tell me she played on the men's circuit. She would have had to tell me the truth—about everything. And it was more important to keep her secret, to keep lying.

The anger crackling inside me catches flame and begins to spread.

"I was never one of the top-ranked players," she says, throwing me a few crumbs to make up for her years of deceit. "I was never going to be a Novak Djokovic. Or a Serena Williams. But I held my own for a little while. I played in a few big tournaments. Then I met Celeste."

And just like that we've rounded another corner. It's a struggle to keep up. She's giving me information, but I don't know how to delineate it. I don't know which parts are the keys that will unlock some bigger picture, and which are nothing more than unfocused ramblings of her guilty subconscious. All I know is that I'm no closer to truly understanding *why*—about any of it.

"So Celeste is why you quit?" I ask, my back pressed against couch cushions that feel far less cozy than they once did. *Where is Celeste? What happened to her?* Too many questions. Too much fog, and not nearly enough beacons.

Mom shakes her head. "No. She'd never have wanted me to . . ." Another pause. She slowly reaches out and places the prescription bottles on the table. *What is going on in her head?* "I loved her, Dara. I want you to know that. We were happy together."

I don't know why this stands out as strange, hearing my mother talk about being in love. It's by far the least strange thing she's said. But she's never showed any interest in men—or women. I've always wondered why, but whenever the subject came up, she would just shrug and say she was too busy to date. I figured it was because after getting pregnant during a one-night stand, she was pretty done with men. But obviously that wasn't it— there was no one-night stand; there was no pregnancy. At least, not *hers*.

My mom is not my mother.

"So you were having sex?" I blurt out. "With your . . . man parts?" I don't know why I feel the need for clarification on this. Obviously, they were having sex if I was conceived.

"Yes."

"Did she know about your . . . feelings?"

"Eventually, yes."

"But you weren't a woman yet."

"That's not how it works—I have *always* been a woman. But you're right in that I hadn't started transitioning yet." She shakes her head. "This is all so strange to say out loud. I don't know if I'm telling it right."

"You're not," I confirm.

Her face contorts. "I'm sorry. You deserve the truth, all of it."

Funny how I only deserve that now.

"What happened to Celeste?" I demand.

"When you were six months old, she was out for a run on South Second Street . . ." Mom takes a breath. "A drunk driver jumped the curb . . ."

A sob leaps into my chest. This morning, I had no idea Celeste even existed. An hour ago, I knew her name but nothing else. Now I'm mourning her loss.

"She loved you very much," Mom says. "She would have been so proud of you."

I had two parents. A mother who looked like me; a father who shared my passion. Two people to love me. Be proud of me.

What the hell *happened*?

As if reading my mind, Mom says, "After Celeste passed away, I began my transition." She runs a hand over her hair. "I didn't really know what I was doing. But I made a few friends in the trans community, and they helped me feel my way through."

"Like . . . with what kind of stuff?" I ask.

"With everything, really. The emotional and the physical. I grew my hair out, and started wearing makeup and women's clothes, gradually at first and then full time. I changed my name. I found a doctor, and began taking hormones."

"What do the hormones do?"

"They've made my skin softer, my body curvier." A whisper of a smile passes over her lips.

I glance at the bottles on the table. She's still taking the hormones, clearly.

It must have been exhausting, hiding the pills and the doctor's appointments and the trips to the pharmacy, all to make sure I never found out. Out of nowhere, a long-dormant memory awakens in my mind. Mom coming to the breakfast table each morning with two pills rolling around on her plate next to her peanut butter–coated English muffin. She'd down them in one go with her first sip of coffee, then munch on the English muffin while she read the paper. I never asked what the pills were for—I barely even noticed them. They were just another part of our morning routine. But by the time I was in middle school, they'd disappeared. She started hiding them when I got old enough to start asking questions.

I glance at her chest. "Did hormones do that too?" She's a C cup—I know that from years of sharing laundry duties. I'm only a B.

"A little. Surgery did the rest."

Surgery? The word makes me flinch. But of course there were surgeries. Look at her—she's a woman. An average, pretty woman. I can't believe this was all happening while I was alive, and I had no idea. "What other surgeries have you had?"

A shadow crosses her face and she looks away. "I know what you're asking."

How? I barely even know what I'm asking. I'm just trying to stay above water here.

"You want to know if I had bottom surgery, don't you?"

"What is that? Like on your . . . butt?"

She looks back at me and blinks. Then relaxes. "No, not on my butt. I thought you were asking if I . . . it's what everyone always wants to know. They're completely unconcerned with what you have below the waist until they hear you're trans, and suddenly, it's all they can think about."

"Oh." Now I get what she's talking about.

"I did have a few facial feminization surgeries." Almost absently, she touches her temple, and then her hand moves to her throat, where I'm guessing her Adam's apple may have once been. "I haven't had the bottom surgery. Our insurance didn't cover it, and there were risks associated with it that I wasn't sure I wanted to take."

"So you mean . . ." My gaze involuntarily travels to her lap. The thing she used with Celeste to make me. She still has it.

She nods. "Honestly, I don't feel like I need that procedure anymore. I'm happy with my body the way it is now. It was more important to me that the general public see me as a cis woman . . ." She pauses again, clears her throat nervously. "Do you know what cisgender means?"

"Someone who . . . someone like me, right?"

"Yes, someone who identifies as the gender they were assigned at birth. The world couldn't know I was trans—for many reasons. I'm grateful that I've been able to pass."

Pass. Another word for *lie.*

I hang my head in my hands, and after a moment something else she said resonates. *Insurance.* Of course—all this stuff costs money. "Does insurance cover everything else?" I ask. "The hormones and the other surgeries?"

"Sometimes. It depends," she says.

"So we've been paying out of pocket for some of this?"

She shrugs tiredly. "You'd think working in a hospital would entitle us to better healthcare coverage, but what can you do?"

The back of my throat swells, making it difficult to swallow, to breathe. All this time, she's been so concerned about money, working overtime, telling me we can't afford my dreams. I have no idea what hormones and plastic surgery cost, but I do know that when I tore the meniscus in my knee a couple years ago and had to get an MRI to assess what kind of damage had been done, we got a bill for over fifteen hundred dollars, and that was after insurance had covered their part. Mom has been living this way for nearly my entire life—the cumulative medical bill can't be small.

The realization that this is where our money has been going, that *this* is another part of why I'm still stuck in this house instead of being able to take the next step in my career like most athletes my age, makes me feel pretty damn insignificant. Embarrassed.

Naïve. Like a scraggly old yard bush watching through a picture window as the houseplants inside get lovingly watered and pruned.

"Where was *I* during all this? The surgeries."

"You were about two at that point. You stayed with my friend Kelly Ann—she was one of the trans women I'd become close with—while I was in the hospital. But it was only a couple nights at the most. There was a lot of bruising, but you didn't seem to mind." She smiles. "Kelly Ann helped me with you for the first week or so after my breast augmentation too, because it was difficult for me to lift you at first."

I don't remember anyone named Kelly Ann at all. "Where is Kelly Ann now? And your other trans friends?" I ask.

"We went our separate ways. It's . . . a long story."

I want to know more, but I also can't let the conversation derail too much. "Who else knows?" I ask. "Like, from our lives now."

"No one." Her voice is a whisper.

"Not even Niya?"

"No."

It should probably make me feel better to know I'm not the only one Mom was lying to, but it doesn't.

"What about Celeste's family? Where were they? Why didn't I stay with them when you had the surgeries?" My history has been shifting with every sentence Mom's uttered. And if I really did have two parents, then something about my severe lack of extended family isn't adding up.

She hesitates, and looks away.

"Mom?"

"They're . . . not good people."

I finally manage to swallow. "What does that mean? Were they abusive like your parents were?"

"No, they . . . they weren't supportive of my choices." Her tone is defensive now. "They were from a different world—old money and conservative values . . ." *Old money?* She takes another moment, and then meets my eyes. She's shutting down again. I'm well-versed in Mellie Baker's art of avoidance. I know her so well and I don't know her at all.

"What aren't you telling me?" I ask.

"We had to leave," she says simply.

"Leave where?" I don't understand.

"Philadelphia."

We lived in another state? In a big city?

"We moved to a few different towns while I completed my transition," Mom continues, "and then settled here."

"Did you tell them where we were going?" I ask.

"Celeste's parents?"

"Yes."

She grimaces. "No."

"Did they have any way of getting in touch with us?"

"No."

"Why not?" I cry, shooting to my feet.

"Dara, you don't understand . . ."

No, I think I do.

The fog lifts. It's like I've stepped outside myself and am looking down at my life from behind a magnifying glass. And all I see
is one giant, unfair mess.

We could have lived in a city instead of this stupid town. I
could have trained at a real tennis center every day with a parent
who could have offered me invaluable advice. We could have been
far better off, financially. I could have heard stories about the
woman who gave birth to me. I could have had family photos, a
family tree. I could have had *grandparents*. Grandparents who had
money, apparently, and might have helped me launch my career.

We could have done all these things *while* Marcus was becoming Mellie. It didn't have to be one or the other. I could have been
her support system, even if Celeste's parents had turned their backs
on her.

But I didn't get that opportunity. Mom didn't like whatever
my grandparents were saying, so she did the most selfish thing
possible: She took me from them, from that life, forever. And she
lied to me about it all, every single day. While we were hustling to
make ends meet. While we were half laughing, half crying over
the Mad Dog 357 hot sauce we poured over our French fries. While
we sat at home together watching old Pixar movies while the rest of
the second graders were at the father-daughter dance.

She didn't do me the decency of considering I could have handled it then, so she sure as hell isn't going to get my sympathy now.

"Why isn't our last name Hogan? Or Pembroke?" My voice
is severe, and my face is growing hot. But I fill in the blank

before she can. "Did you change it because you didn't want to be found?"

She nods, once. Her jaw is clenched.

The lengths she went to, to keep me from my family.

"Mom, *why*? I don't understand! Why didn't you tell me any of this? Is it because you thought I'd react the same way Celeste's parents did?"

She shakes her head.

"Is it because you didn't want me to know I had other family because you knew I'd want a relationship with them? And you didn't want to have to deal with them because they were mean to you?"

She hesitates. Gnaws on her cheek.

"That's it, isn't it? That's how you justified it."

"It's not that simple, Dara."

I get up and pace the room, tugging on the ends of my hair. As more questions leap into my mind, I spit them out: "Where did the name Baker come from?"

She spins her ring around again, runs her gaze over the items spread out on the table. "I don't know. I . . . liked the sound of it."

Wow. Great reason. "Why did you quit tennis?"

She looks back at me with a tired *I'm trying here, okay?* expression. *You're not trying nearly hard enough*, I want to say. "Because I was transitioning. I didn't want to have to do it in public. There was a pro trans player before me, and—"

"Stop," I bite out, before I even really decide to. My mouth knew I'd reached my limit before my brain did. But I cannot listen to another word. "Just *stop*."

She does.

My eyes are blurry with a fresh deluge of tears, but I've never seen so clearly.

It was always about *her* choices, *her* happiness. Every single step of the way. I was just the idiot along for the ride.

Well, guess what? Now I get to make a choice.

I finally let myself do what I've wanted to since she first said the words *biological father.*

I run.

CHAPTER FIVE

"Dara! Where are you going?" Mom is fast on my heels.

"Leave me alone!" I run down the hall toward my room.

I have to get out of here. Go . . . somewhere. Anywhere but here.

I slam my bedroom door in her face, but she opens it immediately anyway. Tears slide down my cheeks, and I don't turn to face her. Instead, I pull my suitcase from under my bed and start throwing things inside. Regular clothes, tennis clothes, shoes, hairbrush, phone charger. I push past Mom without looking at her, go to the bathroom, and grab my toothbrush.

A vague plan starts to form.

I'm going to find my grandparents. Get to know them, discover where I really came from. Maybe they'll even be the source of support I've been wishing for. I'm done sitting around waiting for the approval of a person who has never truly cared about anyone except herself. Now it's my turn to be selfish.

"Dara!" Mom tries again as I stomp back to my suitcase.

I toss the toothbrush in and zip it closed.

With a final glance at my trophies, the twin bed I've slept in every night for the past fifteen years, and the photo taped to the wall above my desk of Mom and me at the high school family picnic, I move to leave the room. But this time, Mom blocks the doorway. "Where do you think you're going?" She tries to be authoritative, but falls short.

"I'm leaving," I tell her.

She shakes her head. "Sit down. We're not done talking."

I meet her eyes, and speak slowly and deliberately. "You don't get to tell me what to do anymore. I'm eighteen. I have a license and a car and money of my own. I'll call Bob and the juice stand and tell them I need some time off. There is nothing holding me here." *Bob.* I hadn't considered him until this second. I shouldn't bail on him like this. But the need to get out of here quickly wins out over any guilt.

I try to push past Mom, but she doesn't budge. I've never felt the effect of the few inches she has on me before now.

Everything is different.

"I understand this is a lot for you to take in," she says desperately. "But I can give you some books and websites to read about gender dysphoria. I . . . I know it's confusing, but we can figure out our next steps together."

I snort. "You really don't get it, do you?"

"I get that it's going to take some time to get used to—"

"I don't need to read a freaking book. And if you think this is about you having *gender dysphoria* or whatever you call it, you're even more self-centered than I thought you were."

She opens her mouth to protest, but I hold up a hand. Tears are marching into formation behind my eyes, and my throat has begun to constrict, but I try to be very clear with my next words.

"You put yourself first without caring about how it would affect me. You erased my father *and* my real mother. You took my grandparents away because they hurt your feelings." I take a quick, barely helpful breath and forge on. "I've sacrificed so much to make something of myself in tennis, and you could have been there for me in ways I never even dreamed of, yet you chose to make me feel alone in all of it—you made me feel *bad* about it. You chose that, Mom. And you lied to me every single day about it all."

From the expression on her face, you'd think she'd been slapped. "It's not a lie to not come out as trans! Everyone has things in their life they'd prefer to keep private. But I'm a woman, and the fact that the world now sees me as one means they see the *truth*."

"You are not listening to me!" I shout. "It's not just the trans stuff. It's everything. Telling me that you got pregnant from a one-night stand was a lie. Not telling me about Celeste or her family was a lie. Hiding your tennis career was a lie." I catch her eyes with mine and hold them there. "Admit it."

She's the one to break the connection; she squeezes her eyes shut. "Yes, those were lies." It doesn't feel like victory. She takes a moment and opens her eyes again. Her gaze is raw, anguished. "But don't you think it killed me to have to keep pretending, after a childhood and adolescence of doing exactly that?"

"I don't believe you. If you didn't want to lie, guess what? You didn't have to! You could have told me the truth at *any* time."

"No, I couldn't!" Her energy is elevated now too, matching mine.

"Why the hell not? I'm your daughter! We're supposed to share things like this as a *family*. You had a million opportunities to tell me. The first time I asked to take tennis lessons, you could have told me you were a tennis player once too. You could have taken me out on the court *yourself*! When I was little and asked why we didn't have any other family, you could have explained that your parents didn't understand this part of you. Any of the times we were doing puzzles or eating dinner or folding laundry or sorting through the mail . . . you could have opened your mouth and said the words." I hold up a finger. "Or, better yet, you didn't have to *tell* me at all—it could have just been how things were. I could have been a part of it from the beginning. Those old family pictures should have been hanging on the wall since the day we moved into this house."

She rakes her hands through her hair, as if trying to hold on to whatever weak excuses have been keeping her going all these years. "You don't understand. I—"

"You *what*?"

"I was scared."

"Of what?"

"Of losing you!"

She says it like I'm supposed to *thank* her or something. Be honored that she cared so much. "You really don't know me at all, do you?" My heart breaks a little more as I say it. "The *only* thing that would have made me leave is *this*. The *lies*. Not the truth."

I push past her again, my suitcase lumbering behind me, and this time, she doesn't block my way. I grab the photos and papers from the living room and shove them in the front zip pocket of the suitcase. When I get to the front door, I hitch my tennis equipment bag over my shoulder. That should be everything. I stop, and turn, keeping my expression blank, ignoring the way the air cools the half-dry tear tracks on my cheeks and chin. "Tell me everything you know about Celeste's parents."

"Why?" she says, slightly panicked.

"I'm going to find them."

Her face crumples. "Dara, please, don't do this. There are things about them you don't know—"

"Well," I say, wanting my words to hurt, "I'm sure you'll understand if I'd rather find out those things from *them*, considering I can't possibly trust a single word you say anymore."

She looks half defeated, half terrified, like a stray puppy being taken into the shelter. "Their names are Ruth and William Pembroke." Her voice trembles. *Ruth*. My middle name. Was I named after my grandmother? "The last time I looked them up, a few years ago, they were still living in the New Jersey suburbs in the house Celeste grew up in. Cherry Hill, the town is called." New Jersey. All this time, we've been not even a half-day's drive from one another. "He was a partner at a law firm, but he may be retired now, I'm not sure. She was the chair of a children's hospital charity. They had another daughter—Catherine. I didn't keep track of her." She holds up her hands, as if to show she's not hiding anything else. "That's it. That's all I know, I swear."

"Thank you," I say and walk out the door.

She doesn't follow, but she does call one final plea after me, her voice raw: "Dara, please don't tell anyone."

The words fall from her mouth and snake around my legs like chains, rooting me in place. I don't turn or say anything. I just stand there on the front path, my back to the house, a final bomb going off in my heart. It's still all about her.

I force myself to move again, and throw the suitcase and tennis bag into the back seat of my car. I'm about to climb into the driver's side, but Sam's house catches the corner of my eye.

I hesitate.

Damn.

A quick good-bye, and then I'm out.

....

The blatant normalcy inside the Alapatis' house feels like an assault. Sam's dad and little sister are in the living room, playing cards and laughing. They wave at me. I run into Niya on the stairs—she's coming up from the basement with a basket of laundry. Her long, shiny black hair hangs over one shoulder in a fat braid, and the delicate stud in her nose twinkles like a speck of fairy dust in the foyer light. "Twice in one day, huh?" she says to me. Without warning, my eyes fill again. Niya is a good mom. She hasn't spent nearly two decades lying to Sam or Annita. Concern mars her features as she notices my tears. "Dara? What's wrong?"

I clear my throat and train my gaze on the floor. "Nothing," I lie. "Sorry, just need to talk to Sam about something."

"He's in his room." We pass each other and then she says, "Ramesh made way too much food for dinner. I'll pack up some leftovers for you to take home."

"Thanks." No use telling her I'm not going home.

I knock on Sam's door and open it. He's at his computer again. Or still.

"Hey! I've been waiting for your call." His eyebrows are raised expectantly.

I straighten up, trying to look like I know exactly what I'm doing, even though it would be so easy to crumple to the floor. "I'm leaving."

"Leaving?" He stands up quickly. "Why? Where are you going?"

"A place called Cherry Hill. It's in New Jersey." Our eyes find each other. His are filled with concern, curiosity, confusion. Mine are wet, and on the verge of spilling over again. I know I'm not giving him much, but I'm afraid I'll start sobbing and won't be able to get myself together enough to get in my car and drive away. I begin to turn.

"Wait." He grabs my arm as if to stop me, like I couldn't just shrug him off if I wanted to. "What happened?"

I take an unstable breath. "Mellie is not my mother," I whisper. It's a little strange, using her first name. But calling her "Mom" right now feels even less natural.

Everything on his face turns down: his mouth, the corners of his eyes. "What do you mean? You *were* adopted?"

"I can't talk about this now, Sam. I'll text you later, okay? I just came to say good-bye."

"How long are you going to be gone?"

"I don't know. At least a few days. Maybe longer." *Depends on how this goes.*

His next words reach inside me, like a salve to the place that hurts the most. "Do you want me to come with you?"

I blink. "Really?"

"I mean, I have to check with my parents, but I don't have anything going on for the next few days."

Maybe he's only offering because of the tears in my eyes. Maybe he just *really* wants to know what happened with Mellie. Or maybe it's because he's Sam, and he would never let me down. I don't care what the reason is. This trip, whatever it ends up being, will be so much easier if I have my best friend with me.

"Yes! Oh my God. Please come. I'll pay for gas and hotels and food."

"Okay, give me five minutes," he says and begins to pack.

CHAPTER SIX

I wait in the car as Sam explains to Niya and Ramesh what's happening. I don't know if they give him a hard time or not, and I don't ask when he gets in the car. I imagine the conversation went something like:

Sam: "*Uhhh*, Mom? Dad? Is it okay if I go on a trip with Dara?"

Niya: "What, right now?"

Sam: "Yeah."

Ramesh: "Where? What are you talking about? For how long?"

Sam: "She said something about New Jersey? For a few days?"

Ramesh: "*New Jersey?* Whatever for?"

Sam: *growing impatient* "Dad, she's leaving town with or without me, and I think it would be better if she had someone with her. We won't stay away too long, I promise. And I'll check in all the time."

Niya: "I don't like this. Let me call Mellie—"

Sam: "No, don't. Dara's leaving *because* of Mellie."

Niya: "What do you mean? What happened?"

Sam: "I don't know. But it must be bad."

Niya: *hesitates*

Ramesh: *looking at Niya* "It's not as though we can stop him. He's going to be off to college in a couple months."

Sam: "We'll be careful. Love you."

Niya: "We love you too."

I squeeze my eyes shut, trying to make the imagination bubble above my head, and the perfect, happy family inside it, pop.

It doesn't work.

Sam and I don't talk as I drive to the bank and take money out of the drive-through ATM. I don't have a lot of savings, and what I do have I had been planning to use for the circuit, but desperate times call for desperate measures.

Everything in Francis shuts down by nine p.m., so the streets are dark and empty. The question lingering in the car is so conspicuous that Mellie herself may as well be perched on the console between Sam and me, crowding the front seat, causing a giant blind spot, and making it difficult to pay attention to anything else.

But Sam doesn't ask just yet, and I don't offer the information. I just want to put Francis firmly behind me. Once we're finally on our *way* somewhere and not simply leaving somewhere, then I'll talk.

The one stoplight in downtown Francis is red. I bring the car to a halt and wait, even though the streets are abandoned and there's no one coming in any direction. It occurs to me that this is yet another example of how I've been conditioned to just go with the flow, not asking questions, not being allowed to make decisions for myself. I could put my foot on the gas right now, drive safely under the red light and into the intersection, and carry on with my journey, and no one would be worse off because of it.

You know what?

Screw it.

I ease the car forward.

A little shot of adrenaline and self-satisfaction surges through me, and I smile.

"Dara!" Sam says, breaking the silence and grabbing on to the inside of his door as if he needs to brace himself against the impact of me going a whopping twenty miles an hour on a deserted street. "The light didn't turn!"

"There was no one coming," I say calmly.

"That's not the point! Someone could have come out of nowhere! Or you could have gotten a ticket!"

"Oh yeah, because the Francis police are out in full force tonight, huh?"

Sam sighs as I pull onto the highway extension. "Okay, what is going on?" he asks.

I shake my head. "First we need to figure out where we're headed." The road we're on now is the only highway around here, so we've got to be on the right track. But directions would help.

"I thought you said New Jersey."

"Yeah. Cherry Hill. Can you look up the address for William and Ruth Pembroke?" I nod toward the phone in his hand.

Out of my peripheral vision, I see Sam's head whip toward me. "Pembroke? Like Celeste Pembroke? From the box?"

"Yes." He seems to sense I'm not ready to elaborate, but I can feel the curiosity radiating off him.

He taps the screen a few times. While I wait, I switch to the middle lane and check to make sure I'm not doing too much over the speed limit.

"Okay, I got the address. Plugging it into the map." He holds the screen up in my line of sight. "Five hours, seventeen minutes. In about forty miles, we're going to merge onto I-81S. I'll let you know when the exit's coming up."

"Perfect."

"It's already late, though, Dara," he says uncertainly. I glance at the clock, surprised to find it's after eleven. "Do you really want to drive through the night?"

I'm wide awake, and itching to put as much distance as I can between Mellie and me. The drive won't be a problem. But he does raise a good point—I probably shouldn't go ringing my long-lost grandparents' doorbell at four a.m. I really want this to go well, and that wouldn't be the best start.

"Yeah, let's keep driving. You can sleep if you want."

"Okay . . ."

"But first can you look for a hotel for us to stay at when we get there?"

Sam opens a new window on his phone, and a few minutes later he's booked a room. It's in Philadelphia, twenty minutes from Cherry Hill, and it had a low rating on TripAdvisor, but it was the cheapest room available on such short notice.

"Are you going to tell me what happened now?" Sam asks. "No more laws to break or Google searches to do first?"

I watch the dotted white lines of the three-lane highway pass on either side of the car. He's going to need to know eventually, and it should probably be before he gets fed up with me and changes his mind about the trip. If the roles were reversed, I don't think I would have been nearly as patient as he has.

I shake my head faintly. "You're not going to believe it when I tell you."

He waits.

I take a deep breath. "Mellie is . . . transgender. Or transsexual. Or both? I'm not a hundred percent sure how it works."

This time Sam's entire body jerks toward me. "She's *what*?"

"She was born a boy. Or . . . that's not how she phrased it, but . . . you know what I mean."

"Whoaaa." The word is a never-ending whisper.

"Yeah."

"But she looks . . . I had no idea. Did you? I mean, did you ever suspect . . . ?"

"Oh yeah, all the time." I shoot him a look.

"Sorry."

But another memory sneaks up on me. An awful heat wave had descended on western New York the summer I was thirteen, and my mom and I spent her days off at the public pool in the next town over. Sometimes Sam would come with us, but on the days he didn't, I would beg Mellie to come in the water with me. I hated swimming by myself, and she knew that. But she refused every time, insisting she was fine sitting under her umbrella with her book, her one-piece bathing suit mostly hidden under her caftan, untouched by water and chlorine. I was so mad at her for not being willing to even wade halfway in. Looking back, I wonder if she refused to go in the water because she was uncomfortable being in a swimsuit in public. There *were* hints; I just never knew how to decipher them.

"She's been lying to me my whole life, Sam. She's been lying to everyone."

He takes a second and then says, "So she adopted you."

"No."

"Oh. Trans women can have babies? I didn't know that."

Oh, Sam. "No. They can't."

"So . . ." He still doesn't get it.

A pair of headlights comes up fast behind us, and I switch to the right lane to let them pass. I'm grateful for the few extra seconds before I have to say . . . what I have to say. "So," I continue once the speeding car's taillights are far in the distance, "she's not my biological mother. She's my *father*. The man in the pictures, the father line on the birth certificate . . . Marcus Hogan. That's her."

I glance at him just in time to watch it all click. His eyes go so wide you can see the whites all around his irises. "Holy *shit*."

My heart is pounding. Sam's reaction has brought it all to the surface again for me. All I say is, "Yeah."

"Tell me everything," he says.

Mom's final request sounds in my ears, but I don't care. Sam and I never keep secrets from each other.

I tell him all I know as I drive. About Mellie being Marcus, and how she was a pro player, and about Celeste and her family, and how Mellie transitioned after Celeste died, how she spent our money on the hormones and procedures, and how she ran away from my grandparents and changed our names so they wouldn't find us.

My phone vibrates with one, then two, then three calls. I ignore it.

"So I was kind of right about her kidnapping me. She stole me away, and lied to me and the world about who I am." Now that I'm talking, it's hard to stop. Every feeling that enters me comes right out again in a rush of words and tears and snot. I'm not even fully talking to Sam anymore. I'm talking to me, the highway, the universe. There's something validating in saying it all out loud, as if somewhere between my heart and the tip of my tongue, between my brain and my lips, these vaporous, unnamed things inside me are given a shape and a name, and made real.

"And you know," I say, wiping my nose on the sleeve of my hoodie, "I think the worst part is, she didn't have one good reason for why. Why it was *so* important that she do all of this. How she was able to justify all the deception. Even as she was speaking directly to my face, confessing this long overdue truth, she *still* wasn't considering my position in any of it."

I glance at the speedometer and realize I'm going thirty miles an hour over the speed limit. Not surprising, considering my whole body is so tense that my foot is practically forcing the gas pedal as far forward as it will go. I ease up, and we slow down a bit.

We're nearly halfway to Philadelphia when Sam asks, "So what are you going to say to your grandparents when we get there?"

"I don't know. I guess I'm just going to introduce myself and see what happens?"

"They'll probably welcome you with open arms. I bet they've missed you."

I consider that. He's right—Mellie didn't only ruin *my* life with her selfishness. She took the Pembrokes' granddaughter away from them. The one thing left to remind them of their dead daughter, gone.

The photos of Celeste, blond and joyful and not much older than I am now, flash before my eyes. I wonder if I'm like her in any other way, if there's anything similar about us apart from looks. Gestures, facial expressions, likes, dislikes. Maybe Ruth and William can help me find those things.

Sam and I lapse into silence again. There are very few other cars out on the road now, and it feels like it's just our little box on wheels and us, pioneering through the night.

"I just can't believe it," Sam says after a while, almost to himself.

"I know," I murmur.

"This is *Mellie* we're talking about."

"I know," I say again.

"Mom's best friend, kick-ass nurse, neat-freak Mellie."

"Yep."

"So weird."

"*So* weird," I agree, though I can think of a lot of other adjectives too.

My phone vibrates in the cup holder again. This time I check the screen. All the calls have been from Mellie. It's 2:30 in the morning; looks like she's not getting any sleep tonight, either. I send it to voicemail, and drop the phone back in its resting place.

"You okay?" Sam asks.

"I'm in top physical shape, Samarjit. Want to have a push-up battle?" I might be more tired than I thought. I'm suddenly feeling a little slap happy.

He laughs. "Yeah, okay, but what about mentally?"

"Not even a little bit."

He reaches over and squeezes my shoulder. "Change of subject?"

I glance at him. There's a hint of my favorite Sam smile there—the one where his right eyebrow lifts slightly higher than the left—and I'm overcome with gratitude that he's here with me right now. "Yes, please."

"Did you know that for every person on Earth there are one point six billion ants?"

I burst out laughing. The shock of it to my system jolts some of the tension loose. *"What?"*

"But!" he continues, grinning. "If you total all the ants together and all the humans together, each group will weigh about the same."

I nod, mock seriously. "And where did you learn this very important fact?"

"Online somewhere. I thought it was a good dose of perspective."

"Perspective about what?"

"I don't know . . . that we're not as significant as we think we are?"

I let that marinate. "Okay, now I'm depressed."

Sam chuckles. "But it got your mind off things for a minute there, didn't it?"

I punch him in the arm. "It did. Thanks."

"Any time."

But I'm a little jealous of those zillions and zillions of ants. They always have one another, and they always have a clear goal. There's not a lot of room for mystery or melancholy or loneliness in their little ant lives. And if they get stepped on, well, then at least they don't die with any regrets.

Sam spends the last hour of the drive asleep, and I have to put on some music to keep me awake. It's amazing how quickly you can go from wired to exhausted. Especially when you're at the end of the longest, hardest day of your life and you're confused about everything, not the least of which is your own place in the world.

We get to Philadelphia—the city where I lived for the first year of my life, apparently—just after four in the morning. I came to Philly once on a school field trip, and had assumed back then that it was my first time there. Yet another instance where Mellie could have told me about our past but chose not to.

I pull into the hotel parking lot and turn off the car. Sam doesn't stir, and I don't wake him just yet. Gingerly, as if it's a baby alligator that must be handled in just the right way, I lift my phone from the cup holder and swipe it on. Eleven missed calls and four voicemails, all from Mellie.

As I debate listening to them, the screen lights up with a new text message.

Please just let me know you're okay.

I sigh, and type back before I can talk myself out of it. *I'm fine. Sam's with me.*

Her reply comes immediately. *Thank you for letting me know. I love you.*

I clench my teeth. She doesn't get to just tell me she loves me and not have to go to the effort of actually showing it. That's what led us to this point in the first place. I think back to what I said to Sam, and my thumbs flash across the keyboard.

You still haven't given me one good reason WHY. Why it was so important that you transition when you did. Why you thought it would be okay to take me from my grandparents. Why you kept it secret from me. It must have taken a LOT of energy to hide it all, and yet you kept making that choice, over and over, for all these years. You must have had a reason. Something more than a flimsy "I was scared" or "My feelings were hurt." But when you had the chance to help me understand, you got defensive. I have my own answers to find now. My own story to track down. Please stop calling me.

I turn the phone off before she can respond.

CHAPTER SEVEN

The hotel isn't horrible, but it's not great, either. The sheets seem clean and the locks on the door work, but it's cramped, with a threadbare, stained carpet, a vague mildew smell, and a window-unit air conditioner that makes so much noise we decide to keep it off. I guess this is what eighty dollars a night will get you.

Sam and I are side by side in matching double beds. He's fallen asleep on the couch next to me tons of times during our movie nights, and our moms used to put us down to nap together when we were little, but this is different. We're in our pajamas, under the covers, in the dark, just feet away from each other, with no one else around. There's something surprisingly intimate about brushing your teeth at the same sink, taking turns changing in the same bathroom, and crawling into bed knowing you're about to sleep through the night in the same room. It's a glimpse into a part of each other's lives that we've never really seen before, despite how close we are. I hadn't considered the logistics of all this when I asked Sam to book us a room . . . but then, I had other things on my mind.

"Good night, Dara," he murmurs, his face mushed up against the pillow. "Dream good dreams." He's asleep again in a matter of minutes, snoring lightly, one leg kicked out of the covers, his chest rising and falling in perfect rhythm.

The glowing red numbers of the clock seem to pulse with the stuttered tempo of my own breaths; I'm too awake to close my eyes, and too exhausted to focus on anything except the uneasiness that has set up camp in my gut.

I roll over to stare at the dark ceiling and walk myself through an exercise that sometimes helps me fall asleep the night before a big match. I go through the alphabet in my mind, taking time to visualize each letter, picturing it so clearly that if I shrunk down and went inside my own head, I'd be able to feel the solidity of the letter's corners, climb up its spine, slide down its slopes and curves. When *A* has been perfectly constructed, I move on to *B*. Usually, by the time I get to *H* or *I*, I've succeeded in distracting myself enough that my body is relaxed, my bothersome thoughts have faded away, and I'm able to sleep. Tonight, I make it to *W*.

....

The next morning, I'm given the gift of one perfect moment. I've mostly made my way out of sleep and am warm and snuggly in bed, fresh, rested, the sun warm on my face. It's a blissful place. My lips curl into a smile all on their own.

It lasts for about two seconds. Then yesterday catches up with me and my eyes fly open.

Sam is awake and sitting cross-legged in his bed, his laptop propped up on a pillow in front of him. His hair is sticking up in a thousand directions.

He smiles when he sees I'm awake. "Morning. I was about to wake you up. We have to check out of here in a half hour."

I check the clock—it's 11:30 in the morning. "Holy crap." I've never slept this late in my life. If I were home right now, I would have already eaten a bowl of granola with almond milk and two servings of fruit, and I'd be at the gym, soaked through with sweat.

But today is not a normal day. *Today is the day I finally get grandparents.* Now that the initial shock of yesterday's events has . . . not faded, but . . . *settled,* the idea of knocking on the Pembrokes' door is a lot scarier than it was last night. Maybe I *should* have turned up in the middle of the night, while I was still high on adrenaline and fueled by fury.

I'm antsy to get up and move. But this hotel doesn't have a gym. And even though the area we're staying in seems relatively safe—lots of office buildings—I can't help thinking about the fact that Celeste was killed while running on this very city's streets. I know it doesn't make sense, but I'm kind of scared to go out there by myself.

"Want to go for a quick run with me?" I ask Sam, not getting my hopes up. He's not exactly the athletic type.

"Ha!" he barks. "You're hilarious."

Yep. Expected that. He'd probably stop every three feet to take pictures of the flowers.

"I really need to work out."

"You can take a day off," he says.

"I can, but I shouldn't."

He gets a mischievous glimmer in his eye, and in one swift action, places his laptop on the nightstand and pops up to his feet on the bed. He starts jumping, his hair lifting off his forehead with each propulsion upward. "Come on!" he shouts. "It's the cool new way to burn calories. All the kids are doing it."

I have to admit it does look sort of fun. I spring up and begin to jump too. As we bounce, something deep inside me, something unfamiliar, starts to glow with delight. I don't know if I've ever done this before, even when I was a little kid.

The beds squeak and groan under the pressure.

We're laughing like crazy now. He jumps from his bed to mine, and back again. I do the same. I switch it up—a cannonball, a toe-touch, a midair somersault. A few times, on a few particularly excellent bounces, the top of my head grazes the ceiling.

"So," I say, out of breath but still going, "what does one wear to meet their grandparents for the first time?"

He slows his jumps and gives me a smile that says he knows I'm a lot more nervous than I'm letting on. "I don't think it matters. I wore jeans and a T-shirt the first time we went to Mumbai to meet my dad's family."

"Yeah, but they knew you were coming. And you'd Skyped together a million times. I'm about to surprise the hell out of these people. I think I need to wear a dress."

He gives me an incredulous look. "Do you even own a dress?"

"As a matter of fact, I do. And I brought it with me, Mr. Know-it-all."

Sam tries to do a cheerleader-type fancy leap from one bed to the other, but doesn't quite stick the landing. His feet catch only the corner of my bed, and he slips and crashes down to the decidedly less-springy carpet.

I end my current bounce on my butt, scoot to the edge of the mattress, and peer down at him.

"You okay?"

He looks embarrassed but unhurt. "I call that maneuver the You Think I Didn't Mean to Do That but I Totally Did."

I laugh and pat his knee patronizingly. "Not everyone can be a born athlete. But don't worry, Sammy, you're talented in other ways."

"Yeah, yeah." He stands up and brushes invisible dirt off the seat of his pajama pants. "I'm hungry." He holds out a hand and pulls me to standing too. He's breathing heavily, and his face is flushed. His *The Secret Life of Walter Mitty* T-shirt is rumpled and snug at the same time, and I notice he actually has some muscles under there. I have no idea how, considering he never works out and last summer at Bethany Milford's pool party (the one he invited me to as his date because Bethany had forgotten I was part of the incoming senior class too) he was still pretty scrawny.

We take turns showering, and I put on the lavender jersey dress I bought months ago on a whim but never wore. I even dry my hair with the blow-dryer attached to the wall in the bathroom. Sam raises an eyebrow when I emerge. It's not like I'm wearing a ball gown, for crying out loud, but this probably *is* the most dressed up he's ever seen me—I didn't go to the prom (latching myself on to Sam and Sarah's date like a superfluous appendage wasn't exactly appealing), and I wore shorts and a tank top under my graduation gown.

"You look nice," he says, but I can't tell if he really means it or if he's just being a good friend.

The man at the front desk says it's no problem to extend our stay another night. I don't know how long things will take at the Pembrokes', or even how it's going to go, so it makes sense to guarantee ourselves a home base to come back to later tonight. One less thing to worry about.

We grab stale muffins wrapped in chemical-smelling plastic wrap left over from the "continental breakfast" in the lobby, and head out.

The day is beautiful. Only a few clouds in the sky, not too hot. The kind of day when street sweepers and jackhammers sound like music. Everyone seems to be in a good mood—even the workers in suits and heels lining up to get lunch from the street vendors. I'd almost forgotten it's a weekday. Just because my world has been flattened and flipped upside down like a pancake doesn't mean everyone else's lives are on hold too.

Oh crap.

"I need to make a couple calls," I tell Sam halfway across the parking lot and pull my phone out. Remarkably, there haven't been any other calls or texts from Mellie. I guess she got the message.

I call the juice stand first.

"Jolly Fruit Juices and Smoothies, this is Arielle speaking, how may I help you?"

Arielle's the manager—just the person I need to speak to. "Hey, Ari, it's Dara." I can hear the piped-in adult contemporary music and sounds of the mall shoppers passing by the kiosk.

"Oh hey! What's up?"

"I'm really sorry for the short notice, but something's come up and I'm not going to make it in for my shifts the next few days."

There's a pause. "Including today?"

"Yeah."

"You're supposed to be here in three hours, Dara. You need to find someone to cover if you have to switch."

"I know, I'm sorry. But I had to leave town unexpectedly. I didn't have time to ask anyone."

"That's not my problem." She's pissed now.

"I've been working there for two years," I say, starting to get annoyed too. "This is the first time I've canceled a shift at the last minute."

"I know that, but your track record doesn't help me today. It's the summer: I have three employees out on vacation, and Jonathan's already worked two doubles this week. If you don't show up, I'm going to have to stay. And that means paying a babysitter to pick Aiden up from preschool."

I swallow guiltily. "I'm sorry—"

"I have a line. I have to go. If you don't show up for your shift, I'll have no choice but to replace you. Permanently."

"But . . . I'm in Philadelphia," I say, stunned. "There's no way I could make it back in time." Even if I wanted to.

"Then I'm sorry. You can come collect your final paycheck any time after Friday." She hangs up.

I realize I've made it to the car, but I haven't unlocked the door. Sam is standing by the passenger side. "Everything okay?"

I stare at the phone. "I just got fired."

"Really? I thought your manager was cool."

"She usually is." I can't believe it. My savings are already dwindling because of this trip, and now I'm out of a job. The pro circuit just got that much further away.

I unlock the car doors and slide into the driver's seat. But I don't turn the car on. I have to call Bob now. Today's Wednesday and my next training session isn't until Friday, but I should give him as much notice as possible. I don't need him to fire me too. Not that I have any idea how I'm going to pay him.

"Dara Baker, my favorite person," he says upon answering.

"Hey, Bob. How are you?"

"I'm doing well! Mary had a productive session this morning, and I just got some terrific tomatoes and fresh herbs at the farmer's market."

I smile. "That's great. So, I actually need to cancel our session on Friday." And maybe next week's too, if things with the Pembrokes go well, but I don't want to jinx anything.

The silence on the other end of the line gives away his surprise. "Are you sick?" It's a reasonable question—I can only remember canceling one session before, and it was when I had a nasty, flu shot–resistant flu.

"No, I . . . It's a long story, but I guess you could call it a family emergency."

"Is Mellie sick?"

"No. Everyone's fine."

"What's going on, then?" he asks.

"It's . . . complicated," I say. I can't get into it right now—and not because Mellie asked me to keep quiet. I just . . . can't.

"I understand." He's clearly displeased.

I hate disappointing him. In a way, Bob's always sort of filled the dad role in my life. Which is ironic, in light of recent events.

The guilt I felt when speaking to Arielle fizzles and reconcentrates here. "Actually, I have good news," I say, hoping to alleviate his disapproval. "I'm going to enter a tournament! Not the Toronto one, because I don't know if I can get a passport in time, but one somewhere." Probably not a good idea to tell him that I have absolutely no idea how I'm going to cover the expenses. Or that today's workout consisted of jumping on a couple of hotel beds.

"You're going to knock their socks off." I can hear his smile. *Phew.* "I'll see you next week. And keep training . . . if you can."

"I will, I promise."

I drop the phone in the cup holder and turn the car on.

"Ready?" Sam asks.

I look over at him, and then straight ahead, not answering.

The GPS app says the drive to Cherry Hill, New Jersey, will take twenty-three minutes. Twenty-three minutes is all that stands between my future and me. Or is it my past?

I don't know what I'm going to find when I knock on the door of their house. Will they recognize me? Will they believe me?

What if they've moved on? Forgotten all about me.

What if they hate Mellie so much that they hate me too, by default?

What if we don't have anything in common, apart from a few genes?

Or . . . what if they *love* me? And what if I don't know how to be in a family? What if I do everything wrong?

A solitary question rings in my ears, a clear soprano, as I back out of the parking space: Am I only rushing into this because Mellie doesn't want me to?

No, I answer. *No, this is for me. I need to do this.*

There's no traffic, no red stoplights, no detours. Nothing is standing in our way. Since when is the American highway system so accommodating?

I try to keep my anxiousness from Sam, try to stay über-confident and focused, like I'm about to begin a match. I don't want to have to admit out loud to being terrified of the one thing that just last night I was so resolute to do. I want to be confident. Fearless. Certain that running away, giving up my job, and letting down Bob were worth it. But I'm not able to stomach eating any of that muffin, and my breaths are becoming a little erratic. Sam can tell. He's always been able to tell when I'm not right.

Once in third grade it was my turn to take the class rabbit home for the weekend, and I completely forgot to feed him. He didn't die, but come Monday morning he wasn't doing so hot, either. The teacher asked, rather unforgivingly, what had happened, and I stood there, stammering and sweaty, reluctant to own up to my own carelessness. Sam had no idea what I'd done, but he got up from his desk, came up to the front of the class, and covered for me anyway.

"I bet Steven has that disease a lot of pet rabbits have been coming down with. It's like the flu. Didn't you hear about it on the news?" he said with a completely straight face.

The teacher looked surprised. "No, I didn't. Poor Steven! Thank you for telling me, Sam." She looked at me again. "Don't worry, Dara; this wasn't your fault. I'm sure you took very good care of him this weekend. You may take your seats." She poured some food into Steven's dish, which he immediately devoured.

I shot Sam the most relieved, grateful smile I could manage through the crushing guilt.

And now he's saving me again. As I drive, he reaches over, places a hand lightly on my arm, and squeezes reassuringly.

"Thanks," I whisper.

The GPS was wrong: Only twenty-one minutes after leaving the hotel, we're driving through a well-landscaped, unmistakably wealthy area, and then we're pulling into a long, circular drive. I stare up at the house, butterfly wings flapping against my rib cage.

I cut the engine. "Are you sure this is the right address?"

"Yep. This is it . . ." There's no mistaking the awe in Sam's voice.

This isn't a house. It's a castle.

The front of the palatial, three-story stone house is shrouded in brilliant green ivy, perfectly pruned around the windows and doorways, and trimmed in a neat line just below the sloping roof. The lawn is as manicured and sprawling as a golf course, and the massive weeping willow in the front yard transforms the property from intimidating to inviting.

I know Mom said the Pembrokes had money, but I wasn't expecting this. It makes me both excited for what might lie ahead and sad about how things could have been. Not that I would have expected . . . I don't know, fancy jewelry and private schools or anything. But there's no telling how far along my career could have been by now if only I'd had the funds to make it happen.

Looking at this house, a picture forms, and the blanks become filled. I don't know how, but I'm suddenly certain I know who the Pembrokes are. The lawyer and his perfect wife. Their beautiful blonde daughters. Family dinners around the table each night, family vacations each summer. Well-dressed, well-liked, well-intentioned. Generous donations to charity and hefty Christmas bonuses to their housekeeper and gardener each year. An old cat who bears a silly name chosen by the girls when they were younger. Grandkids and extended family filling the house on holidays, with at least four kinds of pie laid out on the table for dessert.

They never stopped looking for me. They'll welcome me into the fold of their family like I've been there all along. They'll tell me stories about Celeste and show me pictures and videos. They'll give me something that belonged to her, a doll or locket or hand-made picture frame, something they know she'd have wanted me to have.

Now I'm really glad I wore this dress, even if it is a little uncomfortable. I glance at Sam—I wonder if he should take off his ratty old Converse before entering the house.

"You okay?" he asks.

I nod. "Let's do it."

We get out of the car and I place one foot in front of the other until we're on the stone doorstep. I ring the bell, wipe my palms on the sides of my dress. A few moments later, the door opens. A thirty-something woman with her face perfectly made up and a small redheaded child on her hip stands there.

"Yes?" she asks.

"Hi." My voice comes out squeaky. I clear my throat. "I'm Dara Baker. Or Hogan, I guess. I'm, um . . ." *Spit it out.* "I'm looking for Ruth or William Pembroke?"

The woman's eyes squint in confusion, but her forehead remains unlined. I wonder if that's a result of the makeup, good genes, or some expensive cosmetic procedure.

Shame tugs at me. I've never cared much about traditional beauty. My hypersensitive relationship with my own body has made sure of that—I take good care of myself, but despite that, or maybe because of it, I don't have the typical lithe, waifish physique most people find attractive. I hate that finding out about Mellie has made me start scrutinizing people's faces and bodies in a way I never used to.

"I'm sorry," the woman says. "I think you may have the wrong house."

"Isn't this four-twenty-two Maple View Lane?" Sam asks.

"Yes." She nods.

"And there's no one named Pembroke here?"

"No." Something dawns on her face. "Oh, you know what? Now that I think about it, I believe that was the name of the family who lived here before us." She nods, remembering. "Yes, the Pembrokes. That's right. Very nice people."

All the apprehension and excitement dries up and forms a thick, dull pit in my chest. "When did you move here?" I ask quietly.

"Let's see, I was pregnant when we bought the house, so . . . that was about two and a half years ago now."

"Do you know where the Pembrokes moved to?"

She shakes her head. "We mostly dealt with the realtors. Only spoke to the previous residents once or twice." The kid in her arms squirms and starts to whine. "All *right*, Matthias." She sets him down and he runs away, squealing, into the house. "I'm sorry, I have to go." She closes the door.

Sam and I stand there for a minute. I stare at the door, my reflection distorted in the shiny black paint.

"Well, shit," Sam says eventually, and I look up at him.

"Yeah." The dress, the nerves, all for nothing. We turn and walk slowly back down the path to the car. Once we're buckled in, I grab my phone. "When you looked up the address last night," I ask, "what exactly did you put in the search engine?"

"Ruth and William Pembroke, Cherry Hill, New Jersey."

"Okay." I do a new search, and leave out the name of the town. Just "Ruth William Pembroke." It takes a few minutes, but I find a different address. It's just outside Charleston, South Carolina. There's only one phone number on record for them, and it has a New Jersey area code. Well, maybe it's a cell phone, and they kept the number regardless of where they're living now. I highlight the number and press "call." Immediately I get an out-of-service recording. *Damn.*

I turn to Sam. "How would you feel about next-leveling this road trip?"

He looks wary. "What did you have in mind?"

"I found another address for them. But it's in South Carolina."

He presses his lips together, observing me, thinking. "I'll go, but only under one condition."

"What's that?"

"We have to get Philly cheesesteaks first."

"I'm training for the pro tennis circuit, Sam. I can't eat that stuff."

Something flashes in his eyes. "Seriously?"

"What?"

"We're essentially on the *run* right now, your entire life has been turned upside down, I packed a bag and got in this car with you without even knowing what was going on, we just found out we're going to have to drive a lot farther than we thought . . . and you're not going to have *one freaking cheesesteak* with me?"

I gnaw on my lip. He's not wrong; I *could* use a little comfort food. And I probably do owe him this, as a thank-you for being such a great wingman.

I sigh and start the ignition. "Fine. We have to go back to Philly to get our stuff from the hotel anyway."

....

We park the car and find a street vendor. When Sam and I came to Philadelphia two years ago on that school trip, it was all Betsy Ross House and Independence Hall and bag lunches and following an overzealous tour guide holding a red, white, and blue flag above her head. There's a photo from that day on Sam's refrigerator: him and me and a couple of his other friends—including

Sarah, who wasn't yet his girlfriend but clearly wanted to be, from the way she stood so stupidly close to him—posing in front of the Liberty Bell.

Sam orders for both of us. Street meat, gobs of processed dairy, and refined white flour are as foreign to me as Saturday night dates and million-dollar trust funds. But Sam's aunt lives in Philly, so he's visited with his family a bunch and knows a lot more about the city than I do.

We sit in a park and I take my first bite. My eyes practically roll back in my head as I let out an involuntary moan. "Oh my God, that's the most delicious thing I've ever put in my mouth."

I take another bite, then another. Sandwiches are a staple at home—quick, relatively healthy, and easy for Mom to pack in her insulated lunch bag—but I've never had one like *this*.

After a few moments I notice Sam is watching me, his uneaten sandwich hovering halfway to his mouth.

"What?"

He blinks, and quickly takes a bite of his own cheesesteak. "Nothing. Good, right?"

"It's amazing."

"So, I was thinking . . ." he says. "What if we just spent the rest of the day here in the city? We'll keep the hotel reservation since it's already paid for anyway, and then get a fresh start out on the road tomorrow morning."

I swallow my most recent bite. "I don't know . . . I don't want to lose my momentum and chicken out."

"There's no way you're going to chicken out. Once you put your mind to something, there's no stopping you, Dara."

I bump into his side, a nonverbal *Aww, shucks.*

"I know all of this is super intense. Walking up to that house today was scary for *me*—I can't imagine what you were feeling. And for them to not even be there . . ." He shakes his head. "But that's part of the reason I wanted to come back here and chill for a little bit. You always go, go, go in everything you do. Sometimes I wonder if you put too much pressure on yourself." He says it without looking at me, as if it's hard for him to admit. Then he shrugs. "Anyway, I thought it might be good for both of us to take a breather, clear our heads, have a little fun."

I polish off the last few bits of cheesesteak, using it as an excuse to consider what he said. How long has he thought this? For some reason, I don't want to ask.

So all I say is "Okay."

"Okay?" His face brightens.

"Yeah. We'll get back on the road in the morning."

CHAPTER EIGHT

We spend the rest of the day exploring. You know what's way more exciting than the Liberty Bell? The discovery that I love cookies-and-cream milkshakes even better than the plain vanilla or chocolate ones I've indulged in on special occasions.

Sam takes me to a place called the Magic Gardens, which is basically a plot of land in the middle of a city block that's completely covered in glittering mosaics all done by the same artist.

"This is my favorite spot in the city," he tells me as he guides me through the cavernous walkways. I get why they call this place *magic*; I feel like we're in Wonderland or the Emerald City. Every surface is covered in little mirrors, colored glass, and slivers of ceramic. Some form faces and other images, some just patterns. Some don't have any shape at all, but there's beauty in the chaos.

Sam snaps a bunch of photos. We're in some of them but mostly they're of the art on its own. He brings the LCD screen of his camera close to his face as he studies each shot, and I know he's envisioning the possibilities of what he can do with the pictures when he gets back to his laptop.

"One day you're going to have an exhibit like this," I say as I walk under an archway that reads *Moving* and Sam walks under the one right next to it that says *Picture*.

"I don't do mosaics," he says. "I could never create art with my hands like this."

"That's not what I mean. I mean, one day you're going to have a supercool space where people come from all over to see your art."

"You mean like a gallery? Or a museum?"

"Yeah. Something."

"It's really hard to get to that point."

"Anything is possible if you want it badly enough," I say, and then repeat it again, silently, to myself.

He shakes his head. "I don't have your drive," he says.

"Of course you do."

I catch a glimpse of my reflection in a cluster of silver mirror fragments; the slightly off version of myself looks startlingly like the picture of Celeste from the box, the only one where she wasn't smiling for the camera—she was pregnant and standing at the kitchen sink, staring pensively out the window. I wonder what she was thinking about in that moment.

Sam and I don't talk about Mellie all day, though she's always there, lingering in what goes unspoken. We're only here, in this beautiful place, because of her, after all. I still haven't heard anything more from her. I don't know whether to be glad she's respecting my wishes or hurt that she isn't trying harder. Sam checks in with his parents after lunch; I'm sure Niya will fill Mom in on the fact that we're in Philly. I wonder how that conversation will go—if Mom will tell Niya about her past now.

We go back to the hotel after dinner and curl up on Sam's bed to watch a movie on his laptop. It's exactly what I need. I'm exhausted, and have kind of a stomachache after all that fatty, sugary food. And movie nights with Sam are familiar. Comforting.

"Hey," I say during the opening credits of *Forgetting Sarah Marshall*.

He hits the space bar, and the screen pauses.

"I'm gonna miss this," I say.

"Miss what?"

"Hanging out with you, watching movies."

"You mean when I go to school?" His voice is soft.

I nod. "I don't know what I thought was going to happen—maybe that I would come visit a lot? But look how long the drive was to Philly. You're going to school in *Boston*. It's even farther away."

His brow knits. "Yeah. I've been thinking about that too. It's gonna be different."

"*So* different."

He takes a moment, as if deciding how to phrase his next thought. "But . . . things are already different, you know? School's over, we're on this adventure, you're going to be traveling a lot more . . . Maybe different doesn't have to be bad."

"That's true."

"We'll always be in each other's lives," he says, and he sounds so certain.

"Promise?"

"Of course. I fully expect to be able to use my friendship with you as my claim to fame. Why else do you think I've put up with you all these years?"

I punch him in the arm.

"Aghh!" he groans, grabbing the spot I punched and rolling over onto his side in mock pain.

"Hey, Sam?"

He wiggles back up to a sitting position. "Yeah?"

"Did you tell your mom about Mellie?"

He shakes his head. "I told her you guys were having problems and that you needed some space. But I didn't tell her any specifics. I figured Mellie can tell her if she wants to."

This makes me feel better, though I don't know why.

"Okay. Thank you." I press the button to resume the movie.

I've seen this movie about fifty times—it's one of my favorites. But today it's not holding my attention. All I can think about is what happens if Mellie does tell Niya she's trans. Niya will obviously tell Ramesh. And because it's not the kind of gossip you hear every day in Francis, he'll want to tell someone too, like maybe the guys on his basketball team. And then they'll each tell someone and soon the entire town will know . . .

Sam stops the movie again.

"What's the matter?" he asks gently.

I rub my eyes. "Nothing. Sorry. Press 'play.'" His hand has barely touched the space bar when I blurt out, "I'm worried."

"About what?"

"About what will happen if people back home find out. What if people are mean to her? What if she gets fired?"

Sam is quiet. He's probably running through all the horrible scenarios you hear about on the news. There's a reason everyone knows the term *hate crime*.

He wraps his arm around me. His chest smells like cheese-steaks. "Do you want to go home, Dara? It's okay if you've changed your mind."

I sit up and put a few inches of distance between us. "No. I need to do this."

"Okay. Just checking." He considers something for a moment, then grabs his computer and pulls up Google Maps. He plugs in the Pembrokes' South Carolina address. "Want to see what the house looks like? Might help prepare for tomorrow."

I laugh a little. "That house today was insane, wasn't it?"

His eyes seem to grow three sizes. "Ridiculous. I can't believe your birth mother used to live there."

Birth mother. Is that what Celeste is? Was? I always thought of that as more of an adoption term. But I guess if you consider a "birth mother" being the person who carried you for nine months and gave birth to you, but not the person you grew up calling "Mom," it fits.

Sam hits "enter," and an image of a white house fills the screen. It's not as regal-looking as the Cherry Hill house, but it's just as huge and extremely well taken care of. A large porch wraps around the front, and in the photo, a black cat is asleep on the porch swing. The house looks like it's been restored from a much older version, and like it might even have historical significance. Sam chooses "aerial view," and the whole picture zooms out. Unlike the New Jersey house, which had neighbors on either side, this house is surrounded by vast stretches of green and brown land. When you zoom in you can see a couple of horses.

"It's a *farm*," I say.

"That's pretty cool."

The imaginary image of my perfect family remains intact, with just a few alterations. Instead of the lone cat—which, if this picture was taken since the Pembrokes have owned the house, I was totally right about—more animals enter the mix. Horses, a dog, maybe a cow. Switch the gardener to a farmhand and add some homegrown vegetables, and the picture is complete once more.

Just then my cell phone dings with a new email. It's from Mellie. The subject heading is "You were right," and the preview window shows the message begins with *Dear Dara, I've been thinking a lot about . . .*

I feel Sam reading over my shoulder. "You going to open it?" he asks.

I chew on my lip. I don't want to talk to her. I thought she'd heard me when I said to leave me alone. My thumb drifts from the "expand email" button to the "screen off" button.

But what does she mean by "You were right"? And what has she been thinking a lot about?

I wish I didn't care. I wish I could just delete the message unread and be done with it.

But I'm not that strong.

My thumb floats back to the email.

I click it open.

To: acelove6@email.com

From: Mellie.Baker@email.com

June 20 (8:35 PM)

Subject: You were right

Dear Dara,

I've been thinking a lot about what you said in your text last night.

You're right—I didn't explain any of it properly. I put off telling you everything for far too long, and that resulted in me being completely unprepared when the time came. I'm so sorry.

I'm going to try to fix that now. I know asking for a second chance is already a lot—a third chance is probably out of the question. So if this is my last chance to get the story right, I'm determined not to screw it up this time. I'm going to push past the instincts that have taken root in me over the last seventeen years, even though at this very moment they're telling me what they've always said: *Stay quiet. Protect myself and my family. Never tell a soul.*

I've decided email is probably the best way to do this—it's always been easier for me to organize my thoughts on paper. Maybe I was a writer in a past life. My plan is to start from the very beginning, and take you through everything in chronological order, as

I experienced it. The timeline of my life that brought us to this current place in time. That's the only way I can think of to make sure all the pieces fit together correctly. But please tell me if you have specific questions and want me to jump ahead.

I want you to know I have no agenda in any of this, apart from hoping it helps keep you in my life. I'm not going to try to convince you of anything, or talk you into making the choices I want you to make. Maybe you're on your way to the Pembrokes' right now. Maybe you're already there. It doesn't matter anymore. All that matters is that you finally know our story. What you said is true— you should have been part of this from the beginning. I'm only sorry it's taken me this long to realize it.

I'm going to send another email soon.

You don't have to respond if you don't want to. But please read.

I miss you so much already. I love you. Every time I open the fridge and hear the hot sauce bottles rattle against each other in the door, my heart aches.

Love,
Mom

I look at Sam.

> Hand him the phone so he can read.
> Bury my head under the pillow.
> And let out the loudest, longest wail of my life.

CHAPTER NINE

It's a ten-hour drive from Philly to Charleston.

We check out of the hotel bright and early—after I gave in and went for a five-mile run in a big circle around the hotel block. I didn't check my email this morning, but the little icon says I have nine unread messages. Even if the majority of them are spam, I'd bet money I don't have that one or two of them are from Mom.

I know I said I wanted the whole truth, the full story. But part of that was wanting it to have happened when it *should* have. Days ago, on the couch in the living room with the box of secrets open on the table beside us like tagged evidence during a trial. *Years* ago, each time I stepped onto a tennis court or asked Mom about her past or hugged her and told her I loved her.

A nobler person would say "better late than never" and be thankful that Mom has started to come around. A more compassionate person would argue that she'd been caught off guard the other night and that it wasn't fair of me to expect her to explain everything perfectly and in a way that would make me forgive her on the first try. A smarter person would reason that I should be glad I'm about to get the crucial details I've been asking for.

But getting daily emails on the subject, and being dragged back to Francis and the little yellow house and a lifetime of struggle every time I check my phone, isn't exactly what I meant. Not now, when I'm out here trying my hardest to be brave and find out who I am apart from Mellie.

I said all this to Sam last night. He understood, but he also thinks it's great that she's trying.

A couple hours into the drive, his phone dings with a new text message. "Who's that?" I ask.

He presses a button quickly and turns his phone facedown in his lap. "No one. It was a notification from my game." Sam's obsessed with this stupid Viking game—he's on it all the time, tap-tap-tapping his little men into formation. But I know the sounds that game makes, and I'm pretty sure that was a text message.

Something shifts out of place in my chest, causing a twinge. "Was it Mellie?"

"No. She hasn't texted me. It really was my game."

I glance at him, and he shrugs. I don't know whether to believe him, but he doesn't say anything else.

Somewhere in Virginia, we pass the body of a deer that tried to make it across the road and met an untimely demise. I wonder why the bodies are always on the side of the road, rather than right in the middle of the lanes of traffic, where they were likely hit. Surely the people who hit them don't take the time to move them. Is it that the animals don't die on impact, and instead try to crawl to safety before being unable to go any farther? Do they have families who are waiting for them? Did they have babies who made it across the road, only to turn back and watch their mothers get struck down?

It's as I'm thinking this that the car is filled with a thunderous *bang* and the steering wheel jerks out of my control, the back of the car skirting with it.

"What was *that*?" Sam shouts as I scream and throw a hand over my hammering heart.

"I don't know!" I manage to get the car under control a second later, but it still feels jerky and unstable. "I think we have a flat tire." I got a flat once before, but it was more of a silent ooze and less like a freaking gunshot.

"Terrific." Sam sighs, and shades a hand over his eyes, trying to calm himself down. "Do you have a spare?"

Uh-oh. He's going to be mad. "Umm. I don't think I replaced it after the last flat I got."

"What the hell, Dara?!" Knew it. "And you didn't think this would be important to take care of before going on a *road trip*?"

"First of all, I forgot all about it. Second of all, I didn't think we'd be driving all the way to South Carolina, remember?"

I manage to make it to the next exit. We're in the middle of Virginia. You know what they have here? Cow fields. You know what else they have? Motorcycle bars. That's about it. Not a gas station or car repair shop in sight.

I pull into the parking lot of one of the bars and get out of the car. Yep. The back right tire is deflated like a subpar air mattress after a night of being slept on. I slide back into my seat, not bothering to close the door since we're obviously not going anywhere, and call the number on the roadside service card in my glove compartment. The guy says it will be at least a couple hours before anyone can get here.

"Dammit!" I shout, slamming my hands against the steering wheel. I close my eyes and try to do some measured breathing. Doesn't help. Can't *anything* go right?

Sam doesn't say anything. It's like we've switched—now he's the calm one. Maybe he figures my wallowing is more than enough for one car. After a few minutes, he says quietly, "Well, should we go get some lunch?"

I look up, blinking against the sun. The pub in front of us fits in perfectly with this country atmosphere, with its wraparound front porch and neon Pabst Blue Ribbon sign in the window. It's barely afternoon, but the parking lot is packed with motorcycles and pickup trucks. A tractor is parked in a disabled parking spot. I wonder if someone drove it here. I wonder if that someone is actually disabled. I wonder if you can get arrested for driving a tractor while drunk.

The sign on the building reads THE OUTLAW SALOON. It's not exactly the kind of place Sam and I frequent. I give him a skeptical look.

"What?" he says. "We're from a small town. I'm sure we'll blend right in."

"Funny." But it's either this or sit in the car for hours. And I am kinda hungry. I unbuckle my seat belt. "Let's go."

We walk up the porch steps, and through the door.

Okay, we do *not* blend in. Luckily, it's not like the movies where we walk through the swinging doors and the pianist stops playing, and everyone stops talking and stares at us. No one's really paying us much attention, actually. But Sam starts quietly humming the "One of These Things Is Not Like the Others" song from *Sesame Street*. Apart from us, the dorky teenagers in Old Navy poly/cotton blends, there are two kinds of customers here: Leather and Denim.

Motorcycle riders and horse riders.

Bikers and cowboys.

The haze of smoke is thick and makes my lungs constrict. The sound system is playing country music. I don't recognize the song.

There are only three women, other than me, in the whole place. Two are Leathers. One is wearing a red denim miniskirt, black cowboy boots, and about a half bottle of hair spray, and is dropping off plates of burgers and wings at the tables.

Everyone is white. Except Sam.

"Yeah, my bad," Sam whispers out of the side of his mouth. He takes a slow step backward.

I back up a little too. But then a burst of genuine, easy laughter erupts from a nearby table of Denims, and they clink glasses. I find myself smiling for the first time since before I got Mellie's email. Sam begins to turn toward the door, but I grab his arm. Link it through mine. Hold him in place.

"What?" he asks.

Everything that could possibly have gone wrong these last few days *has*, but there's been a flip side to everything too. Finding out about Mellie has given me hope for things I'd never known to hope for: a family, a history, financial security, a real chance to take the tennis world by storm instead of having to sidle into it with one arm tied behind my back. Going to the wrong address yesterday gave Sam and me a pretty incredible day in Philly. And blowing that tire has led us here, to this half-scary, half-cartoonish bar we'd never in a million years have come to otherwise. I'm beginning to wonder if maybe the universe is telling me something.

Enjoy the ride, for once in your life.

I grin up at him. "We're staying."

Almost immediately, his demeanor turns suspicious. "Why?" he says, like I've led him into a trap.

"Uh, because we have literally nowhere else to go?"

He crosses his arms, waiting for the real reason.

I pull him by the sleeve to a little area away from the entrance and turn to face him thoroughly. "Name something you've done that I haven't." We're directly under a speaker now, and I have to raise my voice to be heard over the music.

His forehead crinkles. "What do you mean?"

"Name something. Anything."

He clearly doesn't understand where I'm going with this, but he plays along. "*Uhhh* . . . flown in an airplane?"

"That's true. What else?"

"Gotten an A on a math test." He smirks.

I roll my eyes. "All right, show-off. What else? Think bigger."

He stares at me and shakes his head. His eyes shine prettily in the light of the neon. "Just tell me what you want me to say."

I sigh. "You've tried beer, right? Gotten drunk?"

He raises an eyebrow. "You know I have. There's nothing else to *do* in Francis. Everyone has—" He stops himself.

"Right. Not everyone." I nod. "You've also had girlfriends, who you made out with and did *other stuff* with." A blush warms my face. I don't like to think about how Sam is much more experienced than I am in that arena. "You've stayed out all night. You got to go on the school trip to Montreal, when I had to stay home to train."

"Yeah, but those things aren't as spectacular as you think they are," he says. "Dating can be awkward. Drinking too much makes you sick. Staying out all night makes you feel like crap. I had to bunk with three other guys on that Montreal trip—you have no idea how bad that room smelled."

I pin him with my gaze. "Do you regret any of it?"

He looks down. "No."

"Exactly. So why shouldn't I get to experience all the normal parts of being a teenager too? The good *and* not-so-good stuff." I push my hair back from my face.

"Because you're *special*, Dara. You have something the rest of us only wish we had."

I scoff. "And I've given up almost everything to get it."

"Wasn't it worth it?"

"Of course. But . . . yesterday was fun, eating junk food and looking at art and jumping on beds. It was like a break in the shitstorm clouds. And I don't really see what's so wrong with making the most of this . . . adventure, like you called it." I think for a moment. "I'm hoping finding my family will mean finding myself, right? The me I never knew about?"

He nods.

"Maybe this is part of that. And I'd like to do it with *you*, before you go away."

Our eyes lock. Finally, he breathes. "Come on; I'll buy you a drink."

I squeal and throw my arms around him. "Thank you."

His arms snake around me and pull me in close. He feels good. Warm. Strong. Protective. I had no idea how much I needed a hug until now.

I pull away and rub my eyes with my knuckles.

"Actually, let me go call my mom first. She texted me this morning asking me to check in. You go ahead and order. Whatever you want, on me." He smiles. "You gonna be okay here by yourself for a few minutes?"

I nod.

"Be right back."

I watch him through the window as he paces the bar's front porch, talking to Niya. I wonder what's going on at home. If anyone knows yet.

Stop thinking about Mellie. Today is not about her.

I spin on my heel, and go up to the bar.

The bartender, a big guy with a leather vest and a greased-back ponytail, raises an eyebrow at me. "You lost?"

I take off my cardigan and straighten up, showing off my defined shoulders and arms. "Nope. I'm exactly where I want to be. Two beers, please."

"You got ID?"

Crap. I didn't think a place like this would card. I stare at him, racking my brain for a believable reason why I wouldn't have an ID that says I'm twenty-one. "I, uh . . ."

Sam slides onto the barstool next to me and hands a driver's license over. "Here you go," he says smoothly. "She doesn't have hers because she locked her keys in the car with all her stuff inside. We're waiting for the guy to come unlock our doors for us." *Saving me again, just like in third grade.*

The bartender looks at the ID and then up at Sam, and back at the ID. My heartbeat tumbles like I'm in the middle of spinning class. Then he shrugs. "What kind of beer?"

I try not to exhale too loudly.

"Whatever's cold," Sam says, taking his fake ID back and tucking it into his wallet.

The bartender plunks two pint glasses in front of us and leaves to serve another customer.

Sam leans toward me. "Two beers, huh? I actually wasn't going to drink—someone's got to be sober enough to deal with the tow truck guy and drive us out of here."

I ignore that. There's no way I'm drinking my very first beer *by myself.* "Where did you get a fake ID?"

He smiles my favorite smile. "Jake Houston was selling them before the end of the year. I hadn't had a chance to use it yet, though."

"My hero." We clink glasses.

....

Two hours later, I think I'm finally understanding what it feels like to be drunk.

At first I wasn't sure I liked beer. It has kind of an earthy taste, with a bite to it that I wasn't expecting. I thought it would be . . . I don't know, sweeter? But now, three pints in, I think it tastes pretty good. Or, more to the point, it doesn't taste quite like anything anymore. I wonder if being drunk changes your taste buds somehow.

Sam is feeling it too—I can tell because his cheeks are flushed and he's got a permagrin on his face. But he's still pretty together, if the fact that he keeps forcing me to drink water in between sips of beer is any indication. Even so, there's no way *either* of us is driving us out of here any time soon.

He spins on his stool and takes pictures of the bar as he goes around. Every time the camera points my way, I make a stupid face and he clicks the shutter release. I grab the camera from his hand, throw my arm around his shoulders, kiss him on the cheek, and take a selfie of the two of us.

"Did Niya say anything about Mellie?" I ask as we separate.

He shakes his head. "She said she actually hasn't been able to get ahold of her. She's not answering the door, and she's not picking up her phone."

Normally, I'd be concerned by that news, but I finally checked my notifications after that second beer—there are three unread emails from her. I know she's fine. "She's avoiding her," I say.

"Probably." He pauses. "Can I say something?" His tone has changed, and his body language is screaming, *I'm not sure you're going to like what I'm about to say.*

"What, are you going to tell me you're transgender too?" Apparently, beer makes me *so* funny.

That makes him smile. "No."

"Are you going to tell me you have a completely different identity and have been lying to me my whole life?"

"No."

"Are you going to tell me this whole trip is a bad idea and that we should turn around and go back to Francis?"

He hesitates. *Don't ruin this for me*, I plead silently.

But then he says, "No."

Good. "Then go ahead. My threshold for surprise has been raised quite a bit these past few days. I'm not fragile."

He nods. "The whole transgender thing . . . Do you really know anything about it? Not just with Mellie, but in general."

"I know everything I need to know."

He frowns. "But—"

"Therapy time is over. Thanks for playing." I straighten up and down the rest of my beer. Sam does the same. The glasses are still frosty, even with nothing in them. We must have finished that last round pretty quickly.

I slide off my stool and march over to the jukebox. The song titles are fuzzy, and I have to squint in order to read what they say. It's mostly country and some rock, and I don't recognize many of the bands. I'm not sure if that's because I don't know much about country and rock, or if these bands are old and that's why I've never heard of them, or if they're new and I've been so out of touch from anything that doesn't have to do with the tennis circuit and *that's* why I've never heard of them. In the end, I choose a few songs at random, and dance back to the bar just as Marla—that's the waitress's name—brings us the plate of mozzarella sticks we ordered.

"I love you," I tell her.

She laughs. "Thanks, sweetie."

I grab a mozzarella stick and take a bite. This place's food is *legit.* The cheese is hot and gooey, and oozes out of the tube of fried goodness. I catch the dripping cheese with my tongue and swirl it around, collecting it all in my mouth.

"God, that's good."

I pick up another stick to offer to Sam, and catch him watching me. It's the same look he was giving me when I sank my teeth into the cheesesteak for the first time. Now I recognize it: It's the kind of look guys give girls who are not me. The kind of look *Sam* gives girls who are not me. It's a lost-in-his-imagination, *that thing you're doing with your mouth is turning me on* look. It makes me excited and uncomfortable all at the same time.

Could I possibly look sexy when I eat this kind of food? Could I look sexy *at all?*

My head is pretty muddled, and before I know it the look is gone and Sam's taking another sip of beer, and I think maybe I imagined it completely. Being drunk makes you feel really good and really loose and really fun, but it also makes things not quite so clear. The clock seems to be skipping entire minutes altogether.

"Want a stick?" I ask Sam, thrusting the fried mozzarella toward him.

He shakes his head. "No thanks. I think you need the food more than I do right now."

"What's that supposed to mean? *Everyone* needs mozzarella sticks."

"I'll order something in a little bit. You eat."

"Sam! I demand you eat this mozzarella stick right this second!" I push it toward his mouth, but he keeps his lips tightly sealed. "Do it!"

He shakes his head in defiance, but I can see the laughter in his eyes.

I switch tactics. "Please, Sammy?" I say sweetly, putting on my best puppy-dog face. He snaps a picture. "Pretty please? Try the mozzarella stick? For me?"

Finally, he rolls his eyes. "Fine." He opens his mouth and takes a bite. "Jeez," he says after only a couple chews. "That's really good."

I jump around in triumph. "I told you."

I feed him the rest of the stick; he doesn't try to take it from me to put it in his mouth himself. His eyes are full of mirth, and I have a feeling mine are too, and we don't break our gaze until the mozzarella stick is completely gone. I lick the grease off my fingers, and he watches—like the mozzarella stick didn't quite satisfy his hunger.

There's that look again. I know I'm not imagining it this time.

We're only about a foot away from each other—Sam's on his barstool and I'm standing. Something is happening. I can't think clearly enough to name it, but it's like the fun, happy beer clouds surrounding each of us join forces to form *one* snug, fun, happy beer cloud. And we're in it together.

Right now everything feels like a good idea. Everything feels like the best idea I've ever had.

I just want to keep feeling good feelings. No Mellie, no flat tire, no reality.

I open my mouth and words come out. They're entirely unplanned, and even I'm curious what they're going to be. "Are you having a good time?" I ask Sam.

He nods. "I am."

"I'm glad you're here with me. Are you glad you're here with me?"

"Very."

"Isn't having fun better than being serious?"

"Yes."

"Are you going to trust that I know what I'm doing from now on?"

He grins and holds up his hands in complete surrender. "Definitely."

Suddenly, the cozy beer cloud around us vanishes, replaced by something more like a giant rubber band. Moving toward Sam is easy. Moving away from him is very, very hard. So I take another small step closer, and smile.

"Good. Because I'm wondering if you'd like to help me check another item off my 'never done that' list." *Where did that come from?*

"What's that?"

I want to kiss you. I don't say it.

But his gaze travels to my mouth, and then back to my eyes, and I know his thoughts are in the exact same place as mine.

It's so weird. This is *Sam Alapati*. My best friend. My neighbor. I've never kissed anyone before, and he knows it.

I'm not thinking this through, but that's just it—I don't want to think. I don't want to talk anymore, either. No discussions, no cutting through the drunk haze to find the words to articulate what's happening, to weigh the benefits and risks and be responsible about it all. I want to just *do*.

So I keep moving forward. With each inch, the rubber band seems to shrink, pushing us even closer together.

"Just one friend helping another out, okay?" I ask.

Sam nods.

"It doesn't have to mean anything."

He nods again.

I try to move slowly, to give Sam the opportunity for an out. He doesn't take it.

And then he apparently decides that slow isn't going to work for him, because he leans forward and crushes his mouth to mine.

That first instant of connection takes me by surprise. Not the action itself—that was inevitable—but the sensation that comes with it. I feel like sparklers have ignited under my skin. Sam's lips are strong and confident and tender. I move mine with his, perfectly happy to let him lead.

I have no idea what I'm doing, but *oh my God, I'm kissing a boy.* I'm kissing *Sam.*

He wraps his arms around my waist and tugs me closer, so I'm nestled between his legs as he sits on the barstool.

Kissing is way better than beer. It's even better than mozzarella sticks and Philly cheesesteaks.

Kissing is the best kind of delicious.

CHAPTER TEN

Sam pulls back first. "Whoa."

I wipe the extra saliva off my bottom lip with my thumb. It's kind of hard to focus on his face; I take a step back and squint to make my vision adjust.

Once he's not all fuzzy, I grin. My whole body—limbs, tummy, mouth—is wired, sizzling and crackling on good-feelings overload. "Another beer?"

"I think maybe we've had enough . . ." he says tentatively.

"What? The night's just getting started! Or day—what time is it, anyway?"

Sam looks at his phone. "It's two thirty in the afternoon."

I pause for a moment, trying to comprehend that, and start to laugh. So much has happened since we stepped foot in this bar that it doesn't seem right for anything less than *days* to have passed. But then again, I should know by now how drastically your life can change in no time at all.

I try to sit back on my barstool, but I only catch the very edge of the seat, so my butt slides off and I stumble a little.

Sam reaches out to steady me. His face, so open just a moment ago, closes off. "Yeah, we're done."

"No way." I do a little dance to show how great I am, and signal the bartender. "More beer, please!" I sit on the stool more carefully this time. Success.

"Dara," Sam says evenly, "I know what you're feeling right now. I've felt it before too. I was even feeling it up until a minute ago. You're in that place where everything feels amazing. But—"

The bartender slides two more full glasses in front of us. Before Sam can say anything else, I take a long gulp, and smack my lips.

"Now you." I point at his beer.

"Dara . . ."

"Sam." I try to mimic his buzzkill tone. We stare at each other, a standoff with no real conviction.

It only takes a few seconds, as I knew it would. For all his posturing, his decision-making skills aren't much better than mine right now. Obviously. We wouldn't have made out like that if either of us were in our right minds.

He sighs and takes a sip.

Just then my phone, lying faceup on the bar, lights up. The flat-tire guy is calling. I tell him we'll be right out, hoping my voice sounds normal.

"I'll go," Sam says, placing two hands lightly on my shoulders as if to keep me in place.

I don't argue.

"Just . . ." He glances around the bar. "Don't talk to anyone."

"Except Marla," I say.

He laughs. "Except Marla."

I grab my credit card from my bag and hand it to him.

"Thanks."

Once he's gone I click my phone on again and pull up Mellie's emails. I've got a pleasantly detached floaty thing going on right now, and confronting her messages doesn't feel quite as weighty as it did a few hours ago.

To: acelove6@email.com

From: Mellie.Baker@email.com

June 20 (10:59 PM)

Subject: The start

Dear Dara,

I haven't told you much about my family. One reason for that you already know, though the details were vague: My childhood was very difficult, and after I left home, it was too painful to revisit that place, even in my mind. But the other reason was because if you knew about my family, you'd surely discover the gaps in the life I'd so carefully constructed for us, and that would have been dangerous. But I'm getting ahead of myself.

My earliest memory is from when my mother was pregnant with my brother Lenny. He's the fourth and final sibling, after Ronald, Joanna, and me. It was 1981—around Easter. To this day, the smell of vinegar egg dye always transports me back to that afternoon at my mother's kitchen table. I don't remember the beginning of the conversation, but I do know it was a "where do babies come from" talk, abbreviated for a three-year-old. My mother must have told me that my little sibling was in her belly, and that I had once been in there too, that the mother's belly is where the baby is put together and grows strong enough to be born. My memory kicks in just as I'm processing this new information. I remember touching her middle, looking up at her, and saying clearly and urgently, "I need to go back in."

She laughed and ruffled my hair. "You can't go back in, baby."

I shook my head. She didn't get it. "I need to go back in and get fixed."

Her smile faded and little lines appeared on her forehead. "Fixed how, sweetie? You're already my perfect little boy."

But I didn't know how to tell her what I meant. I didn't have the words yet. I just knew I wasn't the way I was supposed to be. Everyone thought I was one thing because of how my outsides looked, but I was really something else. How is a three-year-old supposed to explain something so complex? And back then it was mainly a *feeling*—a strong feeling, yes, but not a conscious, articulated *thought*.

I started to cry. I crawled onto her lap and frantically tried to push myself against her stomach, in the hopes that somehow I'd be able to go back in and start over.

She held me at arm's length, her face cross. "Marcus! Stop it. You're going to hurt the baby."

I felt like she'd thrown ice water on me. But her message was clear: The baby was the priority now. My time was over.

It was the first clue I had that I was on my own—and this was long before my parents started to suspect there was something "wrong" with me. It only got worse from there.

Dara, I never want that to happen with us. You cannot know how sorry I am to have hurt you. You are the most important thing—and always have been. I hope these emails will help you believe that.

Love,
Mom

To: acelove6@email.com

From: Mellie.Baker@email.com

June 21 (2:16 AM)

Subject: A dream is a wish your heart makes

Dear Dara,

I was five when I put my feelings into words for the first time. The understanding came after a dream I had, actually. It was the special kind of dream that you only get a few of, if that, during a lifetime. The kind that is so vivid, so perfectly complete, right down to the fibers of the dream carpets and the pores of your dream skin, that you believe—with everything that you are—during the dream and for a little while after, that it's real. But better than real, because in the dream anything is possible. Hearts pulse with unbridled joy, wishes come true, and the world is sparkly and warm and beautiful.

In my dream, Glinda from *The Wizard of Oz*, my favorite movie back then, visited me. Her weightless, luminescent bubble floated effortlessly through my bedroom window, and she alighted to the floor. "You've passed the test, Marcus," she told me, her voice caressing me like a hug. "You've been a very good girl. I know how hard it must have been for you—to be so kind and well-behaved when you've been so sad."

I nodded, soaking up her words. I *was* sad . . . all the time. Every day felt like a trial. And somehow Glinda saw it when no one else did. I knew there was something specific my mom and dad and siblings and teachers wanted me to be; I just didn't know what it was or how to be it. It felt like my whole life was a giant, unsolvable riddle. I thought the wrong way; I felt the wrong things. When I tried to like the things I was supposed to like and act the way I was supposed to act, I still wasn't who they wanted me to be. I got yelled at all the time. But I tried so hard. To be good, to make my parents happy—even though they didn't seem to like me very much at all.

"The hard part is over, Marcus," Glinda said. "Now you will be rewarded."

I reached out and clutched the soft, pink tulle of her gown tightly in my little hand.

"What is your wish?" she asked, smiling kindly.

I opened my mouth to reply, but then I realized: She'd already granted my wish. She'd already given me the one thing I'd always wanted but never knew how to articulate, never knew was even possible. She'd called me a *girl*. It was like I'd put on a pair of glasses with the correct prescription for the first time.

"I want to be a girl," I told her. "A real one."

If I had a girl's body, everything would match. I would like the right things. I would think the right way. My parents wouldn't be mad anymore.

Glinda smiled and nodded as if she'd been expecting me to say that.

"Then a girl you shall be." She smiled kindly, cupped the side of my face in her soft, gentle hand, and floated away on her bubble once more.

When I woke up, it was still nighttime. I grabbed Annie—a tattered old rag doll given to me by my sister when she didn't want her anymore—slid out of bed, and ran barefoot down the short hall to the kitchen. My mother was drying dishes, and my father was reading the newspaper with a glass of brownish liquid in front of him.

"Mommy! Daddy!" I couldn't wait to tell them that I had it all figured out.

"Marcus, what are you doing out of bed?" Mom asked.

"Glinda the Good Witch is going to make me a girl!" I said in a rush, as proud as if I were telling them I got first prize in the county fair potato sack race.

But, for the millionth time in my short life, my parents didn't understand. My mother sucked in her breath and glanced at my father, who pushed out of his chair and crossed the room in two swift strides. He bent down, grabbed my pajamas by the collar, and shouted smelly words in my face. "Don't you *ever* let me hear you say that again. God made you a boy; do you hear me? A *boy*. Knock it off with the queer shit right now or you're going to get whipped."

A frightened sob caught in my throat, and in that instant Glinda's visit faded into nothing more than a stupid dream.

I didn't know what *queer* was, but I knew *shit* was a bad word. And the way my parents looked at each other, the way Dad got so mad so fast, his voice so angry and his face so red, made me think this wasn't the first time I'd done the "queer shit."

Glinda was wrong; I hadn't been good. And I wasn't going to be a girl.

I nodded shakily, and he released me.

His eyes landed on the doll in my grasp, and he yanked her away from me. "Enough of this. I don't know why you've let him keep this damn thing for so long," he said to my mother. Then he threw Annie in the trash and slammed the lid down over her.

"No!" I cried out.

"Go back to bed," he barked, and turned his back on me. I looked at my mother; her mouth was a thin line and her eyes were closed off. She picked up another dish to dry.

I ran back to my room, hid under the covers, and cried myself to sleep.

It's late; I'm going to try to get some rest. I'll write more soon. I love you.

Love,
Mom

To: acelove6@email.com

From: Mellie.Baker@email.com

June 21 (10:11 AM)

Subject: The Hogans

Dear Dara,

My parents—your grandparents—were very . . . limited people. Though they never left our small town, though they barely inter- acted with people who were in any way different from them, for some reason, they thought they knew everything. The beliefs they held, if that's what you can call them, were always dismissive, often cruel, and trumped absolutely everything else, including their actual relationships with actual people in their lives.

It always amazes me how people who have no concept of what gender even is can have such staunch opinions on it. And it wasn't just gender, mind you, that Jack and Mindy Hogan felt they were the authority on—it was all sorts of subjects that are life-or-death situations for other people, but have absolutely zero relevance to the personal experience of the people who are casting the judgment.

My parents knew I was "different," but they didn't understand how or why, and didn't give me the option to try to explain. They assumed I was a boy who liked boys. I guess it made sense. My natural movements and vocal cadence, my attraction toward things that were generally considered "girly," the way I couldn't relate to my brothers and only ever wanted to play with Joanna . . . To someone who has no concept of trans people or gender complexities, who only thinks in terms of sexuality, these traits could, I suppose, be considered "gay."

But not only did my parents misread who I was, they punished me for it. Took away Annie, spanked me, beat me, told me to "man up," punished me in every way they knew how. Because being gay wasn't okay, either.

Dara, I want you to know I'll always support you—no matter what. I know my resistance toward tennis has made you feel otherwise, and for that I will be forever regretful. But know that there's nothing you could ever say or do or feel that would make me love you any less.

Love,
Mom

Sam taps me on the shoulder, startling me away from the words on the screen. I turn to look at him.

After a half hour in the sweltering sun with the tow-truck guy, sweat beads his forehead and his hands are stained with soot. Did the guy make him *help*? "I don't know about you," he says, collapsing, exhausted, onto his stool, "but I'm ready for another round."

I click my phone off and slip it into my back pocket. "Right there with you."

....

"So, where can I drive you guys?" Marla asks when her shift ends at four p.m. She props an elbow up on the bar. This close, she looks a lot younger than I thought she was. The knowing look she's giving us now is the first sign we've had all day that she probably knows we're not twenty-one.

I glance at Sam. He's furiously tapping on his phone screen, wholly focused on winning some battle in the Viking game. A few stray fries lie abandoned on the plate in front of him, the only evidence of the cheeseburger deluxe he scarfed down a little while ago. I didn't eat anything else after the mozzarella sticks—they didn't make me feel too great in the end. Plus, it turns out beer is really filling. And I've had a lot of it. My mouth feels numb and swollen, and it's hard to stand without swaying. I think I'm done.

I was just starting to wonder if there were any cab companies that would be able to come get us, but Marla's offer is even better. "That's really . . . thanks, that's really nice of you," I say. My voice isn't quite right. It's like my words are on a delay, and by the time they reach my mouth from my brain they're all screwy. I concentrate harder. "Is there any hotels?" I don't think that was grammar.

Marla laughs. "Sure, there's a place not far from here. Come on."

The sun is brighter than I remember it being, and the fresh air makes me feel even woozier, like the little bubbles of beer in my bloodstream just got a swift kick of oxygen and expanded three sizes.

"Where're we going?" Sam asks, finally looking up from his screen as we reenter the land of daylight. His voice isn't right either.

"Marla's car. Hotel."

"Oh. 'Kay."

We stumble to my car to get our bags, then follow Marla to her Jeep, which is parked around back.

Sam and I are walking really close, and we keep bumping into each other accidentally. I don't know if I like being drunk anymore. I like being in control of my body. I like when my muscles and bones feel strong and they do exactly what I want them to do. I like when my arms and legs spring into action on a fraction of a second's notice to hit a ball that wasn't there an instant ago.

I give up trying to walk normally, and stay pressed to Sam. His body supports mine like a reinforcement beam in a house.

He crawls into the back seat of Marla's car, and, though Marla reaches over to open the passenger side door, I follow Sam into the back, not stopping until I'm practically in his lap.

"Guess I'm the chauffeur," Marla mutters under her breath.

I drape my leg over Sam's and rest my head on his shoulder. The soft cotton of his T-shirt, the scent of fried food mixed with a slight hint of the Philly hotel shampoo, the very *thereness* of him is a comfort.

"The hotel is a few minutes away," Marla says, pulling out onto the main road. "I've never stayed there, but it seems decent from the outside. I think we only have it because it's not too far from the airport."

"Sounds good," I say. I'm suddenly hyper aware of my jaw. I wiggle it around.

"So where are you guys from?" Marla asks.

"New York," Sam says, facing forward. "Small town you've never heard of."

She smiles in the rearview mirror. "Kindred spirits. So how'd you end up at the Outlaw?"

I open my mouth to say, "I just found out my mother is actually my father." But nothing comes out. I'm not sure if it's because there's still some logic working on autopilot somewhere inside me, or if it's just too much work to form a sentence right now. Either way, it hits me with all the pleasantness of a torn hamstring: People will be asking me some version of "how'd you end up here?" for the rest of my life. An ordinary question for a million situations. And it will always come back to Mellie and her lies.

"Flat tire," Sam says, and leaves it at that.

I tilt my head up and say *Thank you* with my eyes.

He smiles back. *You're welcome.*

The hotel is surprisingly tall and shiny for being in the middle of nowhere. We grab our bags, hug Marla good-bye, and enter the lobby through the automatic sliding glass doors. I link my arm through Sam's and focus on putting one foot in front of the other without tripping over my suitcase or veering off course. He seems to be trying to do the same thing, and by the time we get to the front desk, we're cracking up.

The woman behind the desk begins to chuckle as we approach. It's incredible how contagious laughter is. How total strangers can connect on the most basic level and share in something real without a single word of explanation.

"Welcome," she says, peering at us kindly through sensible, wire-framed glasses. Her name tag says *Sharon.* "Are you checking in?"

"Yes," I say, and make an effort to form my words in my head before speaking them. "One room, please. Just one night." That sounded okay. I think, anyway.

"Of course. The name on the reservation?"

"Oh." I blink. "We don't have a reservation." Sharon's expression falls a little. Crap. If this place is full, it's probably because there aren't very many other options around. Sam and I exchange a glance.

Sharon presses a few keys and studies her screen. "We *should* be able to find something for you . . ." She types for a moment more, and then says, "Yes. We have one room remaining." She sounds as relieved as I feel.

"How much is it?" I ask.

"It's three hundred and nine dollars per night, plus tax."

Yikes. "Um . . ." I have no job and a rapidly shrinking bank account balance. Especially after the unexpected mechanic bill. Who knew tires were so expensive?

"It's our honeymoon suite on the top floor," Sharon explains. She looks up, and her eyes land on the way I'm clinging to Sam. I didn't even realize I was still using him to hold me up. The corner of her mouth quirks up, and she gives us a knowing look. "Would that be all right? I assume you'll be needing only one bed?"

I freeze. Sneak a peek at Sam. His gaze is steadfastly pinned to the floor.

Over the course of the next second, every romantic comedy I've ever seen zips through my memory. Sharon seems like a romantic. Maybe she's got a partner at home who she's desperately in love with. Or maybe she's still waiting for her white knight. Either way . . . *we can use this.*

I pull Sam a little closer and snuggle in to him. "How'd you know?" I say. "We're actually on our honeymoon right now!"

Sam glares at me, a silent *What the hell are you doing?*

I just gaze lovingly back at him. "Right, baby?" I lift up onto my toes to kiss that look off his face. He jolts, but responds as close to immediately as possible. I only meant it to be a quick peck, but he pulls me to him, as if to say, *Whatever game you're playing, I can play too*. We're almost the same height like this, and our mouths line up perfectly. My lips part, and his tongue dances lightly with mine. I fist my hands in the fabric of his shirt and sigh. Why is tasting the insides of someone else's mouth so *good*?

I can't believe we're making out. Again. And right in front of poor Sharon.

God, he's good at this. I wonder if I'm good too. Or if I'm not as good as Sarah or the other girls he's kissed. I wonder if being good at kissing is an innate skill, or something that you get better at with practice. Or maybe it's both, like tennis.

Not a single thing about any of this is real, but it still takes some effort to pull away.

I put some distance between us, avoid Sam's eyes, and turn to Sharon. "Sorry about that! It's just . . . our parents didn't approve, so we ran away together. This is the first time we've been on our own and able to express our love in public."

"Checking things off our list, so to speak," Sam murmurs, throwing my own words back at me.

I yank his arm and tuck it in closer against my side. This has to work. But it won't if Sam doesn't keep his fat mouth shut.

"The honeymoon suite sounds perfect," I continue, "but we don't have a lot of money. The wedding and honeymoon were pretty impromptu, and we weren't able to save much first. We just kind of started driving."

Sharon smiles. "I understand. You can't be much older than, what? Twenty-one? Twenty-two?"

"Exactly," I say. I pinch Sam's back, and he nods.

"I met a man while I was traveling in Europe after college. Rodrigo . . ." Her eyes glaze over a bit, but she snaps out of it quickly. "Anyway, we didn't have a lot of money, either."

Okay, now I'm actually interested. I step forward and place a hand on the counter. "Are you still together?" I ask.

Sharon shakes her head. "I had to come back home because my sister was getting married. And I had this job waiting for me and student loans to repay, and once I was back here it was harder to justify giving up the job and using the last of my savings to get back on a plane with no guarantees of anything. Staying was safer." She shrugs sadly.

There are so many lost opportunities in the world. So many dreams obstructed because of *circumstances*. Sharon's story renews my certainty that I did the right thing in dropping everything to take this chance.

"It's never too late to take control of your life," I tell her gently.

She places a hand on mine. "Thank you." She sniffles. "I don't usually spill my guts to guests like this. There's just something about you two that makes me feel a little nostalgic." She takes her hand back and focuses on the computer once more. "Let me book you that room. I'll give it to you for the same rate as a junior double. One fifty-nine."

"Really?" I say. "That's so nice!" I look back at Sam. *See?* "Isn't that nice?"

He nods. "Very." But he doesn't seem as impressed as he should. I shake my head at him and turn back to Sharon. She swipes my card and prints our keys.

"Have a wonderful evening," she says.

"You too," Sam and I say in unison.

Sharon laughs joyfully at how in sync we are.

The elevator is empty, apart from us. Sam's back is against one wall, and mine is against the other. It's the most space that's been between us in hours.

Sam speaks first. "Really?"

I smile innocently. "What?"

He shakes his head. "I'm finding it hard to know what's real, what's beer-induced, and what's part of a scheme."

"Does it matter?"

"Yeah, I think it does."

"Come on, Sam, don't be such a party pooper."

"Are you serious? No one in the history of the world has ever been more game than I've been the past two days."

"So then why does there have to be an *implication* behind everything?"

He sighs, defeated. "You're right. There doesn't."

Yay. I win.

The elevator doors open and we lug our bags down the hall to room 1407. I slide the key card through the lock and the door clicks open.

Sam whistles.

It's different than our Philly hotel, that's for sure. The suite is huge, with a separate living room, an enormous king-sized bed, two TVs, and a freaking Jacuzzi the size of a small pool in the middle of the room with tiled steps leading up to it and a fake potted plant on the ledge. Floor-to-ceiling windows meet in one corner.

"So this is what a honeymoon suite in an off-brand hotel sort of near the airport looks like," I say, deadpan.

We burst out laughing.

I kick off my shoes, leap up onto the bed, and start jumping. "New tradition," I say in between jumps and gasps of air. "We must jump on every bed in every hotel room we encounter on this trip and rank them from best to worst."

Sam joins me on the vast expanse of white duvet. "This one is definitely the winner so far," he says.

"Soft but not too soft."

"Lots of space in which"—he jumps from one end of the bed to the other—"to make wide-spanned leaps!"

I take a big jump too, and my stomach takes a hard dip as I land. I cradle an arm against it and switch to smaller bounces. I'm probably still bloated from the beer. "And not squeaky at all!" I shout.

He laughs. "Probably because it's the honeymoon suite."

"What do you mean?"

"People must have sex in this bed all the time. The hotel doesn't want a squeaky bed keeping the people in the downstairs rooms up all night."

I stop jumping. "Right." The reality of the little fairy tale I told to Sharon is starting to hit me. Sam and I are going to have to share a bed tonight. And after all that kissing . . .

If I thought the Philly hotel room was intimate, tonight is going to be way scarier.

Sam slows his jumps and collapses to his knees too, shadowing my position.

There's about three feet of soft white bedding between us. Suddenly the bed, and the room as a whole, is feeling a lot smaller than it did a few minutes ago.

"So." I look around. It's still daylight outside. Too early to turn in for the night, even though sleep sounds glorious. "Want to watch TV?" I stretch to grab the remote off the nightstand.

But Sam's fingers graze lightly across the hand I'm using to prop myself up on the bed, and every cell in my body feels like it's fluttering in a warm breeze. I look at him.

"I know you don't want to talk," he whispers. "But can I just say one thing? While we're still drunk and it doesn't count?"

I nod.

"I really like kissing you."

I swallow. "I like kissing you too." Half of me means it one hundred percent. But I'm not as drunk as I was, and the other half is nagging, whispering a sequence of "buts" in my ear:

It doesn't mean anything.

Kissing someone doesn't mean you like *them.*

I needed to try it, and you were there, and it was fun.

So . . . friends, yeah?

But of course there's no reason to say any of it. I'm sure Sam's on the exact same page. If I said this stuff out loud, I'd come off as some conceited, inexperienced idiot who made a good thing weird and jumped to conclusions for absolutely no reason.

Still, he's right here, leaning forward slowly. In the bar, the kissing was part of the adventure. In the lobby downstairs, it was part of the charade. Here, I don't know what it is. Being alone with someone makes everything different. And there's a bed. And we're on it.

But I like the taste of him. Sometimes, I decide, things can be as simple as that.

Our mouths just barely brush each other's, and a breathy noise escapes me.

"Was that a good sigh or a bad sigh?" Sam whispers against my lips.

I open my eyes—I don't remember closing them. His face is as close to mine as it can be.

I hadn't meant to sigh at all. "Good sigh," I tell him.

He smiles—I can see it in his eyes and feel it against my mouth.

My stomach gurgles again.

Sam laughs. "Are you hungry?"

"No." We're still so, so close, and yet still not officially kissing.

But then my stomach makes another sound, and takes a bigger plunge than before, like I'm in a roller-coaster car that's just tipped down a tall slope.

I pull back quickly and freeze.

Worry works its way into the lines of his face. "Did I do something wrong?"

I manage a shallow shake of my head. "No, I—"

My stomach swoops again, and this time I know it's not pangs of desire. *Oh no.* I cover my mouth with my hand, and launch myself off the bed and around the corner to the bathroom. I throw the door open, and fall to my knees in front of the toilet, unable to spare the time to locate the light switch. A couple seconds later, everything inside me—which basically equates to a bucketload of amber-colored liquid and some half-digested mozzarella sticks—comes up. Luckily, my hair was already in a ponytail.

My body keeps heaving until I'm empty, and then a few more times after that for good measure.

I rest my clammy forehead against the side of the tub and flush the grossness away.

"Are you okay?" Sam asks. I don't turn around, but it sounds like he's standing near the doorway.

"Ughhhh" is my only response. I'm sure I look exactly as I feel.

He comes closer and crouches down beside me, placing a hand on my back. It's the complete opposite of the sexy, daring brush on my hand just minutes ago. This is the kind of touch my mom would use to check my forehead for a fever when I was a kid and not feeling well. Comforting. Gentle.

"I *knew* you drank too much," he said. "Or was it the mozzarella sticks?"

I groan. "Sam, please. Shut up."

"Sorry. Can I get you anything?"

I lift my head and push the sweaty strands of hair off my neck and forehead. "No. Thanks." I stand up on shaky legs. "I just want to go to bed."

I brush my teeth, and change into pajamas right in the middle of the bedroom. Sam turns away to give me privacy, but I feel the worst I've felt since I had food poisoning from a bad egg-white-and-spinach wrap when I was eleven, and modesty isn't high on my list of concerns right now.

Neither is the shared bed issue anymore, or the fact that I've spent the day making out with my best friend. Sam and I could be about to share a tiny twin bed for all I care. Nothing else is going to happen.

I pass out as soon as the side of my face presses into the squishy down pillow.

CHAPTER ELEVEN

My head feels like there's a pendulum inside, clanging into one side of my skull, then the other.

My midsection is sore, and my first thought is that I must have pushed myself too hard during a core workout. I sit up slowly. No, this is an unfamiliar kind of discomfort. Someone placed a glass of water on the table next to me. I take a sip. Much-needed moisture returns to my mouth, but the effort it takes to swallow doesn't do my head or stomach any favors.

With the next wave of pulsing inside my brain, my memory comes back, starting with the violent heaving over the toilet—*that's* why my stomach hurts—and rewinding from there.

Oh God. Sam.

I peek to my left. He's lying next to me, on his back, wide awake and staring at the ceiling.

"Hey," I say, rubbing my eyes. Even after the sip of water, my voice is scratchy.

"Hey." He doesn't look at me. After a pause, he asks, "You feeling all right?"

"Not at all. You?"

"Not really."

"Sorry," I say.

"It's my own fault."

There's a tension in the air that I've never experienced before with Sam. It's as if, even though the sky is bright with the morning sun, it's still yesterday in all the ways that matter. Everything that went down is still big and important and here in the room with us.

Why the hell did I kiss him?

That's not what he and I do. Our friendship was perfect. Well-oiled and comfortable and safe.

And now it's weird. I screwed up things with the one person I had left.

He's still refusing to look at me.

I can't lose Sam too. I have to fix this. But short of rewinding time and doing it all differently, I don't know how.

The pendulum makes it hard to think. But slowly, a nugget of an idea starts to form.

Maybe I can give *Sam* a redo? If he wants it. And if he takes it, that could make all of this a lot easier, for both of us.

I make a show of rubbing my forehead and groan, exaggerating the reaction to my very real headache. "So . . . what happened last night?"

That gets him to look at me. "What do you mean?" he asks warily.

"I think I drank too much."

"You *definitely* drank too much. We both did."

I bite my lip. "I remember being at the bar, and drinking a lot of beer . . ."

"And?" Sam sits up, watching me carefully now.

"And the rest is pretty . . . blank."

"Blank?"

Keep going, I urge myself. I blink back at him innocently. "Yeah. I'm sorry. What happened? Do you remember?"

He gapes at me, and I can almost see the machinery working in his head. If he doesn't tell me about the kiss, that means I was right to give him this out. And if he does, well, I guess we'll be back where we started when I woke up.

"Do you remember throwing up?" he asks.

"Um . . . no, I don't think so? When did I throw up?" I don't like this. I don't like lying.

But you have to try. You can't lose him.

"Last night. Do you remember coming to this hotel? Tricking the lady at the front desk into believing we're on our honeymoon?"

I laugh a little, and shake my head.

"Marla? Mozzarella sticks?"

I shake my head again. I'm not even good at this. He's going to see right through me.

No, he's not. Look at him.

He frowns. "You don't remember *anything* else?"

"No," I say. "I'm sorry, Sam. Is there anything else I should know?"

He sighs and seems to consider the question. After a long moment, he shakes his head and says, "No. Nothing important."

Two things happen inside me simultaneously then. One: utter relief. We don't have to talk about all the kissing. We can move on; let things return to neutral. Two: a bizarre, confusing disappointment. He's right—it's not important. It didn't mean anything. He's my best friend; nothing more, nothing less. I don't have the right to want him to think the kisses we shared were at all significant, when I don't. But still. It would have been nice.

I manage a smile. "Okay, good."

"Do me a favor and don't drink that much ever again, okay?" he asks, visibly loosening up now. "You clearly can't handle it."

"Not a problem."

I get up to shower, and once my skin and hair and teeth are clean and I've changed into fresh clothes, I feel a little better.

"Breakfast?" I ask Sam, coming back into the bedroom. He's sitting on top of the bunched-up blankets, fingers tapping away at his computer.

"We can get something on the road," he says. He closes his laptop. "I just need to shower, and then we can get out of here. Or did you want to go to the gym first?"

I shake my head. The thought of getting on a treadmill right now makes me want to puke all over again.

He gathers up some clothes, and skirts around me on his way to the bathroom.

While I wait, I open my email. If this morning has taught me anything, it's that avoiding one problem only causes more.

Two new emails from Mellie.

To: acelove6@email.com

From: Mellie.Baker@email.com

June 21 (6:29 PM)

Subject: Best friends

Dear Dara,

Apart from my family, there was one other person who was central to my childhood. Her name was Kristen Meyer. I fell in love with her in second grade. To this day, she's the only girl I've loved, besides Celeste.

(I know I told you I dated men back when I dated at all, and that's how you were conceived. The truth is, for me, it's only been women. But dating has been complicated. Of course I would have to disclose the fact I was trans to any serious partner, but revealing that information was just not an option. For reasons I promise I'll get to, it was crucial that no one know who I was, or where we came from.)

Kristen had the seat assigned next to mine at our classroom's big table. Her raven hair fell all the way to her waist, and I often had to stop myself from reaching out and stroking it. She wore patterned tights under corduroy skirts, and winter jackets with fluffy, faux fur collars. Her smile made my stomach flip.

But most of all, she was nice to me. She made me feel welcome. Important.

She lent me a pencil whenever I needed one, and sometimes let me use her special silvery one with the purple feathers at the top. We talked about the TV shows and music groups we both liked. We weren't a boy and a girl. We were equals.

The confusing part was that I both loved her and wanted to be her. And I didn't know if that was normal. So I kept my mouth shut on both counts, and for the next several years, Kristen remained my friend. My only friend.

Love,
Mom

I listen to the shower running on the other side of the wall. Sam. *My only friend.*

Just as I think it, his phone dings on the nightstand, the same noise it made yesterday in the car. I can't smother my curiosity. Oh-so-casually, I peek at the screen. It *is* a text message—and it's from Sarah.

I know you said you needed space, but . . . I think about you all the time. Can we please talk?

Immediately, my mouth dries up again. I polish off the glass of water.

It was Sarah who texted yesterday too, I'm positive of it. But why would he hide it from me? Is he thinking of getting back together with her?

I shake my head, even though there's no one in the room to see it. No way. He can't.

Why not? the little "other me" voice in my head counters. *You're not his girlfriend. You just lied to him, for the first time in your life, to make sure of that.*

The shower turns off. I walk to the window and force my attention back to my email. I have more important things to worry about. It doesn't matter whether Sam gets back together with Sarah or not. Anyway, he's probably not. He didn't even reply to her message yesterday.

To: acelove6@email.com

From: Mellie.Baker@email.com

June 22 (12:02 AM)

Subject: Stepping-stones

Dear Dara,

Most of my childhood is blurry, like rough waves sloshing together all around me, significant and unrelenting, but the drops indistinguishable from one another. There are a few moments, though, that stand out as defining, as if they're stepping-stones through the tide, the direct path to who I am today.

The Glinda dream was one.

Another was the day my mother caught me pretending.

Sometimes, when my father wasn't home and I knew my mother was busy with other things and wouldn't be looking for me, I would go into my room and pretend. That's what I called it, though *experimenting* is probably a better word.

Once I "borrowed" some of my mother's makeup from the bathroom cabinet and tried on lipstick and eye shadow. I forgot to bring a washcloth into my room to wash it off, though, so I ended up having to wipe it off using one of my undershirts. And then I hid the shirt at the bottom of the garbage can in the kitchen and prayed no one would notice because I couldn't risk Mom finding it in the laundry.

Another time I put on one of Joanna's sundresses over my pajamas, and curled up under my blankets, taking comfort in the feel of the pretty, flowing fabric around me. I fell asleep quickly that night.

But it was when I was naked from the waist down—eleven years old and standing in front of the mirror, attempting to see what I would look like without a penis—that my mother walked in.

"Marcus!" she screamed, rushing into the room and jerking my arm nearly out of the socket, so that my legs unclenched and all my parts sprang back to their original position. "My Lord, what are you doing to yourself?"

I turned away and quickly pulled on a pair of underpants. I could feel my face and neck burning bright red but I didn't know what to say, so I just hung my head and remained silent.

I had no idea what was going through my mother's mind in that moment. I still don't. All I know is that she called my father home early from work, and when he got there he yanked me from the place behind the bed where I was hiding, terrified, and beat me until I had no tears left and my bottom was covered in dark-purple bruises.

Another stepping-stone, a much happier one, was the day I found out you didn't have to be stuck with what you were born with.

"Have you ever known anyone who changed their name?" Kristen asked me one Saturday afternoon when we were about thirteen. We were at the diner getting smoothies.

"Like a nickname?"

"No, like changed their name completely."

"Like when a woman gets married and changes her last name to her husband's?"

Kristen shook her head. "Michelle decided she's changing her first name." Michelle was Kristen's older sister. She was away at college studying to be an engineer, so I'd never met her, but Kristen talked about her all the time. I think she wished they were closer, but that would have been hard, considering there were several years and hundreds of miles between them.

"She's changing it to what?" I asked. I'd never heard of such a thing, but I was intrigued.

"Corinne." Kristen screwed up her face a little when she said the name, like it tasted bad. "She said she's always hated the name Michelle and thinks Corinne fits her much better."

I didn't understand. Corinne was a pretty name, but it didn't sound anything even close to Michelle. "So you're supposed to call her Corinne now?" I asked.

"Apparently."

"Like . . . all the time?"

Kristen fiddled with her straw wrapper. "Yup. Like forever. She's having it changed *legally*. She said it's been a lot of paperwork, but worth it. And most of her friends and teachers at school already know her by the name Corinne so it's just us who will have to get used to the switch."

I took a sip of my smoothie, trying to make sense of my thoughts, which were suddenly shooting around like a pinball. I'd never heard of anyone changing their identity like that before. Michelle would be Corinne from now on, and that would be that.

"Do you think it will be hard to get used to?" I asked.

"Um, *yes*! She's been Michelle my whole life. It's not just a name; it's *who she is*. I don't know how to just switch who she is in my brain."

"But you're going to try?"

Kristen shrugged. "I have to, right?"

"I guess. Maybe you'll get used to it sooner than you think."

"Yeah, maybe." She sighed, resigned to it already.

What if your identity doesn't have to be set in stone? I wondered. *Maybe "who she is" isn't Michelle? Maybe, inside, she's been Corinne all along?*

If the government had an entire system in place for you to change your first name if you wanted to, this stuff must happen at least sort of frequently. And Corinne's family was going to try to get on board, even though it was hard for them. So people's minds could adjust too, it seemed. Eventually.

Apparently, things like this were possible.

I tucked that information in the back of my mind. Something told me I'd need it someday.

Love,
Mom

Without looking, I click off the phone. I stare out the hotel room window, only vaguely watching the man in the white hat zigzag the riding lawn mower across the lawn fourteen stories below.

I picture Mellie sitting at the kitchen table in her leggings and slippers, her hair back in a braid, typing on her phone or laptop. I bet she has dark circles under her eyes. She always gets them when she's tired or stressed. She's probably not eating much, either.

I've never gone a whole day without talking to her. And now we're at nearly three times that.

My thumbs itch to type a response.

But I can't.

In some ways, the person who wrote those emails sounds like my mother, like the person I knew. Her voice, her phrasing. She's a true writer. Not in a past life—in this one. But the story she's telling is further proof that she's not *her* anymore. This is a person who knows how to bare her soul. And that is something Mellie Baker never knew how to do.

CHAPTER TWELVE

Sharon is at the front desk again today. Her face lights up as we approach. "Did you enjoy your stay?" she asks.

"Yes, very much. Thank you," I say.

"Isn't that suite romantic?" She winks.

I glance at Sam. He's on his phone. I can't make out what he's writing, but Sarah's name is at the top of the screen. My stomach aches in its emptiness.

"Very," I say, turning back to Sharon with a forced smile.

"He's a shy one, isn't he?" she whispers, nodding in Sam's direction.

"Not when you get to know him."

We check out, and I'm about to ask Sharon to call us a cab to bring us back to our car when I remember I'm not supposed to know about that.

"Are we parked outside, Sam?" I say quietly, hoping I don't sound too obvious.

He looks up. "Oh. No, we got a ride here. I guess we'll need to call a taxi." *Success.*

"Can you help us with that?" I ask Sharon.

"Of course!" She seems a little confused, but arranges for the cab, and we wait out front for it to arrive.

"Who were you texting?" I ask Sam, trying to seem barely interested.

He shrugs. "Sarah." As soon as he says it, I realize I was hoping he'd lie. At least then we'd be even.

"Oh. What's going on with—"

"So we're six and a half hours from Charleston," he says quickly, studying the map on his phone. "We'll make a quick stop for breakfast and gas, and then drive straight through. Sound good?"

I sigh. "Sure."

The cab drops us off at the Outlaw. The parking lot is emptier this morning. We toss our bags in my car, and Sam takes the driver's seat this time. My head is still pounding, and my rootless thoughts aren't helping. I could use a break from driving.

The lack of easy conversation as we drive is conspicuous. Almost oppressive. I thought letting him off the hook with the whole kissing thing would allow us to go back to normal. I remember what happened yesterday, and he obviously remembers what happened yesterday, but he doesn't *know* that I remember. So . . . shouldn't that allow us a reset? Why are things still strained? Why can't we just act like we always do?

The email from Mellie about Kristen plagues me. Kristen was her Sam. I'm glad—everyone should have a Sam. I just hope I haven't ruined things with mine.

We stop at a diner around eleven to get food. Sam takes a picture of our plates. His is piled high with pancakes, bacon, and a cinnamon roll. Hangover food, he calls it. Mine has a veggie egg-white omelet with whole-grain toast, no cheese, no butter. I think I'm done with junk food for a while. The omelet is hot and delicious. I feel myself getting stronger with every bite.

Just as in the car, we don't talk much over breakfast. Sam plays his Viking game and texts with Sarah some more; I practice my introduction to the Pembrokes in my head. The clank of silverware against our plates is the only noise at our table.

After using the bathroom and filling the tank, we're on the road again.

I-95 is long, the colors dull. The long strips of grass on the sides of the road have been burned by the Southern summer sun.

The landscape is different, but the closer we get to the farm, the more I'm starting to feel like I did nearing the big stone house in Cherry Hill. In two hours, I'll be knocking on my grandparents' front door.

There are always some nerves at tennis tournaments and qualifiers, but I know what to expect at those. I know how the game is played; I know I have skill; I know I've worked hard. I know that at the end of the match, there will be one winner and one loser. But this could go any of a million ways.

They've been looking for you, I tell myself. *They're going to be so happy to see you.*

My muscles are tight. Now I'm regretting not making use of the hotel gym this morning. I reach into the back seat, pull a tennis ball from my bag, and squeeze it tightly in my right hand, engaging my palm and finger muscles.

We pass an abandoned factory. It's set back from the highway, a squat, gray building with broken windows and an overgrown parking lot. Suddenly, I know what I need to do.

"Pull over."

Sam is jolted out of whatever thought process he was drifting in. "What?"

"Pull over!" I say, louder. The factory is getting farther behind. "Right here!"

He takes his foot off the gas, brings the car to a stop on the right shoulder, and flips his hazards on. "What's wrong? Are you going to be sick again?"

I shake my head, and reach into the back seat for my tennis bag.

"Have you changed your mind about going to Charleston?"

"No. I just need a few minutes." I step out of the car, and the rush and wind of the passing cars shudder through me. I sling my bag over my shoulder and head across the overgrown, sun-bleached field back in the direction of the old building. The day is hot, the sun brutal. But it makes me feel grounded. As if this patch of earth and I are all that exist. I stretch my arms and roll my neck and shoulders as I walk, gripping on to the ball.

I head directly to the north side of the building, past the rusted loading-dock doors, to the place I spotted as we were driving. There's a nearly blank wall here—no windows, no doors, just a large graffiti tag of the word *Believe*—and a good expanse of cracked and weed-ridden but more-than-sufficient pavement. It's a lot more serene this far inland from the highway.

I pull a racquet from my bag and bounce the ball. So many times I hated that I had to practice alone on the racquetball courts, wishing I could afford to play on a real court more than twice a week. Now I'm grateful for the familiarity and comfort of playing against a wall.

My body seems to act on its own, eager to get the chance to do what it does best. Before I fully make the decision to begin, the racquet meets the ball in a crisp forehand stroke.

The ball returns and I do it again. And again.

My anxiety fades. My mind quiets. Effort and exhaustion thrum pleasantly through my flesh. Exercising—training—is the one thing that never lets me down. It's the one thing that's the same everywhere, any time, no matter what else is going on. It's the one way I know how to stay centered.

Some part of my mind registers Sam pulling the car around the building and parking about fifteen yards off to my left. I don't look. I hit the ball again, hard, falling more securely into the most beautiful rhythm in the world, a never-ending volley.

I know I told Sam I only needed a few minutes, but it turns out I need more than that. They say it takes ten thousand hours of practicing something to become an expert. I check one more hour off that goal at this almost-too-perfect place.

Even though I can't seem to trust my mind lately, my body never fails me. I know when I'm done, sure as I know my left foot from my right.

I let the ball whiz past me and drop to the pavement, pack my gear up, and toss it in the back seat. I grab my hairbrush and deodorant out of my bag. I probably shouldn't have gone and gotten myself all gross before arriving at my grandparents', but . . . I really needed that.

"We still have that bottle of water?" I say, sliding into my seat. It feels more comfortable now. I wonder if this is how other people feel after a really good therapy session.

"Yeah." Sam reaches into the compartment in his door and hands the water to me. It's warm, but I don't mind. "You okay?" he says after I polish off the last drop.

"Better now."

"Ready to get back on the road?" He's speaking cautiously, like he's trying to prepare for another outburst of unpredictability.

"Yes. Thank you," I add.

He nods and pulls back onto the highway. I turn the AC way up and aim the vents toward me to dry the sweat. Then I set about fixing my hair and making myself as presentable as possible.

We take the exit just before Charleston proper and follow the GPS's directions for another fifteen minutes down narrow side roads shaded by canopies of green. I turn off the AC and open my window—the air is fragrant with hay, fresh-cut grass, sunflowers, and cow manure. We make another turn, this time onto a worn gravel road, and the trees open up to reveal blankets of farmland. Large, round bales of hay are scattered over gently rolling hillsides. Horses graze; sheep with short coats sunbathe.

And then there it is. The house. It looks just like it did in the photo. Inviting, well-kept, and cushioned by sprawling farmland on all sides.

I'd love to know what made the Pembrokes decide to move here. Not that it's not beautiful and incredibly peaceful. Or that it doesn't show off their wealth. It's just so different from that fancy mansion in Cherry Hill.

We pull up to the house, but can't park in the driveway because it's already filled with cars, trucks, and trailers. I wonder if they all belong to the Pembrokes or if some of them belong to visitors or farm staff.

Sam turns off the car, and I get out and stretch. The air is humid, but we're parked under the shade of a large tree so it's not too hot. I didn't put the dress back on, but at least I don't feel quite as out of place in my tank top, leggings, and tennis shoes here as I would have at the Cherry Hill house.

We leave all our stuff in the car and wordlessly walk side by side across the grass toward the porch. I'm glad Sam's here, regardless of the subtle shifts between us that haven't managed to right themselves just yet.

Just then the screen door opens and a guy comes out. He's wearing cargo shorts, sneakers, and a gray T-shirt that says, *Animals are people too*. His dark-blond hair is pulled back into a sloppy bun at the nape of his neck, and he has the kind of smile that makes you wonder how any one person could have possibly lucked out with such an exquisite arrangement of DNA.

The back of my neck warms when I realize I probably shouldn't be checking him out—we could be *related*.

"Hello," he says, apparently as surprised to have found us out here as I am to be faced with a guy around my age instead of my grandparents.

"Um. Hi. Are William and Ruth at home?"

It takes a moment for the names to register. "Oh! Our gracious benefactors. No, they're not here right now."

"Do you know when they'll be back?"

He shakes his head. "They actually don't spend much time here. Their main house is on Hilton Head Island, I think."

Hilton Head? Google said nothing about that! They're supposed to be *here.*

For the second time, I'm standing outside a house that's supposed to be inhabited by the Pembrokes, but isn't. Embarrassing tears prickle my eyes, and I look down. "I can't believe this," I mutter. There's a rock at my feet. I kick it as hard as I can, and it plunks into the grass several yards away.

Sam speaks up. "Do you know how we can contact them? We've come a really long way."

"Sure, man. I can get you their number." He jerks a thumb back at the house. "Actually, their daughter is here. Maybe you'd want to talk to her?"

My head snaps up. "Daughter?"

He nods. "Catherine. She's the best. She's the reason we're all here, actually."

Celeste's sister. "Yes!" I say, my words nearly stumbling over his. "I'd love to talk to her!" It's not the family reunion I was expecting, but it's something. A start.

The guy waves a hand, indicating we should follow him into the house. I give Sam an anxious smile. He raises his eyebrows and gestures for me to go first, then follows the two of us inside. Two rambunctious yellow dogs scamper over to us, tails wagging and drool flying.

"This is Vincent and Walt," the guy tells us, dropping to his knees and rubbing vigorously behind their ears. The dogs flop over and expose their bellies. I give them both a pat.

The interior of the house is incredible. Open floor plan, wood paneling, and exposed rafters holding up the vaulted ceiling. My gaze drifts like a bee, touching briefly on the baby grand piano in a corner, the matching floral pattern of the upholstery, the hand-woven throw rugs strategically scattered over the shining wood floors.

The guy leads the way to a room in the back of the house with tall windows overlooking the landscape. There's a desk and computer and couch, and papers everywhere. An office.

"You can wait in here," he says. "Catherine's out back. I'll go get her."

Outside, a few workers are busy hammering together a wooden fence near the barn. Chickens wander around freely, pecking at the ground, and a goat stands by, overseeing the action. I hear a door swing shut, and Sam and I watch as the guy crosses the grass to a large pen occupied by several enormous pigs and speaks to a woman with cropped blonde hair. She nods, removes her gloves, and walks toward the house.

"Are you ready?" Sam asks.

An anticipatory shiver rolls over my skin. "As I'll ever be."

When she enters the room, my heart throws itself against my rib cage. She looks so much like the pictures of Celeste, only older, and with a slightly larger nose and wider-set eyes. She's not wearing makeup, but her face is sun-kissed and glowing. I wonder if the little lines around her eyes are indications of a life of laughter or sadness.

"Sorry to make you wait," she says. "It's been mayhem around here today." She blinks at Sam and me, as if really seeing us for the first time. "How may I help you?"

"Hi," I say. My mouth has gone dry, and I take a second to swallow. "My name is Dara Baker. Or you might know me as Dara Hogan. I think . . . I mean, I know . . . um . . . my birth mother was Celeste Pembroke?"

Her entire face goes slack, and she places a hand on the wall to steady herself. "Dara? Oh my God, is that really you?" Her voice is soft, as if she's afraid I'm a hologram and if she disrupts the energy in the room too much I'll shimmer away.

I nod.

Another beat goes by, and then, so fast it forces a startled gasp from my lungs, she throws her arms around me. Her embrace is strong, and she pins me against her so tightly it's a challenge to breathe. I stand there, trying my hardest to be in the moment, to feel her warmth and her joy, to soak up the emotional impact of what's happening. But the only adults I've ever been hugged by are Mom and Bob. Catherine's hug is unfamiliar. Awkward. Which makes sense; she's essentially a stranger. I guess I just thought, when coming face-to-face with my flesh and blood, everything would click into place in an obvious way. Definitive. Undeniable.

It feels like entire minutes pass before she steps back.

"I can't believe it," she whispers finally, her eyes roving over my face. She chews the corner of her bottom lip. "How are you here?"

I glance at Sam, overwhelmed. I don't know what to say. I should have planned this out better.

"Hi, I'm Sam, Dara's friend," Sam says, stepping up and holding out his hand. "We drove here together from New York. We thought this was where your parents lived, actually."

Catherine shakes it. "So nice to meet you, Sam. And yes, this is my parents' farm. They let us use it for our organization." She gestures to the couch. "Come, sit. We have so much to talk about. Would you like something to drink?"

"Oh. Um, no, that's okay," I say.

Catherine grabs my hand and holds it fast with both of hers. "You know, you aren't an easy woman to find." Her face is flush with emotion.

I suck in a breath. "You've been looking for me?"

She seems appalled that I'd even ask that. "Dara, we looked for you nonstop for *years*."

My heart pangs. *I knew it.*

"And even after the trail went cold, we kept searching, doing checks at least once a year on person-finder databases. What did you say your last name is?"

"Baker."

She nods slowly, taking that in. "And you must be, what, eighteen now?"

"Yes. I just graduated from high school."

"Wow . . ." She trails off, then seems to shake off whatever sadness had been about to descend. "Please, please, tell me everything! Where have you been? What has your life been like? What brought you here now?"

I glance at Sam again. I need to know, now that the moment is here, after all the buildup, that it really is okay to merge these two worlds.

He gives me an encouraging smile, as if to say, *Go ahead. This is what we're here for, isn't it?* It's the first smile I've seen from him all day.

But I don't know. Wouldn't it be better to ease into it? Besides, I have so many questions of my own. "I noticed you biting your lower lip," I say, testing the waters. "Do you do that a lot?"

Catherine chuckles and looks heavenward. "It's my worst habit. Celeste used to do it too. Drove our mother crazy." She tilts her head. "Why do you ask?"

"Because I do the same thing. Don't I, Sam?"

He nods. "All the time."

Catherine clasps her hands together in glee. "Proof that you're a Pembroke girl through and through!"

"It isn't one of my mom's habits, so I always did wonder if I got it from the other side of the family."

Her smile cracks. "What do you mean, your mom?"

Ugh. So much for delaying the inevitable.

"Yeah, um . . . I have a lot to tell you."

Catherine listens, silent as the country air, as I begin the story.

CHAPTER THIRTEEN

Turns out Catherine isn't all that surprised about Marcus being Mellie now. She says she always suspected "he" would go that route, after her parents told her what he had told them about his feelings.

I know Mom said she told the Pembrokes about her plan to transition seventeen years ago, but it hurts all over again, getting the confirmation from Catherine. I *hate* that she told them and didn't tell me.

"My parents always refused to consider that he would have transitioned fully," Catherine says. "I think that was part of why they weren't able to track you down. They didn't understand this stuff. They thought Marcus was having an extreme reaction to losing Celeste. They thought he was having a mental breakdown."

I wonder if those were the "bad things" they said to Mellie when she came out to them.

"I can't believe he didn't tell *you*, though." She shakes her head in disbelief.

"Me neither," I mumble.

It doesn't escape me how she keeps saying "he," even though she says she's the one in the family who understands trans issues. I'm not an expert on the subject, but even I know you're supposed to use the pronoun the person uses for themselves. But on the other hand, Catherine doesn't owe Mellie anything. To Catherine, Celeste is, and will always be, my mother. The person she knew as

Marcus is my father. I can't imagine the strife Mellie taking me away must have put the family through. All things considered, I guess I can't blame her for her word choice. I'd be pissed too. I *am* pissed too.

"You poor thing," she says, reaching her arms around me again. Since she arrived in this office, she's barely broken a physical connection with me. Hugs, hand-holding, fingertips on arms. I don't know how to feel about it. I want to tell her it's okay; I promise I won't disappear for another two decades. "All this time, not knowing we were out here. Not knowing about your real mother." She shakes her head, and her voice has an edge to it now. "I'll never forgive him for taking you away from us."

I'm right there with her on this one. "We deserved a chance to be each other's family." I get a little misty as I say it, and Sam, who's been sitting there quietly, hands me a tissue. I sit up and wipe my eyes and nose.

"You're absolutely right about that." She gives me a questioning look. "Should we call my parents now?"

I suck in a breath and nod eagerly.

She lifts her office phone and dials. I wring my hands, wishing I had that tennis ball to occupy them. But after a few seconds Catherine shakes her head and whispers, "Voicemail."

Of course. Because I haven't been forced to wait long enough.

"Mom, Dad, call me as soon as you get this." There's a hint of teasing in her tone, like someone giving the birthday girl a hint about a surprise party. "It's important." She hangs up, then explains, "They're retired now, and they take their boat out most days, which means they're often out of cell range. But they'll call back tonight."

Boat? On top of this incredible farm and what is surely a state-of-the-art home in Hilton Head? I add a long, glistening sailboat with silk pashminas, chilled bottles of champagne, and platters of fresh fruit to the composite in my head.

"Okay," I say. "Thank you."

"No, Dara. Thank *you*. For coming to find us. It's been hard without Celeste here, but it's been even harder knowing you were out there somewhere but we couldn't talk to you or watch you grow up." She claps her hands on her thighs and stands up, full of purpose. "Now. You must be hungry after your journey. Shall we have some lunch?"

The three of us go to the kitchen, where there's a ton of food spread out on the breakfast bar. Sandwich bread, hummus, all different kinds of vegetables, olives, chips, several different salads, fruit. I'm impressed by how healthy it all is.

Handsome Man-bun Guy is in the middle of making himself a wrap. He puts his plate down and holds his hand out to me. "I'm Matt. I'm one of the staff members here."

"Dara." His grip is somehow soft, despite his rough, farmworker skin. I feel my cheeks flush. He shakes Sam's hand too, and Sam begins constructing a sandwich.

"It's nice to officially meet you, Dara," Matt says with a flirty grin as I select a carrot stick and take a bite. We were in that office for a long time, and I'm suddenly starving. It probably helps that I'm no longer hungover and the nerves from the drive are mostly gone now.

Now that I know that Matt just works here, and we're not related, I'm feeling better about the fact that I seem physically unable to take my eyes off him.

Catherine points to something behind me. I turn to find a group of people, none of them much older than Sam and me, sitting around a table with plates of food in front of them. I didn't even notice them when we came in. "That's Gabby, Meadow, Ezra, and Jane."

I immediately feel more comfortable knowing the spread of food isn't only for us. This may be my grandparents' house, but I'm still a guest.

"Guys, this is Dara and Sam. Dara is my niece."

Matt quirks an eyebrow at me. "But you never met before today?" he asks.

I shake my head. "Long story."

He doesn't ask anything else, though he does seem curious. "Well, like I said, Catherine is the best. You couldn't have gotten a better person for an aunt."

"I hope to learn more about her." *And Celeste too.* I say hi to everyone at the table.

They wave. It's obvious they're paired off. Gabby, a freckled white girl with a pierced eyebrow, is helping Meadow, a beautiful Asian girl with two long braids, remove a splinter from her palm. She succeeds, then kisses the spot. Jane, a brown-skinned girl with bright eyes and short hair, has one leg draped over tall, fair, skinny Ezra's lap. They're all tanned, and their clothes are covered in dirt.

I help myself to some food and join the group. They smell of hard work and sweat. The wooden table is flanked by two long benches, and large enough for all of us, plus everyone else still outside and probably a couple of the goats too. Walt and Vincent sit on the floor, patiently waiting for scraps. Everything about this kitchen is welcoming, including the people in it. I always pictured farms being run by young boys who milk the cows before the sun comes up and old bearded men in overalls. These people are nothing like that.

"Where are you guys from?" Ezra asks.

"New York," I say. "Upstate; not New York City."

"Are you in college?"

"No, we just graduated from high school. Sam's going to college in the fall, though." Sam's mouth is full, but he raises his sandwich in a toast. "How about you all?"

"We go to NYU," Gabby says, indicating herself and Meadow. "And they"—she points at Ezra and Jane—"go to Clemson. We're all on summer break right now."

"Oh, I know Clemson," I say. "Good sports school."

"So we've heard," Ezra says with a goofy shrug.

Jane laughs. "Yeah, we don't really follow that stuff. Aren't college sports *so* bizarre? The way the football and basketball games are nationally televised and how bookies run betting rings and all that. Why do grown-ass adults get so obsessed about a bunch of *kids* playing a game for no pay at a place where they're supposed to be getting an education? It's entirely unethical, if you ask me."

"I see your point," I say after swallowing a spoonful of bean salad. "I've played sports my whole life, but it's always been a personal goal kind of thing. There wasn't any pressure from the outside." *No pressure, but also no support.*

163

"What sports do you play?" Matt asks. We're sitting side by side, and even though there's plenty of room on the bench, his leg is only an inch from mine. He's taller than I am, more muscular, and I like the way our bodies relate to each other's. I feel dainty next to him, feminine, not like a big, strong athlete.

"Tennis. I'm beginning my pro career this year, actually."

Every single person at the table looks up from their food. I can't help the little gleam of pride I feel at knowing I've impressed them.

"That's wonderful, Dara!" Catherine says. "I guess your father passed down that particular passion to you."

"No, I . . ." I'm not sure how much to explain. Do I want all these strangers knowing why I'm here? Not that it's a secret; it's just sort of . . . personal. "I came to it on my own, actually." But I take this as an opportunity to get one of my questions in. "Did Celeste ever play any sports?" I ask Catherine.

She thinks about that. "I don't think so. She ran a lot, for exercise. But no team sports. We were never really a sports family, now that I think about it."

"I do yoga," Meadow says.

"That's the understatement of the year," Gabby says. "She's *obsessed* with yoga."

"I played soccer when I was a little kid," Matt says, "but that's about it."

I switch my attention back to him. "You look good, though. I mean, like you're in shape. I mean—" I clamp my mouth shut, and immediately want to sink beneath the table and die.

Everyone laughs. Except Sam. His gaze lands on the space—or lack of it—between me and Matt, then travels up to Matt's face and over to me. His lips press together.

"We know what you mean," Jane says, pushing her short hair back from her eyes. "Everyone reacts that way to Matt when they first meet him. Even us—and three out of the five of us don't even like guys."

Ezra, Meadow, and Gabby exchange a look and a shrug. "What can I say, the boy is pretty," Ezra says.

"Speak for yourselves!" Catherine says. "I'm his boss *and* old enough to be his mother."

The word catches me in its net. *Mother. Is* Catherine a mother? Could I have first cousins out there? I want to ask, but everyone's laughing again, so I join in instead.

Matt doesn't seem embarrassed. "Thanks. I do a lot of manual labor, so that's how I get my exercise."

"Right. The farm." The image of him with his shirt off, riding a horse or milking a cow, floods my vision and I grow even warmer. I don't think I've ever had this kind of reaction to another person before, unless you count the massive crush I developed on John Boyega after seeing *The Force Awakens.* I clear my throat. "Do you work here all year round?"

"Yup. I decided to follow my passion instead of going to college too." He smiles, and I know it's just for me.

"But it's actually not a farm," Catherine says. "Not in the traditional sense, anyway. We're in the process of turning the property into a farm *sanctuary.*"

"What's a farm sanctuary?" Sam asks. Look at that. He remembered he has a voice. I can't tell if he's being so quiet because this is my thing and he doesn't want to get in the middle of it, or if he's still weird because of last night.

"We work for an organization called DFA. Dignity for Farm Animals. We help save and rehabilitate abused farm animals raised for meat and dairy. There are two other locations, in Georgia and Arkansas. This one is the newest, though; we're just getting it off the ground."

"That's incredible," I say. Now the absence of meat and cheese at lunch makes a lot of sense. "Did William and Ruth buy the farm for that reason?"

"No." Catherine shrugs. "They actually thought they were going to retire here. But after about a year they realized they'd rather live closer to the water, and other people their age. They were going to sell the land, but I convinced them to sign it over to me. I'd been working with DFA for a while and was ready to take the next step."

"And we're so glad she did," Matt says.

"So they just *gave* you the farm? That's amazing."

"No one could ever accuse my parents of not being generous," Catherine says.

They're generous. That fits in with my picture too.

"You got here just in time for the real action," Meadow says. "This morning we intercepted a factory farm truck on its way to a slaughterhouse. And now we're the proud parents of twenty nine-hundred-pound pigs."

"Whoa," I say. Those must have been the pigs we saw through the window. I knew they were big, but *nine hundred pounds*? "How did you get the people on the truck to give them to you?"

"We had to buy them," Catherine says. "But that's okay. We do a lot of these, and often no amount of money or protesting or getting arrested is enough to save the individuals on board."

"Getting arrested?" Sam asks.

"Well, it depends on the level of assholery of the security guards and truck drivers," Matt says. "If they call the police, that's when things get dicey. The cops can't arrest us for protesting peacefully, and they know it, but sometimes they're in the pockets of the slaughterhouse owners, and they find excuses to bring us in anyway."

Sam whistles. "That's crazy."

"Yeah, but it's worth it," Gabby says, and they all nod in agreement.

"Did you and Celeste have pets growing up?" I ask Catherine. I don't care if I'm hogging the conversation. I want to know everything.

"We had two hamsters named Trixie and Pixie," she says. "But we never had any dogs or cats because Celeste was allergic."

"She was?" As far as I know, I'm not allergic to anything.

Catherine nods, then smiles. "I always resented her for it. I wanted a dog so badly; I've always loved animals. I like to think she would be proud of the work I'm doing now." She calls Walt and Vincent over and feeds them each a potato chip. "Good boys."

"Do you think Ruth and William will be calling back soon?" I ask, trying not to sound too impatient and failing completely. So far, this family is everything I'd hoped they'd be and more, and I can't wait to be part of it. But I feel like it won't be official until I meet my grandparents.

Catherine reaches across the corner of the table and cups my cheek in her hand. I wonder if Celeste would have done something similar if she'd lived long enough to get the chance to be my mother. "I know you're anxious, sweetie. This reunion has been a long time coming. I suspect they'll get my message tonight, and leave for the farm first thing in the morning. They're not the kind of people who like to sit around waiting—they like to take action." She smirks, the kind of knowing look that only a daughter who knows her parents very well could make. "In the meantime"—she looks out the back window—"we have to be getting back to work. Do you want to come help?"

"Really?"

"Sure."

"Um, okay? I don't think I've ever seen a pig in real life before."

"Oh my God, they're so sweet!" Jane says. "You're going to love them."

"What will we be doing?"

"The vet is out back checking everyone out right now, and after each pig is given a clean bill of health, we're giving them baths to wash off the factory-farm smell. Plus we have more hay beds to make, food to chop up, and fences to build."

Sam clears his throat. "Dara, can I speak with you for a minute, please? Privately?"

I place my napkin on my empty plate. "Yeah." We leave the kitchen and walk through rooms until we're out of earshot. "What's up?"

"You're really going to go out there with them?"

"Why not? They need help."

"Yeah, but you don't know anything about working with animals—especially not ones that can crush you with a single step. What if you get hurt? What about tennis?"

That brings me up short. But I regroup and lift my chin. "I'll be careful."

He watches me carefully. "Since when do you care about animals, anyway?"

"Since today." I cross my arms.

"Says the girl who practically had an orgasm over a Philly cheesesteak."

His words have me flashing back to the moments when I caught him staring at me with lust in his eyes as I moaned with pleasure—first over the cheesesteak and then later with the mozzarella stick. And those images bring me right back to the kisses we shared. But it was a drunken mistake, that's all. An ill-advised blip in our otherwise stable friendship.

Yeah, today's felt real stable, taunts the other half of me.

"Well," I say defiantly, "maybe I'm changing my ways."

"Is this sudden drive for activism because of *her* . . . or because of *him*?"

My eyes narrow. "Who?"

"Mr. Movie Star over there, the one who had you practically sitting in his lap."

"I have no idea what you're talking about."

Sam searches my face as if he's trying to find a button that, if pushed, would make me start making sense to him again. "I'm worried about you," he says finally.

Never before have such kind words felt like such an insult. "Why?"

"This is a *lot* to be dealing with, Dara. Look where we are right now!"

"I *know*, Sam."

He blows out a breath, and it lifts his hair off his forehead. "We just got here. You just met these people. And now you're going to follow them into a pigpen with absolutely zero training and hope for the best?"

Why can't he just be happy for me?

"You said last night you would trust that I know what I'm doing." My words are sharp.

He freezes. "You remember that?"

Oh no. My mind starts to backpedal, but not fast enough. I have to say something. "Um . . . yeah?"

"So you do remember some things." His face has gone pale.

"Not a lot. Just a few fragments here and there." I shrug as if it's nothing, as if most of the night is still blank.

"What else do you remember?" he presses.

I force myself to look directly at him. "Nothing big."

His eyes say so much, I can almost read his thoughts: his panic that I remember we spent half the day making out with each other, his uncertainty about what I feel about it all, his worry that I might be lying about not remembering and that I know that he knows. My eyes, on the other hand, are hopefully saying nothing.

I lied so things would stop being awkward, and look where that got us. Fighting in a room filled with vegetarian cookbooks.

He takes a breath and opens his mouth to say something, but I jump in ahead of him. "It doesn't have anything to do with Matt," I say quickly, truthfully. "It's Catherine. This is her life. And she's inviting me to be a part of it." Sam has to know how huge this is for me. Until now, my only family was Mellie, and she never invited me to be a part of anything.

That does it. The fight goes out of him. "Fine. *Fine.*" He throws his hands up in acquiescence.

"Thank you." I hug him, and he squeezes me back. It's the first sign that the unease following us around since this morning might not be permanent. "Are you going to come with? You don't have to if you don't want to . . ."

"I've stuck with you this long, haven't I?" he says with a sigh. "Why stop now?"

Together, we go back to the kitchen, where they've started to clean up.

"All right," I say, "let's go meet some pigs!"

CHAPTER FOURTEEN

"I hope you guys don't mind sharing a room," Catherine says, leading Sam and me upstairs. She insisted on carrying my suitcase, so all I have is my tennis bag slung over my shoulder. "Normally we'd have plenty of extra space, but we've got more volunteers here than usual right now because of the new arrivals."

I glance behind me in time to see Sam's eyebrows knit together. He's thinking about last night again, I know it. What may have happened on that big bed if I hadn't gotten sick.

I turn back around. "Not a problem at all," I tell her. "We've been sharing hotel rooms the whole trip."

"Are you two a couple?" she asks.

Some spittle gets caught in my throat and I cough. "No, no, just friends."

Sam mutters something but I don't catch it.

Catherine opens a door at the end of a long hall, and we go in, dropping our bags on the baby-blue carpet. The room is nice, with a big bed in the center covered by a patchwork quilt, and an en suite bathroom. The window overlooks the horse stable, beyond which the sun is starting to set, causing the land to take on a golden glow.

"This is great. Thanks," Sam says. He grabs some clean clothes from his duffel. "I think I'll go take a shower. It's been a long day."

"I'll go after you," I say.

We're both filthy, but he's a lot dirtier than I am. The pig adventure ended up being far less exciting than I'd expected—and that was just fine with me. Up close, the pigs kind of freaked me out. They're really, really big, and they have gnarly teeth and tiny little eyes. I decided to help construct the new fence instead of doing any of the jobs that involved more direct pig-to-human contact.

Sam got right in there and helped bathe them.

He disappears into the bathroom, and I decide to unpack. But when I unzip the front pouch of my suitcase, the papers and pictures from Mellie's secret box stare up at me. "Catherine!" I catch her just as she turns to go. "I almost forgot." I leave the birth certificate and other documents in the pocket, but I hold up the photos.

She gasps and scurries to my side. We sit on the edge of the bed and flip through the stack together. With each picture, she looks from it to me and back again, as if trying to find hints of me in that baby and vice versa. "Until today," she says softly, "any time I thought of you or wondered where you were or what you might be doing, this was the image that came to mind. This baby. That was all I knew you as. No matter how hard I tried, I couldn't come up with a clear picture of what you might look like today."

I nod. "I understand that. This"—I gesture with a photo of Celeste—"is all I can picture Celeste as. I didn't know her before this moment in time, and I'll never know her after."

Tears fill Catherine's eyes. "It's not fair, is it?"

"No. It's really not." I gaze down at a picture of Celeste holding me.

"You look just like her, you know," Catherine says, putting an arm around me.

"You think?"

"I do."

We silently sift through a few more photos. "Catherine?" I say, needing to give voice to the question in my mind.

"Yes?"

"Was Celeste happy? Was she glad she had me?"

"Dara." She grabs my shoulders and rotates me so we're facing each other. "She adored you. You were the light of her life. You were the light of *all* our lives."

I nod. "Okay. Thanks." But the nerves are creeping in again.

All I want are people in my life who will support me and be proud of me and won't lie to me. People who I can always count on to be on my side, no matter what. I think the Pembrokes are as close to perfect as I could ever hope to find. They're kind and generous, and they clearly love each other. And they've been searching for me. But, like Catherine said, they only ever knew me as that little baby. A lot has changed since then. I come with a lot of baggage.

What if I don't live up to *their* expectations?

....

After Catherine leaves to go get some more work done, I open my email. One more letter from Mellie.

To: acelove6@email.com

From: Mellie.Baker@email.com

June 22 (11:20 AM)

Subject: "I am."

Dear Dara,

I often think I should write to Stephen King and suggest he write a book about a transgender kid going through puberty. Because, at that point in my life, I couldn't imagine anything scarier.

The body that I already had such a complicated relationship with was betraying me, propelling me forward into something I desperately did not want. Something irreversible.

Things were happening all over me, all at once. My voice was changing, my body was becoming taller and broader, and the hair growth kept on coming. The mirror told me "man" more and more each day. And, in direct response, my brain screamed, *No.*

I watched the girls at school turning into women. They were experiencing things I wished I could. They were turning into someone I'd never be, while I was turning into something I hated.

My mustache seemed to grow in overnight. I don't know why it was the mustache that did it; maybe because it was unhideable. I could choose to not speak, and no one would hear my voice. I could keep my body covered under clothing, and no one would see what was happening there. But facial hair was plain as day, on display for the whole world. I couldn't go through life wearing a mask, though in many ways it did feel like I already was. Regardless of the reason, it was that morning, when I looked into the mirror and saw that dusting of dark hair above my lip, that the sentence passed my lips for the first time. "I am a girl." Not "I want to be a girl," or "I wish I were a girl." I *am* a girl.

I didn't know how I knew it. All the evidence was to the contrary. But I was certain. And I was the only one who knew.

Another stepping-stone.

You're probably thinking how ironic it is that it took me until that moment, when I looked the least like a woman than I ever had, to define it. But it was like a door in my brain had finally been unlocked, and all the feelings and ideas that for years had been leaking out piecemeal through the crack under the door came rushing out in their glorious, honest entirety. It made me under-stand why people have faith—I now knew what it was like to be so sure of something you can't see, something that should make no sense at all.

I slid to the bathroom floor and whispered it to myself over and over. "I am a girl, I am a girl, I am a girl." I tried a variation: "I am a woman."

I'd known it for a long, long time. When I was three and telling my mother something had gone wrong while I was being baked and I needed to go back into the oven to be fixed, this was what I'd been trying to say. Ten years later, I was even surer of it. It had just taken me a while to put the words together in the right order.

The relief was immense and indescribable.

But it barely lasted a minute.

Panicked, I grabbed my father's razor and shaving cream, and got rid of the new, soft hair on my lip as quickly as possible.

I wiped my face with a towel and stared at my reflection. The hair was gone, but a shadow remained, a sure sign it would be back. There was no stopping what was happening to me.

As long as I live, I will never forget that moment.

It was the first time I considered suicide.

It wasn't the last.

I'm so sorry if this is hard for you to read, Dara. I can't tell you how hard it is to write. I'd always hoped that, even when you learned my whole story, I could shelter you from the darkest parts. But like you said, knowing the *what*s is not enough. You need to know the *why*s behind them. And my wavering mental health is a very big part of it all.

Speaking of which, you should know that I've decided to take some time off work. Just a few days, hopefully. But I can't be there right now, floating around the corridors, distracted, checking my phone a thousand times a day, waiting for you to call or email or text. It's not fair to the patients or the other nurses, and it's not fair to me. I'm not in a great place right now, and I need to focus on getting better. But I promise I'm working on it.

I'm here if you want to talk. I miss you.

Love,
Mom

Suicide? Not in a great place? What is she talking about? My mother is the strongest person I know. Often to a fault. How could she even *consider* . . . ?

My chest tightens and my throat starts to burn, that horrible thing your body does when sadness comes on too quickly and it needs time before it can produce a cry.

And the puberty stuff. How she was jealous of the other girls. Did she feel that way when I went through puberty too? Did I make these feelings worse for her then?

Did my leaving make it worse for her now?

Sam comes out of the bathroom, all clean and good-smelling and escorted by a puff of steam.

I stare at him, stricken.

He halts. "Now what?"

I hold the phone out. "Mellie's emails."

"She's been sending them?" He takes the phone and starts scrolling.

"Start at the beginning," I say. I don't know what I'm feeling. Shaken? Numb? I'm still pre-cry, and I'm not really sure if tears are going to come at all.

I can't tell if these emails are a good thing or a bad thing. I'm glad she's finally opening up, trusting me—*respecting* me—enough to tell me the whole truth, but they're just making things even more confusing and upsetting. One minute I'm mad as hell that Mellie took me from this family, the next minute I'm sick to my stomach over the development that my mother has periodically considered killing herself.

Why does everything have to be so hard?

Leaving Sam with the phone, I go into the bathroom to change into a sports bra, then manage to duck out of the house without seeing anyone. They're all still working out back.

I head straight for the gravel road, push every last thought out of my mind, and force my tired body into a run.

Without my phone, I don't have music, but that's okay. When you really focus, even the most quiet of places becomes filled with sound. Wind zipping past your ears. Trees rustling. Cows mooing. Birds singing. Fallen leaves crunching. Planes flying high above. Add to all that my sneakers beating a steady rhythm as the gravel turns to pavement, and I've got more of a soundtrack than I'll ever need.

As the miles pass, my muscles begin to groan. The groans turn to screams, and eventually I have to give in. I stop. Lean forward with my hands braced on my thighs. Breathe. Look around.

I've made it to a town. There's not much in the way of pedestrian traffic, but a supermarket is up ahead to the left, and a small post office is to my right. I have no idea what this place is called, but in getting here, I've managed to return to myself.

Dusk will be setting in soon. I straighten up, redo my ponytail, and turn back the way I came.

CHAPTER FIFTEEN

When I get back to the house, Sam is waiting on the front porch, petting the black cat from the Google Earth photo. His phone and mine are resting next to him on the swing.

"What's his name?" I ask, dragging my tired feet up the porch steps.

"Her."

"His name is Her?"

Sam rolls his eyes. "*Her* name is Yoshimi."

"Oh." I sit next to him, on the side with the cat, not the side with the phones. I scratch under Yoshimi's chin and she lets out a purr.

"Mellie emailed you again," Sam says. "I hope you don't mind, but I read it."

I shake my head. I'm actually glad he read it. He can prepare me for whatever is about to come next. "Is it about suicide again?" I mumble. I don't know if I'm ready to read another of those.

"No."

"Good."

"Yeah."

We sit there in silence, listening to the gentle creak of the swing's chains. This silence is better than the silence in the car and at breakfast.

"It's about tennis," he says after a few moments.

I blow out a breath. "Terrific." I hold out my hand, and he drops the phone into it. Might as well get this over with.

To: acelove6@email.com

From: Mellie.Baker@email.com

June 22 (6:17 PM)

Subject: The greatest game ever played

Dear Dara,

So. Tennis. In some ways, keeping silent about my history with the sport feels like the biggest transgression of all. We had this shared passion, this shared skill, and you didn't know. You felt alone. Misunderstood. Unsupported.

So many times I wanted to tell you. To grab a racquet, get on the court with you, and volley for hours and hours. But I made a choice a long time ago: Leaving my old life behind meant leaving *all* of it. It has been incredibly hard, but it was also without a doubt the right thing to do. Allowing myself to slip back into that place now, even a little, would be too painful, too confusing. Besides, how would I ever be able to explain my ability to you? As far as the world knew, Mellie Baker had never played a match in her life.

I'll never forget the day tennis started for you. You were fifteen months old, and the women's finals of Wimbledon were on the TV. Sitting there in your high chair, a dish of Cheerios in front of you, your eyes caught the movement on the screen. In that instant, your chubby hand froze halfway to your mouth, and the Cheerios were forgotten—you were enraptured by the ball flying back and forth over the net, by the grunts of the players, the swish of their skirts, the sound of the ball connecting with their racquets. When the match ended, you cried. You wanted it to come back. And I knew that was it. It was in your blood, just as it was in mine. I was equal parts overjoyed and saddened. I knew it meant a lifetime of walking a fine line, trying to be supportive of you but all the while being reminded of what I'd lost. I guess I haven't walked that line very well. I'm very sorry for all the times you felt alone.

I lower the phone to my lap and stare out across the uninhabited land stretching for miles beyond the farmhouse. Mellie's first memory of tennis and me is different than mine. I don't remember that day with the Cheerios and the Wimbledon finals. But that obviously came long before the day I begged her to buy me the red plastic racquet. Mom knows everything about me—even things I didn't know about myself. And yet she never allowed me to know anything about her.

The phone feels heavier when I pick it up again. I keep reading.

Here's how tennis started for me:

Kristen introduced me to it, actually. She took tennis lessons every Saturday morning. I didn't know what she loved more—playing tennis or talking about playing tennis. She was always telling me about the techniques she was learning and how many matches she'd won, her voice taking on a special kind of excitement reserved only for tennis talk.

It made her so happy, and I began to wonder if maybe it could do the same for me. At that point I was willing to try anything.

My parents kept pushing me to do sports, but it had never gone well. One year my father forced me to join the Pee Wee Football team, but not only wasn't I any good, I was *terrified* of getting tackled by the boys. The coach and I came to an agreement: I'd show up for practices and suit up for the games, but he wouldn't put me in to play. Dad had words with him for not playing me, but in the end even Dad couldn't argue that I wasn't doing the team any favors when I was out on the field.

After the failed football experiment, Dad tried to get me to play basketball and baseball. I tried so hard to get just one basket or hit one ball—do *something* right, be the kid my parents wanted—but it was clear I didn't fit in there, either.

But tennis could be the perfect thing. My parents would be happy that I was taking up a sport, and I wouldn't have to suffer through being on a boys' team. Men *and* women were allowed to play tennis. It was good enough for Kristen, and she was the litmus test by how I measured pretty much everything. And, best of all, it actually looked fun.

"Can you teach me how to play tennis? The rules of the game and stuff?" I asked her one day during eighth grade gym class. It was easier to broach the subject with her rather than my mom and dad. I was so used to being a wantless, needless half person around them that I didn't know how to express things like this. I was more myself with Kristen, braver.

She beamed. "Yes! I bet you'll be so good at it!" I didn't know about that, but it felt good to know that she had faith in me.

The following Saturday, I went to the tennis club with her family and watched her lesson. After, she took me onto one of the practice courts and showed me the basics. On my third try, I managed to serve the ball correctly.

I'd never felt anything like watching that ball soar through the air, knowing it was going to go over the net and land exactly where I wanted it to. This, I thought, was what confidence felt like. Pride. It was entirely new.

The ball bounced to the ground, and Kristen shrieked in celebration and threw her arms around me. "You did it, Marcus!"

"I did," I echoed, still staring at the other side of the court.

"Try to do it again." She stepped back to give me room.

I hit another ball, and it too went over the net. Then a third and a fourth.

I was *good* at this.

That was all it took. I was hooked.

At the end of the day, Kristen's mom dropped me off at home and told my parents how well I'd done and that they should consider putting me in lessons. I remained still as a statue during the entire conversation, hanging on to every word they said, too scared to even breathe. They had to say yes. They had to.

That night, I crept into the hall and listened to my parents' hushed discussion at the kitchen table.

"Do you know how expensive private tennis lessons are?" Dad asked.

"I know," Mom said. "But she said he has talent. Maybe he could be a real athlete."

"Why couldn't he have had talent for one of the sports the kids play at school for free?"

"Jack. I know money is tight, but think about it. This could get him back on track."

I knew what she meant. It was exactly what I knew they would think: *Normal boys like sports. This is the first regular boy thing he's ever shown an interest in. Maybe this is our chance to fix him.*

There was a pause, and then Dad said, "You're right. Of course. We have to."

I resisted the urge to whoop and punch the air in triumph. I didn't care that they were only agreeing because they thought it would straighten me out, or that my actual happiness hadn't factored into their decision at all.

Intentions didn't matter. For the first time in my life, my parents and I were actually on the same page.

Tennis quickly became everything to me. When I had a racquet in my hand, I turned into someone else. Someone confident. Someone talented. Someone strong. Someone who had parents who were proud of them. When I wasn't at a lesson I was on the practice courts, and when I wasn't on the practice courts, I was shadow swinging in front of the bathroom mirror or doing string catches with a ball and racquet in my room. I started setting goals, and then did everything I could to reach them.

Sound familiar? ☺

Love,
Mom

"Ugh, that smiley face," I groan.

One corner of Sam's mouth quirks down sympathetically. "I know."

"So, what, is she trying to say that we're the same? That because she was good at tennis too when she was younger and we all of a sudden have that in common I should just go ahead and forgive her?"

He scratches between Yoshimi's ears. "I think maybe she's trying to relate to you. To show that she understands you, not that she expects *you* to understand *her*."

I grimace. "I knew you were on her side."

"*What?*"

"You keep finding good things to say about her, or asking me if I know much about trans stuff. It's like you're trying to get me to not be mad at her anymore."

"Dara, obviously I'm on your side if I'm here with you right now. You *have* to see that, right?"

I shrug.

"Well, it's true. But . . ."

I give him the side-eye. "But what?"

He lifts his hands in a sort of defeated shrug, and drops them in his lap. "You can't stay mad at her forever. Even if things go absolutely amazingly with your grandparents tomorrow, Mellie is still your mother. Your closest family."

"Just because she's my parent doesn't mean she gets to do whatever the hell she wants and I automatically have to forgive her."

"No, but she's trying to fix it." He nods at the phone. "She's confiding some pretty heavy stuff in you now. Stuff that maybe she's never told anyone. Yes, it's way too late, but it has to count for something, doesn't it?"

"I don't know." It's not exactly an answer, but it's also the most honest thing I can say right now. I *don't* know. I wanted the truth, and then I didn't, and now that I'm getting it I'm not sure what to feel or do about it.

I *hate* that she's considered suicide. And there are still so many blank spaces: Has she actually attempted it? And what does "I'm not in a great place right now" mean?

I get that those feelings are part of the reason she felt she had no choice but to transition. I do. But on the other hand, should that give her a free pass for the rest of it? Should I just give up and go home and tell her everything's fine, because I'm scared of her hurting herself?

Maybe I should call her. Not to forgive, but just to . . . check.

I lean my head on Sam's shoulder. I'm sure I don't smell great after my run—and building the fence and hitting balls for an hour in the southern sun—but he doesn't seem to mind. "I don't know, Sam."

He lets out a breath. "Yeah."

"Yeah."

....

We're building a fire in the front-yard fire pit when Catherine's cell phone rings. My bundle of wood falls from my arms, and I hold my breath as she checks who's calling. When Ruth and William didn't call by dinner, I was beginning to think it wasn't going to happen.

She looks to me eagerly. "It's them!"

I try to let the breath out, but I can't seem to make my body work right. My heart is racing, and the sound reverberates in my head.

She answers the call and waves for me to follow her. "Hi, Dad," she says into the phone. We go inside and into the kitchen, which is clean and quiet post-dinner. A single light is on over the stove, and the dogs are curled up in their beds in the corner by the table.

Catherine closes the kitchen door behind us and switches the call to speakerphone. "Did you have a good day sailing?" We sit on the benches, and she grabs my hand.

"Oh yes. Not too much wind at all." That's him. My grandfather. His voice is deep, with a hint of a Southern accent. I wonder if he's picked it up from living in the South for the past couple years, or if maybe he's from the South originally. "Your mother finished the novel she was reading, and I caught a nice four-pound flounder."

Catherine winces. "You know I've asked you not to tell me about that stuff, Dad."

"Fish isn't meat, Catherine. Everyone knows that."

She rolls her eyes in good-natured exasperation; it's clear this is an argument they've had many times before. *They even bicker like the perfect family.* "Anyway, is Mom nearby? I have news."

"Yes, she's right here."

"Put the phone on speaker so I can hear both of you." There are a few beeps as he apparently tries to figure it out.

"Okay, got it," William says.

"Hello, dear," Ruth says. Her voice is higher pitched than I imagined, but it folds around me like a blanket. *They're really real. I finally found them.* "Is everything all right? The farm is okay?"

"Yes, the farm is great. Everything is great. *Better* than great, actually." Catherine grins at me and squeezes my hand. "You'll never guess who's sitting next to me right now."

"Who?" Ruth asks.

"Dara."

The silence that follows goes on for a long time. I know they're still there because I can hear the ambient noise from their end of the speakerphone, but neither William nor Ruth says a word.

"Mom? Dad?"

"What do you mean, Dara is sitting next to you?" Ruth whispers shakily.

"She came to the farm today, looking for you both!"

"Oh my goodness. Oh my goodness, oh my goodness," Ruth says. "Put her on the phone!"

"She's on speaker. Go ahead, Dara, say hi."

I clear my throat. "Hi," I say. This is so weird. Exciting, but incredibly bizarre. I don't really know what to say. I don't need to introduce myself, because they already know who I am, and I can't shake their hands or give them hugs because they're not here. "I'm sorry I didn't come sooner. I only just found out you existed this week."

"Marcus didn't tell her anything about us!" Catherine says.

"Oh my goodness," Ruth says again.

"Where have you been living, Dara?" William asks. "We looked for you for so long, but never found a single clue."

"Um, a small town in western New York called Francis," I tell them.

"New York?" Ruth asks in dismay. "We assumed Marcus would have taken you farther from home. How could we have missed it?"

"It's okay," I say. "It's not your fault."

"It's not *your* fault, either," Catherine assures me.

We sit with that, without a doubt all thinking the same thing: It's Marcus's/Mellie's fault.

"But we're very glad you're here now," Catherine continues after a beat.

"Praise the Lord," Ruth says. "It's a miracle. Our granddaughter home with us at last."

"Speaking of which," Catherine says, "Mom, Dad, do you want to come here tomorrow? We can all properly catch up then."

"Of *course* we're coming," William exclaims. "We'll get on the road at sunup and be there by eight."

"Sounds good."

"I'm really looking forward to it," I tell them.

"Oh, sweetheart," Ruth says, her voice breaking. "We've been waiting for this day for a very long time. Thank you for coming to find us."

CHAPTER SIXTEEN

The fire Matt and Gabby built is roaring impressively. The flames dance off our faces, arms, legs, matching the warmth I feel inside after talking to my grandparents. Sam sits to my left, snapping photos of the fire. Matt's on my right, significantly closer to me than Sam is.

Catherine went to bed a little while ago, and it's just the seven of us now.

We can't see the pigs in the darkness, but we can hear them—they're snoring. Loudly.

We've been waiting for this day for a very long time, Ruth said. I keep hearing her voice in my ears. My grandmother.

Ruth and William. Catherine. This farm. This *family*. The enormity of it all, the fact that my grandparents are probably packing a bag at this very moment, preparing to come meet me, is a lot to process. I need to not think about it for a little while.

"Too bad we don't have any marshmallows," I say to distract myself. "S'mores would be amazing right now."

Jane shakes her head. "It's hard to find vegan marshmallows around here."

"Oh." I had no idea regular marshmallows weren't vegan. For someone who's spent her whole life watching what she eats, I don't know very much about this stuff.

Matt places a hand on mine, and my skin ignites even hotter than the fire. "It's okay, a lot of people don't know that. I even ate marshmallows and gummy worms and stuff for a while after becoming vegetarian, because I didn't know, either."

That makes me feel better.

He holds out an Oreo, and I take it from him. I make sure to use my left hand, because I don't want to remove my right one from his grasp. Our fingers have somehow become interweaved, and our grip is active, as if we're both sending all our energy to the places where we're touching. I watch as Meadow and Gabby take notice and exchange a look. It's not clear what exactly they're saying to each other, but they've got matching smirks on their faces.

I purposely don't look to my left. If Sam has realized that Matt and I are holding hands, I don't want his opinion about it.

I turn my attention back to Matt and the cookie in my hand. "Wait, Oreos *are* vegan?"

He laughs. "Pure sugar and chemicals, but not an ounce of gelatin or dairy in sight."

Ezra passes around a couple six-packs of beer and a bag of candy. I shake my head when the beer comes my way. I don't need a repeat of last night. Sam, however, takes one.

Now I look at him, incredulous.

"What?" he says, and tilts the bottle against his lips almost defiantly, taking a long pull.

"Nothing."

"Let's play two truths and a lie!" Meadow says, undoing her braids and running her hands through her hair.

"What's that?" I ask.

"It's a game. It's really fun. We go around the circle and each person shares three facts about themselves that the rest of us might not already know. Interesting things, like, 'I drove cross-country once' or 'I won a pie-eating contest.' But only two of them should be true—the other one is completely made up. And we all have to guess which one is the lie."

I want to say, *I've had enough lies to last me a while.*

Meadow goes first. "Let's see . . ." She chomps on a Sour Patch Kid as she thinks. "Okay. I've been to all the continents except Antarctica, I have a twin brother, and I hate eggplant."

"*Oooh*, good ones!" Jane says. "I think . . . the continent one is the lie."

"I agree," Ezra says.

"Eggplant," Matt says.

"Eggplant," I say.

"Twin brother," Sam says.

Everyone waits for Gabby to guess. She laughs. Her silver eyebrow ring, shiny in the light of the fire, is a miniature version of the half moon hovering high above us. "You really want me to play? She's my girlfriend—of course I already know the answer."

"True," Matt says. "Okay, you won't get the point, but tell us the answer."

"Meadow does not have a twin brother," Gabby says confidently.

"Sam gets the point!" Meadow reaches over to fist-bump him.

"You seriously don't like eggplant?" Matt asks. "How did I never know this?"

Meadow makes a *yuck* face. "Ew. So gross." She claps her hands. "Sam's turn!"

"Oh. Um, okay. I'm allergic to shellfish, I used to have really long hair, and Sam is actually short for Samarjit."

So easy.

"Long hair," Meadow says.

"Yeah, long hair," Gabby says.

"Shellfish," Ezra and Jane say in unison, and then laugh.

"The last one," Matt says. "The name one."

I'm the only one left. "I'm the Gabby this time. I mean, we're not dating like Gabby and Meadow, but—" *Stop babbling.* "I just mean it wouldn't be fair for me to play this round because I already know the answer."

Sam holds his hand out in a *please do the honors* gesture.

"Sam is not allergic to shellfish," I proclaim. "But he did have hair past his shoulders in ninth grade, and Samarjit is a Hindu name meaning 'victorious in war.'"

"The lady is correct," Sam says into his beer bottle.

Jane takes a piece of candy from the bag and pops it in Ezra's mouth. "Do you think you know me as well as Gabby knows Meadow and Dara knows Sam, babe?"

I feel my face go red, and I hope it blends in with the firelight so no one can tell. *Sam and I are not a couple!* I want to shout. But that probably wouldn't help.

Ezra licks the flavored sugar from Jane's fingertips, their eyes locked on each other's. "Whatever I don't know I look forward to learning."

She leans in, kisses him full on the mouth, and lingers there.

As if they share a brain, they stand up at the same time and gather their trash. "We're going to turn in for the night," Ezra says.

"Already?" I say. "But the game's not over."

Sam snorts, and I glance his way in time to catch him rolling his eyes.

"What?" I ask. Am I missing something?

"They're going to go have sex," Matt leans in and whispers, loud enough so everyone can hear.

Right. I knew that.

Meadow and Gabby dissolve in a fit of laughter, and Jane says, "Nuh-uh! We just have to get up early tomorrow. You should all be going to bed soon too." But it's a half-baked effort—she's giggling nearly as much as the other girls. She and Ezra disappear across the lawn and into the house.

Not two minutes later, Meadow and Gabby say their goodnights as well. Surely they're also going to . . . do what couples do. I won't be making that mistake again.

And then it's just me, Sam, and Matt. My attention zeroes in on my and Matt's clasped hands once more, but now it's more of a self-conscious awkwardness than a light, buzzy feeling. Sam's stare is weighty. I slide my hand out from Matt's.

Matt and Sam take another sip of beer, almost in unison.

"So how many of those . . . what would you call them? Rescue missions?"

"That works," Matt says.

I nod. "How many have you been on?"

He shrugs. "I've lost count. I started volunteering for DFA when I was in high school, with the group back in Arkansas, and have been working full-time for them ever since graduation. That was three years ago now."

"How many have been successful?" I ask.

"Not as many as we'd like. The meat industry is gargantuan, and they work hard to make sure meat eaters don't think twice about where the food on their plates comes from. We often feel like David battling Goliath."

Sam snickers.

Matt and I turn to him. "What?" I ask.

He looks up from his beer. His expression is flat, and the shadows from the fire dance mysteriously on his skin. "Nothing. Never mind." His voice is nearly a mumble, but there's an edge to it.

"If you have something to say, man, you should say it," Matt says.

Sam glares at him, or maybe through him, for a beat. "Fine. That David and Goliath metaphor is not only clichéd, it's wrong."

"How do you mean?" Matt asks.

"Everyone always talks about how amazing it is how, in the story, David won the battle and took down Goliath, since Goliath was so much bigger than he was, and had armor and a sword when all David had was a slingshot. But actually, David would have been a huge favorite to win, because he had a projectile weapon and was highly skilled at using it. All he had to do was stand out of stomping range of Goliath and aim carefully. The fight was over before Goliath could even attempt an attack." He gives Matt a smug look.

"The people who use that metaphor don't have the slightest idea what they're talking about." He might as well be saying, *You're an idiot. Go read a book.*

"You know what he meant," I say. "The point was to illustrate how hard it is to be the little guy fighting the big guy. Right, Matt?"

Matt nods. "And how much it sucks when ethics and right and wrong don't have a place in the argument at all."

I turn my back more firmly on Sam. "How many times have you been arrested?"

"Four."

"Four?"

He shrugs.

I shake my head. "I can't believe I never knew about any of this."

"Yeah, it's hard. That's why we need all the help we can get." He takes my hand again and scoots even closer. My fingers itch to reach out and stroke the dusting of stubble on his cheek and chin. "I'm really glad you're here, Dara." God, even his voice makes me want to float toward him.

"I'm really glad I'm here too," I whisper.

The moment is broken by the sound of Sam cracking open another beer. I sit back and clear my throat. Sam has moved down several feet and is nearly on the other side of the fire from us now. He stokes the firewood with a stick. His gestures are punctuated, severe.

"Anyway . . ." I begin, without the slightest idea what to say next.

"So, how is it that you've never met the Pembrokes before now?" Matt asks, steering the conversation back on course.

"It's a long story."

"I don't mind," he says, then adds, "But you don't have to tell me if you don't want to."

I do want to. I trust him. And it's not like everyone's not going to catch wind of the story by tomorrow anyway. "Well, the gist of it is that I just found out my mother is transgender."

Matt's eyes go huge. Clearly, he wasn't expecting *that*. "Wait, back up. Like she's decided to become a man?"

"No, no." I shake my head. "She was born male—"

"Assigned male at birth," Sam interjects.

"What?"

"That's what you're supposed to say. Not 'born male.' "

"How do you know?"

"I've been reading about it."

I don't know why, but that rankles me. *"Anyway."* I turn back to Matt. "She was *assigned male at birth*, and started living as a woman when I was little. Biologically, she's my father. My mother was Catherine's sister, Celeste."

Matt's eyebrows pull together. "The one who died?"

"Yes."

"Whoa. And you didn't know any of this?"

"I had no idea until a couple days ago. I thought Mellie was my mother. I mean, I thought she gave birth to me."

He whistles. "This story has *got* to be good."

"I wouldn't call it *good*, but I guess it is interesting, if you're not the one living it." I go on to recount exactly what happened. Matt is riveted. "I figure getting to know the Pembrokes is a good step in learning about the life I should have had if Mellie hadn't taken me away from it."

"That is *major*," Matt says, caressing the back of both my hands with his thumbs. I don't remember him taking my other hand—or did I take his? "And not okay. I'm so sorry he did that to you."

He. Matt's doing the same thing Catherine did. But he's never met Mellie, so it's not a personal vendetta that has him using this pronoun.

Sam reacts to it too. He was so quiet as I relayed the insanity of the last few days that I sort of assumed he'd fallen asleep, or was maybe lost in the Viking game on his phone again. But apparently he's been paying attention, if a tiny, two-letter word stirs a response in him. *"She,"* he says. "Not *he.*"

Matt turns his palms out and shrugs, as if to show he hadn't meant to be combative. "Dude, don't get me wrong. I'm sympathetic to the plight of the LGBT people—two of my best friends are lesbians!" He jerks a thumb toward the house as if to indicate Meadow and Gabby. "But do you really think Mellie deserves our sympathy after what he-she did to Dara? If you ask me, he got off easy."

"Thank you!" I say. Finally, someone backing me up.

Sam continues to stare him down, unimpressed. *"Dude,* you have absolutely no idea what you're talking about, so just stay out of it."

"I don't have to answer to you, man. Who are you, anyway? She's made it clear you're not her boyfriend. So why don't *you* stay out of it, or give her the support she clearly needs?"

I'm not sure how I feel about them talking about me like I'm not even here, but I *am* glad to have someone completely on my side, with no caveats. Even if it's someone I just met and not the one person who *should* be in my court.

Sam shifts his gaze to me. His countenance is flat, but there's something bubbling under the surface. "Dara? Sidebar, please?"

Again?

I stand up and brush the grass off my butt. If he wants to throw down, I'm all for it.

Sam walks toward the gravel road. If not for the light of the stars, it would be pitch-black out here. There's a distinct chill in the air now that we're away from the fire too.

When we reach the road, Sam spins around to confront me. "This isn't you."

"What isn't?"

He waves a hand around, indicating all of me. "None of it! The trash-talking Mellie, the over-the-top flirting with the pretty boy, the sudden attachment to the aunt you never met before today. I went along with the drinking plan yesterday because you seemed to be . . . I don't know, searching for something, but that wasn't you, either."

"Maybe it *is* me, Sam. All of it. Maybe this is who I was supposed to have been all along."

The constellations reflect in the darkness of his eyes. "No. I know you. You're unraveling."

The word grazes me in just the wrong way, and I feel like I've tripped and gone down hard, face-first, on a brand-new clay court. *Unraveling.* He really thinks that? When all I've been trying to do is rebuild some semblance of a life? "That's a really messed-up thing to say."

"What's messed up is you listening to that guy. 'He got off easy'? *Really?* He has no business having an opinion on any of this."

I bark out a laugh. "I suppose I should listen to you instead?"

"No! I have no idea what it's like to be transgender, either! But I'm guessing it's a pretty big deal."

"So?"

"So maybe you should stop being so selfish."

For the second time in as many minutes, Sam has managed to strike me down without laying a finger on me. "How am *I* being selfish? *She's* the one who ruined *my* life. What did I ever do to her?"

"Dara, she didn't do anything to you, either." His voice is suddenly oddly calm, his words patient, measured.

And that's when I realize: Everything that's coming out of Sam's mouth right now is something he's been bottling up since the beginning of our trip.

He continues. "You said that when you first found out, you didn't run away, right? You tried to listen to what Mellie was saying, and think it through logically?"

"And?"

"You didn't run or scream or cry because you knew that what she was telling you was real. And it was hard. You were mad, but you weren't packing a bag yet, either. Even when she told you about tennis, you stayed put. It wasn't until she told you about taking you away from Philly, and the people and resources and *money* associated with that, that you snapped."

"Get to the point."

"The point is that you're not thinking about *her* at all. Not really. You're focusing on how *your* life could have been so different, and how dare *she* do this to *you*, but don't you think she probably made the best choices she could have within a really hard situation? She didn't ask to be a single parent. She didn't ask to be transgender."

"No, but she didn't have to change our names and leave everything behind and pretend she hated tennis and lie to me about it every day, either." It's a good thing there's nothing breakable around, because I'm suddenly feeling the need to smash something.

"You have no idea what it was like to have to make the choices she did!" His voice is rising again. "I'm not saying she should have lied to you, and I'm not saying you shouldn't be upset that you had to find out this way, or that you shouldn't feel sad about Celeste dying or not getting to know your grandparents. I'm not even saying that you don't have the right to be completely freaked out about the fact that your mother is actually your biological father. That's a *lot* to get your head around."

"So what *are* you saying?" I snap.

"I'm saying, consider the fact that Mellie lost those things too!" he cries. I've never seen Sam this mad. I'm glad the darkness is hiding most of his face. I don't think I'd like what I see. He takes a shallow breath. "And that what she was going through was so brutal that she considered *suicide*, and that maybe this isn't all about *you*. You're so mad at her for what she did to you, but she must have had reasons. And she's trying to be honest with you now in her emails, confessing some of the most brutal shit I've ever heard, and you won't even email her back."

I can't believe he's defending her. "Her reasons are useless to me. She betrayed me in so many ways, so many times! I have zero interest in listening to her excuses."

"Oh my God, take yourself out of it for *one* minute," he shouts. "She's your mother. You love her. You've had eighteen years together. Doesn't that count for something?"

"Not when those eighteen years weren't *real*! She told me stories about my 'father,' the guy who knocked her up and then left. But *she* was my father the whole time! She told me when I turned fifteen that if I wanted to continue playing tennis I had to get a job to pay for it because we didn't have enough money. Meanwhile she was spending our money on hormones that she hid from me in a secret box under her bed. She even . . . helped me decide between pads and tampons when I got my period for the first time. Every single thing I went through, *every memory* I have is discolored now. Destroyed. She's nothing but a liar." Sam's tirade backfired—not only am I really freaking angry now too, but the sympathy I *was* feeling for Mellie has evaporated. "I can't believe you're seriously telling me *I'm* the bad guy, when I need you to—"

"What, be on your side? Jesus, Dara! How many times do I have to say it? The fact that I'm here with you right now—"

"Well," I cut him off, "now I wish you weren't."

The silhouette of his shoulders falls in defeat. He gives a weak, short nod.

I have to ask, though it can't possibly make things better. "If we'd had this conversation back at your house, would you even have come with me?"

He's silent for a long minute. And then, finally, he says, "I don't know."

CHAPTER SEVENTEEN

I leave Sam standing in the dark. But a distance had already formed between us, even before I walked away.

Tears grip on to my lashes as I run back to the fire and into Matt's waiting arms.

"I don't know why he's being so mean," I sob. Matt's hold tightens around me, and I breathe in the heady combination of campfire smoke, sweat, and a hint of eucalyptus—must be his soap.

"He doesn't get it," he whispers against my ear. "But I do. It's not about her being transgender. It's about her deception and her lack of consideration for you. She didn't allow for the possibility that you might not have wanted to live her lie, and that's not fair."

I nod and sniffle. "Thank you for saying *she*."

"You're welcome. I can admit when I'm wrong."

My eyes are closed, my cheek soft against his chest, and I vaguely register the crunching-leaves sound of Sam making his way back to the house. I don't open my eyes until I hear the distant clap of the door closing.

"You know," Matt murmurs, "I know what you're going through, in a way."

I pull back just enough to look up into his eyes, and rest my chin on his strong torso. "You do?"

"I mean, not the exact same thing, but I've had a lot of family shit to deal with too. I don't talk about it a lot."

"You can trust me," I say.

His eyes soften even further. "I know I can." He takes a deep breath, and my belly moves with his intake of air; we're that close. "My father left my family a couple years ago. He and my mother were married for twenty-three years. But for the last year or so of their marriage he'd been seeing another woman, someone *way* younger than he was. I think she was, like, twenty-five or something. I know, how original." He sighs, his eyes skyward, and I squeeze him tighter. "The worst part is, my mom found out but didn't leave him. She depended on him too much— emotionally, financially, everything. So she kept it from my little sister and me; she *protected* him. But one day we were all sitting at the breakfast table and out of nowhere he got up and left. He didn't pack any of his stuff or anything. It was as if he couldn't bear even one more minute in the house with us. And he never came back."

"Oh, Matt, I'm sorry." I don't know what else to say. "That's awful."

He shrugs, trying to make it seem like he's not that bothered. "He's an asshole. We're better off without him."

"Yeah." I nod.

"But anyway, I get it. I get why you're upset with your mom. My dad did the same thing. He lied, and was only thinking of himself, and the rest of our lives were affected because of it. And he doesn't seem to care."

I haven't even known Matt for a full day and already he understands me better than my supposed best friend.

We cling to each other in silence.

Then he leans down slowly, and lightly grazes his lips against mine.

Even though we're already pressed against each other at nearly every place along the length of our bodies, it's that feather-light touch of his mouth that electrifies me.

An involuntary sound of want escapes me, and for a nanosecond I'm embarrassed, but apparently it's the encouragement Matt was waiting for. He lets out a groan of his own and deepens the kiss. His tongue dips into my mouth, dancing with mine, tasting me. His lips move both thoughtfully and passionately.

It's different than kissing Sam. Just as good, but more . . . loaded. A promise of things to come.

The whole world is dark, and this boy is my lighthouse. He listened to me, he trusted me. He's on my side. There's no past between us, nothing to turn bad.

I want to lose myself in him.

The urge to keep going ignites in my blood, and my body takes over. I wrap my arms around Matt's neck, pulling his face even harder against mine. I slip the cloth band from his messy bun around my wrist and run my fingers through his hair. My knee slides between his legs.

I have no idea what I'm doing, but Matt seems to be responding.

His hands creep up my back, under my shirt, grazing my bra strap. No one's ever touched me there except doctors and sports massage therapists. But it feels good, his confident touches somehow even better than an expert masseuse's strong strokes. His hands are warm, and I shiver as they glide across my skin, which is still chilled from my excursion away from the fire with Sam.

Don't think about Sam right now.

"Let's go to my room," Matt says, low, and nips at my bottom lip.

I remember Jane and Ezra, and Gabby and Meadow. I know what will happen if I go with him.

My body screams, *Yes!*

My mind says, *No.*

The echo of Sam whispers, *You're unraveling.*

That wakes me up.

Matt is nice and gorgeous and says all the right things. The newness, the novelty of him, was exactly what I needed today. But this, I don't think I need. Not tonight. This isn't what I came here for.

Somehow, I make my body get on board with my mind. I take a step back and look down at the ground in front of me while I try to catch my breath.

"What's wrong?" Matt asks.

I shake my head. "I'm sorry. I . . . I think we should stop."

"I'm sorry if I assumed something I shouldn't have. You just . . . were so into it." He seems genuinely confused.

"I am," I say. "I mean, I was. I just . . ." How do I explain? Eventually, I just say, "I have a lot going on right now," and leave it at that.

He nods. "I get it." I can tell he's disappointed.

"I guess . . . we should get some sleep?"

"Good idea."

He throws some dirt on the fire, and we go inside. I realize I don't have a room to sleep in. No way am I going to share a bed with either Matt or Sam tonight. I say good night to Matt, then go into the living room and curl up on the couch, pulling the soft cotton throw over me.

The house is silent, still, and very, very dark. There are no streetlights outside, and the moon and stars are blocked by clouds now. I'm the only one downstairs. I can barely see my own hand in front of my face. It's a little scary.

With nothing to distract me, my thoughts start tumbling down a slide.

Sam hates me.

Matt is probably mad at me.

I have no idea what's going to happen tomorrow.

And Mellie's considered suicide. She had to take off work this week for mental health reasons. Fuck. *Fuck fuck fuck.*

I sit up. Hands shaking, I reach into my pocket for my phone. The light from the screen is shockingly bright, like a spotlight has been turned on me.

"Dara?" Mom answers before the first ring is complete. "Are you okay?" She sounds . . . not herself. But I don't know if it's because she's having a hard time, or if I'm just hearing her voice differently now.

"Yes, I'm okay."

I can hear her exhale all the way down the line. "Thank goodness. Where are you?"

"In South Carolina."

"South Carolina? Why?"

"This is where the Pembrokes live now."

There's a brief pause. "So you're with them."

"Sort of. I'm with Catherine. William and Ruth are coming tomorrow."

I wait for her disapproval, her protest. It doesn't come. Instead, she asks, "Is Sam okay?"

Physically, yeah. Emotionally, I think I screwed everything up. Big time. "Yes, he's fine. Mom, listen. Are *you* okay?"

"What do you mean?"

"That email you sent today. It scared me."

"Oh, honey." Her voice is softer, less frantic now that she knows we're alive and in no imminent danger. "Don't worry. I promise you I'll be okay."

I exhale. "Are you sure?"

"Absolutely. Dara?"

I wait.

"I'm sorry."

The simplicity of the statement, with no *buts* or *ands* attached to it, makes me falter. "For what?"

"For everything."

"Oh."

"I wish you'd come home."

A flash of my own bed and a plate of extra-spicy noodles appears in my mind. After everything that's happened today, it sounds better than I would have imagined. But I can't. "Not yet," I say.

She sighs. "I understand."

"You do?"

"I know I hurt you, Dara. I know none of this is fair to you."

A lump forms in my throat. I swallow it back. "Thanks for saying that."

"Thanks for calling."

"Bye." I end the call before she can say "I love you." I'm not ready to say it back.

CHAPTER EIGHTEEN

I awake to the sound of an actual rooster crowing.

I stretch and rub my eyes. I know exactly where I am this morning. The couch wasn't bad, but I never fell deeply enough asleep to dream. It's still mostly dark out, with only the tiniest hint of gray beginning to work its way into the sky.

I shuffle into the kitchen.

"Good morning!" Catherine says, way too chipper for this early in the morning, and gives me a side hug. I'm starting to get used to her affinity for physical affection.

"You're up early," I say.

"My day to do the breakfast shift."

I look around the kitchen. "Where?" All I see is coffee. I pour myself a cup and add some almond milk.

"For the animals, silly goose."

I take a sip. "Oh yeah."

"My parents texted—they're on the road," she says.

My heartbeat stutters. This crazy journey is about to end, and something else is about to start.

After finishing her coffee, Catherine goes to feed the animals, and I head upstairs. All my things are in Sam's room, and I need to get ready to meet Ruth and William. I might put the dress back on after all.

But when I try the door, I find it's locked. I knock lightly. "Sam?" I whisper.

The only answer is his snore.

Terrific.

I go to the bathroom downstairs and wash my face. There's some mouthwash in the cabinet, so I swish with that, and go out front to check my email. There are four new ones from Mellie. And some of them are long.

When did she have time to write these? After we got off the phone last night? She must not have slept at all. That can't be a good sign. Mentally healthy people don't take off work and then stay up all night frantically composing emails, do they?

To: acelove6@email.com

From: Mellie.Baker@email.com

June 22 (11:34 PM)

Subject: Thank you

Dear Dara,

Thank you for calling tonight. You have no idea how nice it was to hear your voice. And good luck with the Pembrokes. I truly hope you find what you're looking for.

I love you.

Love,
Mom

I take a breath. She seemed normal enough in that message. I have to have faith that what she said last night was true. That she'll really be okay.

To: acelove6@email.com

From: Mellie.Baker@email.com

June 23 (2:09 AM)

Subject: Saying good-bye

Dear Dara,

Freshman year of high school, I entered my first regional teen tournament. It was held at a college two hours away. I placed third in the boys' competition. Kristen placed fifth in the girls'. It was a good day. Until it wasn't.

"It's not normal for a teenage boy to only have girl friends," my mother said as we buckled into the car and waved good-bye to Kristen and her parents.

My parents had muttered similar sentiments many times in the years since Kristen and I had become close, but there was something in her voice this time that made me think she was about to say something more on the subject than usual.

I waited.

"We thought tennis would be good for you . . ."

"Tennis *is* good for me." I held up my trophy as evidence.

"Yes, but you haven't made friends with any of the other boys. We thought if you were involved in athletics, you'd make friends, take an interest in . . ."

She trailed off, but I knew what she was getting at. "In *what*?" I pressed. The lingering endorphins from my last match had me feeling brave.

"I don't know, Marcus." Mom sighed heavily, as if I was exhausting her. "Team sports. Video games. Cars. Girls. Normal boy things!"

I had so much to say in response to that, but I knew the only thing that would help my case would be to tell her that I *was* interested in girls in the way she was talking about. I could have so easily told her I had a crush on Kristen and that was why I liked hanging around her so much. But it wasn't the whole truth. I liked hanging around Kristen for lots of reasons. She was my best friend, and it didn't feel right to use her that way. So I said nothing.

When I didn't reply, Mom continued. Her voice was quiet, and she kept her eyes pinned to the road. "Your father and I have decided you are not to see that girl anymore."

"Don't be ridiculous," I retorted, and was met swiftly with a hard slap across the face. The car didn't even swerve.

I sucked in a breath and cradled my cheek in my hand. Tears raced to my eyes much quicker than even the possibility of a verbal response. I turned my face toward my window, gulping back tears, wishing again I had long hair—this time to hide behind. The car seat, the seat belt strap, the armrest built into the door all felt like they'd sprouted millions of piercing, ruthless daggers, and my body begged me to get as far away from my mother and this suddenly cramped car as possible.

My father was the one who hit me, not my mother. I'd always maintained hope that she was different than he was. That, if she could just be allowed to form her own opinions, she'd be nicer. But it was now startlingly clear that she hated me as much as he did.

For a moment I considered opening the door and jumping out, but we were going too fast.

I was trapped. In this car, in this family, in this body.

Mom spoke first. "I'm sorry. I didn't mean to . . ." She shook her head and squared her jaw. "You are not to speak to me like that. And our decision is final. No more Kristen."

Over the remainder of the weekend, a yellowish-purplish bruise formed on my left cheekbone, with a scab precisely in the center from where her ring had split the skin. Like the dark, thick hair on my lip and chin, there was no disguising it.

"What happened to your face?" Kristen asked on Monday morning.

She didn't even know about the time my father had beaten me to the point where I'd had trouble sitting down for days. How could I explain that my mother had taken up the family pastime as well?

But this affected her too. She deserved to know. "I talked back to my mother," I said simply. "This was her response."

"Oh my God, Marcus!" Kristen pulled me into a hug. "Are you okay? We have to tell someone!"

Her body was small and soft, but also athletic, strong. Her hair smelled like fruit salad. I pulled away.

"No," I said, drawing small circles on the hallway tile with my toe. "I don't want to dwell on it."

"What were you arguing about?"

"They don't want me to hang out with you anymore."

Her face crinkled up. "Did I do something wrong?"

I waved my hands as if to clear her assumed meaning from my last few words. "No, of course not! It's me. They think I . . . they think I don't act right." Throughout all the years of our friendship, Kristen and I had never spoken directly about *it*. Me. The non-gender-specific elephant in the room. This was the closest we'd ever come. "They think I shouldn't hang out with girls so much."

"That's so unfair!" She was mad. But her unhappiness made me feel better—she cared about me. "Is it because you're . . ." She trailed off. But she didn't need to say it. I knew she thought I was gay.

"I don't know," I said quickly, not wanting to get into it. "But don't worry; we'll still see each other at school and tennis. And there's always the phone."

She nodded, unsure, chewing the inside of her mouth.

"It'll be fine." I tried to sound reassuring, when inside, I was embarrassed and angry that I'd been forced to have this conversation at all. "Basically no difference, okay? I just had to tell you because you can't call the house anymore unless you know my parents aren't home, and I won't be able to go to the mall or things like that."

She nodded again.

"I'm really sorry," I said.

"Me too."

For a little while, things weren't horrible. I still sat with Kristen at lunch, and next to her in English class. We still saw each other at the tennis club café for a few minutes after our lessons. But it was hard work. My parents hadn't been kidding about making sure Kristen and I weren't associating. They started keeping closer tabs on me—picking me up right after school, and staying at the club to watch my lessons from the stands. They roped my siblings in to helping them too, so even if Mom and Dad weren't home, there was always someone watching to see if I was on the phone, and sneaking onto another receiver mid-conversation to try to catch who was on the other end.

It was exhausting, and unsustainable. Especially for Kristen. Why should she go out of her way to try to keep being friends in secret when she had plenty of other friends to occupy her time, and parents who let her have more freedom than mine?

So, inevitably, we drifted apart. My parents saw the shift—I stopped fighting to get to tennis early in hopes of seeing Kristen, and I stopped using the phone altogether—and they were glad. But they only got half their wish. Just because I'd lost my friendship with Kristen didn't mean I'd changed personalities. The boys at school and at tennis still didn't have any interest in being friends with me, nor I them. The result was that I was the same broken, nervous, strange kid, only now I was completely friendless.

High school crept by slowly, like that winter when you were eight and Francis was trapped under six feet of snow. Remember how bored and cranky we were, stuck in the house for weeks, eating a lot of spaghetti and doing the same six puzzles over and over? The difference here was, the sun never came out and melted the ice away.

Love,
Mom

I hate that she lost Kristen. I mean, I knew something must have happened, because Kristen has never been a part of our lives, but still. It hits way too close to home. If Mom grew apart from her best friend, who's to say the same won't happen to me?

Before this trip I never would have questioned the stability of Sam's and my relationship. But a lot of things happened this week that I never would have predicted.

To: acelove6@email.com

From: Mellie.Baker@email.com

June 23 (4:33 AM)

Subject: Renée

Dear Dara,

If you wouldn't mind, could you give Sam a hug from me? I've been thinking about Kristen a lot this week, more than I have in years, and it's made me so grateful that you have Sam, and that he's on this journey with you. He's a good friend.

Anyway.

Once my parents were satisfied I wasn't friends with girls anymore, they stopped Big Brothering me. I could come and go as I pleased and spend my time however I wanted to, as long as it didn't break their rules.

I spent a *lot* of time at the tennis club. And I was getting very good. I started collecting first place trophies. Our paths have

222

been similar in that way—tennis was for me, as it is for you, the most important thing. The only thing. Sometimes it pains me, Dara, to think about how much you've given to the game. How much you've sacrificed. But then I remember that though our situations may resemble each other's, they are not identical. Your dedication to tennis is a choice you've made out of love and passion. Mine was a reflex, a desperation.

Sometimes I saw Kristen at the club; we'd smile and wave, or exchange small talk, but it wasn't the same. She stopped competing in tournaments in eleventh grade, and in twelfth she stopped coming to the club altogether. She started dating Mike Fallon, one of the big, muscle-bound guys from the football team. Maybe those were her kind of people all along.

I began to read a lot. Books became my friends. I took out several from the library each week and read in bed at night and during downtimes at the club. It was one of these library books that completely changed my life.

I'd picked up a book about tennis in the 1970s, in an effort to learn as much about the history of the game as I could, and there was a long chapter about a player named Renée Richards. I'd never heard of her before. But I quickly saw myself in those pages.

She'd been born Richard Raskind. Unlike me, she'd been good at all sports, and had played for the football and baseball teams in high school. She'd even been invited to play for the New York

Yankees. But, like me, she loved tennis best, and stopped playing everything else. Soon she was one of the top college tennis players in the United States, and she continued on to the pros. The problem was, she was playing in the men's circuit, and despite what the world assumed, she wasn't a man. So, not knowing what it would mean for her career, she began to transition. Publicly.

The tennis community flipped out. They refused to let her play as a woman, saying that regardless of the hormonal and physical changes she'd gone through, she had still been "born male" and therefore would be at an advantage over the other women players. She was prevented from playing in all the major tournaments, and eventually she sued the United States Tennis Association. And she *won*.

Can you imagine my seventeen-year-old self reading this? Barely breathing, my eyes unable to take the words in fast enough, my fingers slippery with sweat as they tried to turn the pages.

Transgender. Transsexual. It was the first time I'd seen those words, but they instantly filled a long-vacant part in my heart. There was a *name* for what I was. And there were more possibilities than just name changes and being "a man in a dress." There were medical treatments, options. There was at least one famous person—a tennis player, no less—who had gone through what I was going through. And the government validated her.

The tennis community didn't embrace her as easily as the law did, nor did the media or the public, but the courts said she was allowed to compete, so she did. She went on to win more titles. She became Martina Navratilova's coach. I watched as she was inducted into the USTA Eastern Tennis Hall of Fame, and later the National Gay & Lesbian Sports Hall of Fame.

She was a trailblazer. Pro sports—and the *world*, really—have so much to thank her for. *I* have so much to thank her for. Not the least of which is the basic fact that if it weren't for her, I have no idea how much longer I would have gone on thinking I was the only one.

Love,
Mom

Catherine joins me on the porch. She has a book with her. "My parents just called. They're only a few minutes away."

The space under my ribs seems to shrink, pinching my organs together. "Oh wow. Okay."

"What are you up to out here?" she asks, opening the book to a dog-eared page. It's a novel. I add that to my mental picture: a family of readers.

"Just catching up on some emails," I say.

"Anything exciting going on back home?"

I know she's asking about friends, not Mellie. "Not really." I shrug, and casually pick up my phone again.

To: acelove6@email.com

From: Mellie.Baker@email.com

June 23 (5:27 AM)

Subject: The beginning and the end

Dear Dara,

I don't know if you have any questions about any of this. I think it's important that these emails be solely about my story—*our* story—not about definitions and studies and statistics. I already fear the story's been going on too long, and I don't want to get off track too much, so I won't stop to explain the technical terms. I'm far from the authority on it all, anyway, and everyone's experience is different and I don't want to speak for anyone else. From our conversation, I know you know a little about what transgender means, so I'm relying on that here. But please, if you do have specific questions about it or gender dysphoria or anything at all, ask me. Or, if you're not ready to talk to me about this yet, Google knows all.

After learning about Renée Richards, I made a list of every book in the library about gender identity and sexuality, and read them systematically, cover to cover, not starting the next until the previous was completed, its contents sufficiently digested. There wasn't nearly as much published about the topic then as there is now, and our little local library barely had anything on the subject, but at the time I felt like I'd stumbled upon a diamond mine. Each new bit of information slotted perfectly into a hollow in my mind, making me more whole.

I read while at the library, crouched in a corner at the end of the Medicine and Science aisle—I didn't want the librarians noticing the types of books I was checking out, and I couldn't risk anyone in my family finding them. The librarians didn't ask why I never checked anything out; I think they suspected I needed the library itself more than the books inside—a refuge from home—though they never brought it up directly.

Eventually the library got dial-up internet, and, tentatively, I started exploring online. The internet wasn't the wealth of information it is today, but it was certainly better than out-of-date library books. I found a website called Susan's Place, which was, miraculously, a networking resource for trans women. I spent time on there almost every day, making sure to delete my browsing history every few minutes.

One Saturday evening when I was exactly your age, shortly after high school graduation, I arrived at the library, after yet another dinner with my family where I sat there quietly and listened to my sister and brothers talk, to find things were different. Instead of the usual empty aisles, low lights, and quiet din of computers running and pages turning, tables and portable shelves had been set up in the entryway, the overhead fluorescents were blazing, and a fair-sized crowd was milling about, sipping coffee from small paper cups and eating cookies and brownies they'd purchased from a baked-goods table. Propped up on an easel by the front door was a large sign that read "Book Sale." The tables and shelves were piled high with old books, each with price stickers on them. Twenty-five cents, fifty cents, one dollar.

I asked Marjorie, my favorite librarian, what was going on.

"Oh, hello, Marcus, dear," she said, her apple cheeks shimmering with freshly applied berry-pink blush. "No one told you?"

I shook my head.

"We received a grant from the state to purchase thousands of new books, and they've just been entered into the system. So we're holding a sale to get rid of some of our older and lesser-read titles to make room for the new ones."

"Wow," I said. "Congratulations."

"Thank you!" She beamed. "We're thrilled. Why don't you take a look around and see if any of your favorites are up for grabs?"

I hadn't thought of that. The internet had largely replaced my book research, but those dusty old volumes had saved me. Given me hope. My bookmarks were still in some of them. The books were my friends, and I didn't want to have to say good-bye to them too. Frantically, I began to scan the tables. I was able to take inventory pretty quickly—I knew the spines and covers of my books by heart—and breathed a sigh of relief when it became apparent that none of the medical journals were on the chopping block.

As I headed toward the computers, I noticed all the shiny, new, just-delivered books stacked all over the library. Curious, I veered down my usual aisle.

Like magnets to steel, my eyes were drawn to a book, faceup on the top of a pile, with a woman on the cover. Looking back, I probably only noticed it because of how stunning she was, with her dark skin, platinum hair, and long legs peeking out from her gown. She was pretty, and I was a hormone-ridden teenager who was attracted to female humans. Nothing more complicated than that. But it was the book's description that had me clinging on to it for dear life. The woman on the cover was a *drag queen*. Drag queens aren't necessarily trans—many of them are cis men, RuPaul included—but it rocked my world to discover that this beautiful woman spent much of her life presenting as male.

The book was RuPaul Charles's autobiography. I hadn't heard of RuPaul before, but I was desperate to know more about her. She was anatomically male but looked like *that*—and she was *famous*. People admired her. She was important enough for this little suburban library to buy a copy of her story.

I had to read it immediately.

To this day, I still don't know how I gathered the courage to walk back up to the desk, place the book on the counter, and hand Marjorie my library card.

But I did, and the librarian just smiled and thanked me.

The book might as well have been a tube of lipstick, or one of the lacy bras I used to covet during my shopping trips with Kristen.

I felt like I'd just taken a huge step. Toward what, I didn't quite know, but it felt good.

I hid the book in the back of my closet, under piles of clothes and tennis gear, and only read it at night after everyone had gone to bed.

Barely two weeks later, I got home from practice to find my father waiting for me on the front porch. There was a fire in his eyes I had never seen before.

"What's . . . going on?" I asked hesitantly.

He crossed the porch, grabbed my upper arms, and threw me into the side of the house. The breath went out of me and my shoulder stung. He yanked me forward and pushed me against the wall once more, even harder this time. He didn't retreat; he was in my face, his expression a mask of blind rage, clearly hoping I'd fight back.

I stared at the ground, shivering in my father's shadow.

Then I heard a noise, a crack. I glanced to my right to find a metal bucket off to the side of the porch, a small but brilliant fire roaring inside. I can only imagine I didn't notice it earlier because I was too frightened of my father to properly take in my surroundings, but now I realized that the fire I'd seen in his eyes was only a reflection of the very real blaze just a few feet away from us. Or at least, that's what I told myself. It helped to have an excuse for his inhuman appearance at that moment; my fear level dropped just a notch.

He must have sensed it, because he let go of my arms, and the places where his grip had been pulsed, desperate to reclaim their blood flow. I took a slow step toward the fire and peered over the edge of the bucket, confirming what I'd subconsciously already known. The RuPaul book, or the shrivels of what was left of it, was inside.

Turned out my parents' suspicions hadn't decreased post-Kristen after all. I wonder if they'd been *looking* for an excuse to hit me, punish me, change me, throw me out, whatever it took to remove the blemish from their otherwise perfect, God-fearing family.

They were about to get their wish.

I looked back up at my father. The fire-eyed monster was gone, but in its place was something worse. A very real human staring directly at me with such definitive, blinding hatred I had to look away.

That was the last moment I laid eyes on him. My heart throbbing against my rib cage, my throat tight, my arms and back and shoulder aching and bruised, I walked into the house, past the living room where my mother and all three of my siblings had been sitting quietly, watching my father beat me up in front of our home, and into my room. I packed some clothes and my tennis gear, and left. My movements were methodical, robotic. It must have been some sort of survival instinct kicking in, which is strange, because I was pretty sure I thought about harming myself even more than my father dreamed about harming me.

No one said a word. That's maybe what's haunted me the most over the years—that we never spoke about the issue at hand. They hated me, but they never even *knew* me.

When the front door swung shut behind me, I swear I heard a collective sigh of relief. I never saw them again.

So. Now you're caught up on the Hogans. You know everything I know. Maybe someday, when we're both ready, we can find out what became of them . . . together.

Love,
Mom

No thanks, I think. *They sound awful. Not anything like the Pembrokes.*

I consider writing back, but just then a car turns onto the gravel road. It stops in front of the house, and an older man and woman get out. Yoshimi runs to greet them and leaps right into the man's arms.

Catherine takes my hand and grins at me. "Ready?"

"I think so," I say with a shaky laugh.

I slip the phone in my back pocket and smooth out the front of my shirt and shorts. I'm not as dirty as Catherine, who's been out back with the animals all morning, but I wish I weren't still in the clothes I slept in. And it would have been nice to be able to brush my teeth.

Ruth and William run straight to me. They're both fit and tanned. William is gray-haired; Ruth is blond, like her daughters. Like me. They look exactly as I pictured them, right down to the neat, tailored clothing.

"Hi," I say, holding out a hand. But Ruth throws her arms around me and hugs me as if she's trying to make up for the last seventeen years. It's as awkward as it was being hugged by Catherine the first time, but I concentrate on hugging her back, trying not to let go or pull away too quickly.

"Oh, Dara," Ruth murmurs in my ear. "My sweet, sweet baby girl."

William stands beside us and places a warm, large hand on my shoulder; he pulls it away after a minute to wipe his teary eyes.

When the hug ends, I realize Ruth has been crying too.

"It's nice to finally meet you," I say, a little shy.

Ruth flinches, but recovers quickly. "Of course. You were too young to remember. We *have* met before. We were actually a big part of one another's lives for a year or so, until . . ."

"Right," I say quickly, filling in the blank. "Sorry."

"Shall we sit?" William asks, gesturing to the porch. He sets down Yoshimi, and she chases after a fly.

Ruth sits next to me on the swing, and Catherine and William pull up chairs.

"Tell them the story, Dara," Catherine urges.

I know it's still morning, but today already feels like it's lasted for ages. I'm worn out, in every way, and I don't particularly feel like going into the whole Mellie-betrayal story yet again. But of course I have to. Ruth and William are waiting expectantly. Everyone's staring at me.

So I tell them. They hang on my every word. Then they ask about tennis and school and friends. If we've ever traveled, what sorts of books and music and films I like. They ask about our new last name and what Francis is like. They ask what "Marcus" does for a living, what procedures he's had done and what he looks like now. I show them a photo on my phone of Mom and me from graduation.

Ruth gasps, and a hand flies to her mouth. "Oh my . . ."

"Are you *sure* that's him?" William says, squinting and bringing the screen closer to his face as if searching for a clue.

"I'm sure," I say.

"Unbelievable," he whispers. He and Ruth exchange a long glance. There's a lot being said, but I don't know them well enough to decode it. He turns back to me. "Those documents and pictures you were telling us about. The ones you found. Do you have them with you?"

"Yes."

"May we see them?"

I stand up, but Catherine stops me. "I'll go."

"Oh. Okay, thanks. They're in the front zip pocket of my suitcase. If Sam's not awake yet, bang on the door until he gets up."

Catherine laughs. She thinks I'm being funny; she doesn't know about our fight.

"Can I ask you guys some questions?" I ask while we wait. We've been talking for a while now, and I'm feeling more comfortable. Just like I'd hoped, just like Catherine promised, they made me feel welcome from the start. Not only welcome, but really, truly *part* of it. The family. Like I've been on an extended vacation, but I'm back where I belong now.

"Please do!" Ruth says, pleased. "What would you like to know?"

"Well . . ." I think about which question to ask first. "What was Celeste like?" I've gotten Catherine's account, but I want more.

Their faces grow sad, and I wonder if it's because they're remembering and missing her, or if they're thinking how tragic it is that I never got to know her on my own.

"She was the kind of person who made friends everywhere she went," Ruth says. "Everyone loved her. She wasn't like Catherine, who's always known what she wanted to do with her life, but that never seemed to concern her. I think she would have been truly happy doing anything. That was just who she was—adaptable, easygoing, always finding the good in things."

"She was prelaw at U Penn," William says. "She would have made a fine lawyer, if given the time."

"She was still in college when she had me, right?" I ask.

They nod.

"What did you think of that? Of her getting married and having a baby so young?"

"Honestly, we were thrilled," Ruth says. "We thought Marcus was a lovely boy . . ." Her jaw tightens, and she very subtly rolls her shoulders back. "And they seemed very much in love. We were excited to be grandparents, and of course we insisted on helping out financially so she could finish her schooling and start her career."

"Do you have any other grandchildren?" I ask, realizing I never asked Catherine if she had kids.

Ruth looks down, and William shakes his head. "Catherine here doesn't seem all that interested in motherhood." He gives her a disappointed look just as she returns with the papers.

"Not true!" Catherine retorts. "I'm mother to four horses, two dogs, a cat, three goats, nine sheep, and now twenty enormous pigs."

He pats her knee patronizingly. "I know, darling."

Apparently, Catherine is the black sheep of the family. But the fact that they gave her this entire farm, and probably money too, to pursue her dream proves how much they care about her, even if they don't always understand her.

"Was Sam up?" I ask.

"Yeah, he was on his computer." She hands her dad the stack of documents and photographs. William takes his time looking through it all, then passes them to Ruth, who grazes her fingertips reverently over the photos of Celeste.

I have to ask. "What happened back then?"

They all look up at me. "You mean . . . ?" William says.

"I mean what made my moth—Mellie run away? How was she even able to? How did it all go down, from your perspective?"

Ruth and William share another look.

"It's okay," I assure them. "You can tell me."

"What do you think happened?" William asks slowly.

I shrug. "All Mellie said was that you weren't supportive of her transition, and it reminded her of her bad relationship with her own parents, and that's why she left. I don't know what was said, but Catherine mentioned you thought she was having a breakdown?"

"Marcus didn't tell you specifics?" William seems surprised by this.

I know it's all they knew her as, but it's still weird to hear them calling her *he* and *Marcus* when I've clearly been calling her *she* and *Mellie*.

"No." I don't mention that she's trying to now, with the emails. "But I honestly don't see what could have been *so* bad that she thought changing our names and going on the run was a reasonable option."

"Neither do we," he says. "That's part of why the last seventeen years have been so difficult. We don't know what we did to deserve this." I look from him to Ruth to Catherine. They look so helpless. Broken. "We may have reacted . . . unfavorably. But I'm sure anyone would react the same way when their daughter's husband starts wearing dresses and makeup with no explanation. Before we knew it, you were gone without a trace."

"I'm so sorry," I say.

"What do *you* think, Dara?" Ruth asks. "You must have some strong feelings about it all."

"I think it sucks," I say bluntly, and they smile. "You're really nice people. I wish I could have had you in my life this whole time."

My nose prickles. I rub it with the back of my hand. "I wish we'd stayed in Philly, where I could have trained at a real tennis center . . ." I sniffle, and wipe under my eyes. "I wish none of this had ever happened."

Ruth circles an arm around me and cradles me against her. I never knew the comfort of a grandmother's embrace until this moment. "Us too, sweetheart. Us too."

....

Catherine has to get back to work, but William, Ruth, and I take a long walk around the property together.

"I went to the house in Cherry Hill first," I tell them as we stroll. "I hadn't realized you'd moved."

"I'm sorry. Of course we would have told you if we had known how to contact you," Ruth says.

"Oh, I know that. I wasn't blaming you or anything. It was actually nice to get a chance to see the house where Celeste grew up."

"It's where your parents got married too, you know," William says.

"It is?" Mellie didn't say anything about that.

"Oh yes. It was a beautiful wedding."

"I'm sure it was. The house is incredible."

"We have the wedding album at home," Ruth says. "If you'd ever like to come see it."

"I'd love that."

She smiles.

"What made you decide to move to a farm?" I ask.

William chuckles. "We'd recently retired, and had grand illusions of country life. Riding horses, collecting fresh eggs from our own hens, all that business."

"It does sound nice," I say, taking a deep breath of the fresh air.

"It was. But it didn't take us long to figure out it wasn't for us."

"It was really cool of you to give the place to Catherine. She seems so happy doing this work."

"Yes, she's our little do-gooder." Ruth lets out a wistful sigh. "I do wish she'd find a husband to join her in her ambitions, though. It would be nice to know she's taken care of."

We come upon the pigpen. Catherine is working diligently to file down each pig's hooves to a more comfortable length. I never knew pigs needed their toenails cut like humans do. Some of them resist and pull away, but she's patient with them, rubbing their bellies and murmuring soothing tones in their ears until they allow her to continue.

She doesn't look like she needs anyone to take care of her. I glance at Ruth as she watches her daughter perform this unusual task. She shakes her head, ever so slightly, in amazement.

Matt, Jane, Ezra, Gabby, and Meadow are all here. Sam's probably still in his room. Avoiding me.

Matt nods at me. I wasn't sure what it would be like seeing him again, but the light of day has reinforced that I did the right thing in walking away. He made me feel wanted and understood, and last night I really needed that. But he was a mere moment, and moments can't last.

"Have you met Maybelline yet, Dara?" William asks as we continue our tour.

"No, I don't think so."

"She's our five-year-old American Quarter Horse. We bought her when we moved to the farm."

We walk a little ways to the horse paddock. William calls out for Maybelline, and moments later a shiny, muscular brown horse with black legs and a black mane and tail comes trotting over. "And how have you been, my lovely?" he asks her. She nuzzles her face against his, and he pats her side.

"Do you ride?" Ruth asks me.

"Me?" My eyes widen. "No, I've never been on a horse before."

She looks saddened by that. "That's a shame. I grew up riding, as did my daughters." Horseback riding. It was part of my vision of the family at the farm. I was right about so much.

"For me it's been strictly tennis," I say.

"Yes." She nods thoughtfully. "Will you be playing in college?"

I bite my lip, remembering what Ruth said about making sure Celeste continued her education even after she had me. College is clearly important to them. "Um. No, actually. I've decided to pursue a pro career instead."

William pulls his eyes away from Maybelline for a moment. "That's very impressive."

"Thank you." A sense of vindication blooms within me, rich as the farm earth. "It's my dream. Traveling this week has made it hard to keep up with my training, but I'm really looking forward to getting back on the court."

"Oh!" Ruth says, her eyes lighting up. "We have a tennis court!"

I look around. "Where?"

"At home in Hilton Head. The previous owners had a court built on the property. It's blue. We've never used it, but we keep it well-maintained. For aesthetics, you know."

"Wow," I say. "There isn't even a tennis court in all of Francis. I have to drive to Rochester to train with my coach, and most days I practice on a racquetball court at the rec center. And you have a court at your *house*?"

Ruth takes my hand in both of hers. She glances at William, and he nods. "Dara," she says, almost breathless. "We'd love it if you came to stay with us. The court is all yours. We'll hire a pro from the club to come practice with you if you like, since your grandfather and I won't be much help in that arena." She laughs. "How does that sound?"

Came to stay. Could that mean what I think it does? "Um . . . how long were you thinking?" I ask carefully.

"As long as you'd like! We've missed out on nearly your whole life up to this point. We'll take all the time we can get now."

Their eyes brim with anticipation and hope.

My thoughts start spinning, slowly at first, but picking up speed as they go. My long-lost grandparents just asked me to come *live* with them. In their guaranteed-to-be-super-fancy house on the water with *its own private tennis court*. I could train every single day. And we could get to know one another—*really* get to know one another, in the way that only happens naturally over time. Share our stories, the almost-forgotten ones that only emerge in your memory when triggered. This scenario is beyond anything I'd allowed myself to imagine.

"Would—" I begin, but my mouth goes dry. I want to ask the thing that's been on my mind since Mom mentioned they had money. I want to know if they'd consider sponsoring me. If they'll help me build a real career. After getting to know them a bit, I'm certain they'll say yes. Still, it feels cheap—wrong—to ask even more when so much has been taken from them already. But I have to know—before I agree to live with them. I can't let one dream thwart another. I need to find a way to develop a relationship with my new family *and* get out there on the circuit as soon as possible. "The thing is," I say, fighting the urge to avoid their eyes, "I've been planning on signing up for some pro tournaments this summer. It's important for me to earn ranking points. But the expenses involved have made that tricky—"

Ruth waves a hand, as if she can't imagine being bothered by such a thing as money. "We'll cover anything you need."

I chew on my lip, not allowing my hopes to get up just yet. "That's . . . wow. Thank you. That's incredibly nice of you. But you should know that starting a tennis career can be very expensive. There's a lot of travel and training and equipment involved—"

"Dara," William cuts me off. "It's not a problem. Like your grandmother said, we've missed out on too much of your life. Let us spoil you now." He grins.

I almost don't trust my own hearing. This is the one thing I've been praying for, and the Pembrokes just offered it up as if it's the simplest thing in the world.

"Really?" I whisper.

"Just one question," Ruth says. "Are there tournaments you can play in near where we live?"

"Yes—well, not *too* far away." I mentally run through the schedule I memorized while stalking the ITF website. "There are a few coming up in Winston-Salem, North Carolina; Sumter, South Carolina; and Charlottesville, Virginia." And the deadlines to register for them are fast approaching.

"Wonderful!" Ruth collects my hands in hers and squeezes. "You let me know the dates and I'll have our travel agent arrange everything. Perhaps we can even find some spas to stay at. We'll make a holiday out of it!" She's absolutely radiant with the idea.

"Well . . . okay then!" I'm grinning now too. "When do we leave?"

CHAPTER NINETEEN

"Sam!" I cry, out of breath, throwing open the door to his room. I ran at top speed all the way from the horse paddock. "You'll never guess what just happened."

"What?" He's coming out of the bathroom, toothbrush in hand.

"My grandparents have a tennis court! At their house! And they're giving it to me. They asked me to come stay with them and said they'd pay for me to travel to tournaments and whatever I need to make a career happen!"

"That's great. I'm happy for you." His voice says otherwise. He walks past me and tosses his toothbrush into his duffel, which is lying open on the bed. Then he goes to the dresser and starts packing his clothes too.

"Wait," I say, feeling like someone just pulled an emergency brake. "What's happening here?"

"I'm packing."

"Why?"

"Because I'm leaving."

"Leaving?" I repeat, stunned. "Where are you going?"

"Home. My bus leaves in a couple hours. Gabby said she'd drive me to the station." He hasn't shaved in a couple days, and he's got a smattering of dark stubble across his chin and cheeks. It makes him look older. Or maybe it's the exhaustion in his eyes that's doing that.

"Is this because we had a fight last night?" I'm starting to panic. "Everyone fights sometimes. It doesn't mean we're not friends anymore."

"That's not what this is about."

"What is it about, then?"

He looks at me. Cold. Detached. *He's already gone*, I think. "You don't need me here." He finishes packing up his clothes and zips the bag shut. "Honestly, you probably haven't needed me in a while. I just didn't want to see it."

"Of *course* I need you!" I cry.

Sam shakes his head vehemently. "You don't."

"No, really, I—"

"Dara!" He scrubs his hands down his face in frustration. "Listen to me. There's a difference between needing *me* and needing *someone*. You knew how I felt about you, and you used it, dragging me from place to place, expecting me to go along with all this, taking advantage of my presence when you needed it, tossing me aside when something—some*one*—more interesting came along. It was never me you needed. I was just a warm body to keep near when you didn't want to feel alone."

"That's not tr—" Hold on. "Wait, how you *felt* about me?"

He blinks, like he hadn't realized he'd said that. But the pause lasts barely a second—he seems to surrender to the turn the conversation has taken. "Don't act like you didn't know," he says, trying to be confident but looking more vulnerable than I've ever seen him.

"I didn't!" I cry.

Sam likes me? Like, *like* likes me? And *that's* why he's mad today? Not because of the fight but because he thinks I spent the night with Matt?

How did I not know this? I know I've been distracted this week, but the way he's talking, I think his feelings have been going on for longer than that.

"Tell me something," he says. "And don't lie."

I bite my lip and wait.

"Do you remember kissing me the other night?"

All the air leaves my body. I have no choice; I have to answer. "Yes," I whisper.

He shifts his weight. "Did you black out at all or was that just a convenient way to pretend it never happened?"

I don't answer. But I don't need to. He knows.

He slings his bag over his shoulder and walks around from the other side of the bed. "You know, just because you're going through a hard time doesn't mean you get to treat me like crap."

"Sam . . ." *I didn't spend the night with Matt. I lied to you because I thought I was saving our friendship.* I want to say it, but I know it won't change anything.

Instead, I ask a question of my own. Maybe I'm playing into his accusations of selfishness. I don't care. "Are you getting back together with Sarah?"

His face goes hollow. "Why would you ask that?"

"Because you've been texting her. I saw one of her texts when it came up on your phone—she said she thinks about you all the time."

His hand drifts to the pocket in his jeans where he keeps his phone. "I don't know. Maybe. She wants to."

"But what about college? All the reasons you broke up with her are still there."

"She wants to try to figure it out." He shrugs. "I think maybe I should try, too. There's no reason not to anymore." He pauses. Looks me in the eye. "And at least I'll know she'll be with me for the right reasons."

I don't know what to say to that. So I just . . . don't say anything.

His shoulders slump. "Bye, Dara." He turns toward the door.

"I called Mellie," I blurt out. It's a coward's move, but it's all I have.

He stops. Turns back. "You did?"

"Yes."

"When?"

"Last night."

"What did you talk about?"

"Not a lot. She said she's sorry."

"That's good."

"And I told her I was reading her emails."

"Why did you decide to call her?"

"Because I was sad and worried about her." I smirk. "I guess all that mean stuff you said to me last night got through after all."

He smiles, and it's like my chest has been lifted by the power of a thousand helium balloons. "I'm proud of you, Dara."

"Thanks."

A few moments pass.

"But I have to go." He comes close to me, gives me a heart-breakingly detached kiss on the cheek, and then walks out the door.

CHAPTER TWENTY

The rooster only has one job, and he does it well.

I slept on the couch again last night, because William and Ruth needed a room to stay in. With everything they're doing for me, it was the least I could do for them. But man, I'm tired.

I shower in Catherine's bathroom since she's already out with the animals. Then I get dressed, and zip my suitcase—I packed most of my things yesterday. When I come back downstairs, the sounds of the house are more awake.

"Good morning!" William greets me as I'm sitting on the couch tying my sneakers. "Ready to get on the road?"

"Sure. I just need to go say good-bye to everyone first."

"You got it." He picks up my bag and takes it out to the car.

I make a quick stop at the kitchen to grab an apple, and eat it as I head out to the farm. It's all hands on deck with the pigs this morning. I watch from the fence as the farm crew fills bowls, shovels poop, and re-hays the bedding. Jane fills a kiddie pool with water for the pigs to cool off in. One of the goats trots up next to me. I scratch between his little horns and give him my apple core. I'm going to miss this place, but it's time to move on.

In some ways, whatever's about to happen next is more of an unknown than what lay ahead of me after I left Francis. This isn't a fly-by-night adventure anymore. This is an informed decision, a calculated deviation from the path I've been on for most of my life.

This is what I want. But there are new things to be unsure of. What will it be like living with my grandparents? Will I manage to make friends there? How long will I stay? Will I go back to Francis to get my stuff? What will Sam say . . . if he's even speaking to me? And the hardest question to answer of all: How am I going to tell Mellie?

I ignore the way the apple seems to be turning to acid in my gut. The Charlottesville tournament is only a few weeks away, and registration closes in a couple days. I need to get training again.

Catherine turns around and sees me standing by the fence. She points me out to the others, and they all come over to say good-bye.

"Thanks for letting me help out," I tell them. "It was pretty interesting."

Meadow laughs. "Good interesting or bad interesting?"

"Definitely . . . enlightening," I say.

I give Jane, Meadow, Gabby, and Ezra each a quick hug, and they go back to work.

Catherine stands off to the side squinting up at the clouds in a not-so-discreet attempt to give Matt and me some alone time. I kind of wish she wouldn't—Matt and I have been tiptoeing around each other since the other night, and I don't really know what to say now that I'm face-to-face with him. This is what I imagine breaking up with someone and then having to see them every day at school feels like.

"So," I say, leaning back on my heels.

"Good luck with tennis," he says. "I'll be watching for you on TV. ESPN—that's a sports channel, right?"

I'm relieved for the excuse to laugh. "Yes. And thanks."

"And I hope everything works out with your mom."

I clear my throat. "You too—with your dad, I mean."

He brushes his toe across the dirt. "That ship has sailed, I think. But thanks." He pauses, as if considering whether to say something else.

"What?" I press.

He sighs. "Sam's a good guy. You two would be good together."

It's the last thing I expected him to say. Does he think that's why I stopped things between us the other night? "That's not . . . what this is."

He raises a skeptical eyebrow.

I frown at him. He might be only the second boy to kiss me, but that doesn't mean he *knows* me.

Matt leans down and kisses me lightly on the mouth. A good-bye. Sam's kiss on the cheek yesterday contained volumes, and this one, though far more intimate, is empty. But I force a friendly smile as Matt steps back. I'm sure the only reason I'm even thinking of Sam right now is because Matt brought him up.

"See ya around, Dara," he says.

Catherine walks me to the cars and gives me a big bear hug. I hold on to her fiercely. I'm suddenly scared, standing next to my open car door with no Sam in the passenger seat. Can I really do this on my own?

"Call me anytime," she says. We exchanged phone numbers last night, and I believe her when she says to use it. But I think it would help to know that I'll see her again before too long.

"Maybe you can visit Hilton Head soon?" I ask. "Or can you come to one of my tournaments?"

She gives an unconvincing smile. "We're negotiating with a dairy farm right now for some of their older cows, so I'm not sure when I'll be able to get away . . ." I feel my face fall, and Catherine sees it. She tacks on: "But I promise I'll try."

"Okay."

With a few final waves and *Drive safelys*, my grandparents get into their car, I get into mine, and we drive away.

CHAPTER TWENTY-ONE

About halfway into the two-hour drive, I hit a stretch of traffic.
There's roadwork going on, and the three highway lanes are being
funneled into one. I'm at a dead stop for several minutes, so I use
the time to check my email.

There's one new message from Mellie.

To: acelove6@email.com

From: Mellie.Baker@email.com

June 24 (9:59 AM)

Subject: Celeste

Dear Dara,

After I left home, my first instinct was to go to Kristen's house and
ask if I could stay there while I figured things out, but we hadn't
been close in years and I was scared of being turned away. So
I went to the bus station. The next bus was headed to Philadelphia.
I bought a ticket. Philly sounded as good a place as any.

I still hadn't showered after the day's practice, and I hoped the
people sitting around me hadn't noticed. Seven hours on a
cramped bus with strangers is bad enough without being sweaty
and smelly too. But I couldn't worry about it too much; I had more

pressing things to figure out, like what I was going to do when the bus reached its destination.

Before that afternoon, my plan for the future had been to get a job in town, go to community college, and eventually transfer to a bigger school where I could play tennis. I'd tried to get a scholarship right out of high school, but my grades hadn't been good enough. A smile of satisfaction ghosted across my lips when I thought of how my father had already put down a nonrefundable deposit on my first semester at the community college. But the glimmer of levity faded fast.

As I watched the road blur outside the bus window, I came to a decision. I was going to make whatever sacrifices I had to, do whatever it took, to make my family regret the way they'd treated me. We'd reconnect in the future, after I was a successful, rich tennis star, and they'd realize that all this time *I* had been better than *them*, not the other way around. They'd beg me to forgive them, and I'd be the one with the power this time.

The image fueled my determination and helped ease the enormity of what had just happened. *This won't be forever. I'll show them.*

Determination quickly became an obsession.

I had a little money saved, so I used it to rent out the cheapest room I could find. There was no kitchen—just a sink and a microwave—and the shared bathroom was down the hall, but it was fine enough. I took the first job I was offered—a gig at a shoe store. My days were spent hauling shoe boxes from the stock room to the sales floor and back again. After rent and food, the rest of my money went to a cheap membership at the YMCA. I played as many pickup games as I could get there, and eventually was noticed by the right people. I was offered a job teaching adult beginner tennis clinics at a swankier, better-equipped athletic facility across town. That led to an opportunity to train with a coach. Finally, though I was still struggling to make ends meet, I had enough flexibility to start playing in tournaments.

A year after leaving home, my solitary goal was still to be the best. To achieve higher levels of success, to prove my parents wrong. I didn't stop to think about anything else, including my own happiness. I was now playing professionally—I wasn't winning any titles, but I was ranked, my name was out there, and I was making some money—but I hadn't heard a whisper from any of my family members. No matter. I kept pushing.

The result was that my body was in the best shape of my life and my mind was in the worst.

The suicidal thoughts came back, louder and more insistent now. I'd started to shave with a straight razor, because it was the closest shave I could get, and I began to be careless with it, shaving rapidly, flinging the razor around my face with minimal focus. During times like these, a small part of me acknowledged that I was almost hoping the blade would slip and slice open a jugular vein and I'd be dead without ever fully having had to make the decision to be so. The thought actually brightened my mood temporarily.

It was in the midst of all this that I met Celeste. Your biological mother. The love of my life.

We met at a Lady Foot Locker, of all places—I'd been having a particularly difficult day and, in a moment of weakness, had wandered in to admire the display of women's tennis shoes. Celeste was sitting on one of the padded benches, trying on a new pair of running shoes. They were lime green with neon-pink laces and a pink Nike swoop. Colorful—just, as I would learn, like her.

"Those are nice," I said without thinking. I usually kept to myself when I went into women's stores—I always felt like the childless old man at the playground: creepy and completely out of place. But I was tired, and my filter was down.

She looked up, and her smile beamed new life into me. She was beautiful. Chin-length blonde hair, sparkling eyes, and dimples that looked like they'd been carved by Michelangelo himself.

"You think so?" she asked. "I didn't know if they were too much."

I shook my head, and felt my face contort into the unfamiliar stretches of a smile. "If you don't get them, I will." I immediately wanted to clamp a hand over my mouth and take the words back. I never said things like that, even in jest. I didn't even let myself think things like that too often. Transitioning wasn't any more an option now than it had been when I lived with my parents. Tennis was the most important thing. I couldn't lose sight of that.

But Celeste just giggled and said, "You've convinced me. Thanks." She held out her hand and I shook it. "I'm Celeste."

"I'm Marcus."

"What are you doing in a Lady Foot Locker, Marcus?" She was teasing, not accusatory.

I swallowed. "Looking for . . . a gift."

"For your girlfriend?"

I shook my head. "No. No girlfriend."

"Glad to hear it." She bit her lip. "Do you go to U Penn?"

We weren't too far from the university's campus. "No. Do you?"

She nodded. "I'm a sophomore." We were the same age.

"What are you studying?"

"I haven't declared a major yet." She gave an unconcerned shrug. "I've just been taking a bunch of different courses and try-ing to figure out what I want to do. My parents want me to be a lawyer, so I'll probably end up doing that."

"Right." I didn't know what else to say—I didn't have much to offer in the "parents caring about your future" department. The lull in conversation shifted into a full-on silence, and I knew I should duck out before I said something else stupid just to fill the gap. "Well, I'd better be—"

I jerked a thumb toward the exit and began to turn that way, when Celeste said, "I was going to grab some kimchi mandu at the Korean place next door after this. Any interest in joining me?"

I stared at her. *Did this gorgeous, perfect ray of light just ask me out?* I'd gone on a couple of dates since living in Philly, but I hadn't had half the connection with those women that I felt with Celeste after one minute. If anyone had been watching, they wouldn't see anything particularly noteworthy: a guy and a girl engaged in a few smiles and some small talk. But the flips of my stomach, the sweat on my palms, the frenzy of my heartbeat were telling a very different story. I knew if I said yes, this one was going to stick.

The thought terrified me. I hadn't been truly close with another person since Kristen. And she and I had never been more than friends, no matter how much I had wished for it. There were so many places—emotionally and physically—we hadn't gone. I was nineteen now. An adult, for all intents and purposes, though I hadn't yet had my first kiss. I didn't know what having a girlfriend entailed, not really, but I knew it would be big and exciting . . . and very tricky.

This angel in front of me did not deserve to be pulled into my web of shit.

Say no, I lectured myself. *Say no.*

But Celeste had me caught in her smile, and all I could possibly say was, "I love spicy food."

Love,
Mom

....

I follow my grandparents' car into their driveway a little after eleven a.m. I'm tired and hungry, and can't quite believe I'm at my new home.

This house is different still from the ivy-covered Cherry Hill house and from the sprawling white farmhouse. It's imposing and pristine, with tall columns and curved staircases. It looks like it should be the setting for a Civil War–era debutante ball. The property, William tells me, used to be a plantation. That information doesn't make me feel great, but I try to remember that there are no slaves here now, and there haven't been for a long time, and the Pembrokes didn't have anything to do with it when there were. I hope.

"I noticed you have an accent, William," I say as they show me around the house. "Did you live in the South before moving to New Jersey?"

"Very astute! I grew up in Georgia, and lived there until Yale Law came calling."

"Is your family still there?"

"My parents are gone now, but I do have one brother who lives outside of Atlanta. You'll meet him someday."

"Meet him *again*," Ruth corrects.

"Yes, of course. You did meet him when you were a baby."

"Oh." I nod.

We climb one of the staircases. They point out a shiny bathroom that they say is all mine, the laundry room, and the upstairs sitting room.

"And this," Ruth says, opening another door, "is your room."

It's like something out of a magazine. Windows on two sides, four-poster bed, enough space to hold a cardio kickboxing class, and French doors leading onto a private terrace. The view overlooks the Harbor River. I run my fingertips over the intricately embroidered white duvet, the gauzy curtains.

"Of course, we can change the décor if it's not to your tastes," she says.

I shake my head. "It's perfect. Thank you. For everything."

"We'll leave you to get settled in," William says. "Lunch will be in the dining room at noon. And then"—he gets a gleam in his eye—"what do you say to going to look at the tennis court?"

I grin. "Can't wait."

....

Lunch ends up being more of a "luncheon." Even though it's just the three of us, it's a sit-down meal in the formal dining room. Ruth and William are already seated when I arrive—William at the head of the long table, Ruth just to his right. Glistening white place settings rest before them, though there's no food on the table. The chandelier is lit, as are two tall candles in the center of the table.

"I'm sorry; I thought I was on time," I say, sitting quickly in the seat across from Ruth.

"You are right on time. Not to worry!" she says warmly.

I'm still wearing my outfit from earlier in the day—my standard leggings and tank, plus a hoodie I threw on because the central air in this house seems to be cranked up to museum levels—but both Ruth and William have changed. William is wearing a suit jacket and Ruth is in a maroon short-sleeved lace top. Her makeup looks freshly reapplied too. They don't say anything about my appearance, but I'm suddenly feeling like I've done everything wrong. I zip the hoodie up to my collarbone.

A maid in a gray uniform serves us a soup course first. I never knew soup was supposed to be a "course"—on the occasions we've made it at home, it's always been the main event.

The bits of vegetable and shrimp slide down my throat and warm me. "Wow, this is so good," I say, trying not to slurp. "Do you have lunch like this every day? Or is it a special occasion?"

They laugh, as if I've said the cleverest, most delightful thing in the world. "Both!" William says. "We've worked hard for the things we have, and we don't think there's anything wrong in enjoying them. But today is absolutely a special occasion as well. You being here with us, Dara . . ." He gets a little choked up, and takes a moment to collect himself, patting his cloth napkin against his mouth. "Well, it's a dream come true."

"Thank you," I say. "It is for me too. I've always wanted a big family, but never knew it was a possibility for me."

Ruth and William clasp hands on top of the tablecloth.

The main course is a spring risotto with asparagus and shelled edamame. The texture is perfect, but the flavor is a little bland. "Do you have any hot sauce?" I ask the maid as she comes around to refill our glasses of iced tea.

Ruth answers for her. "No, we don't. That stuff is all sodium, and it completely defeats the chef's intent for the meal. Is your risotto not to your liking?"

"Oh, no, it's delicious," I say quickly. "I just prefer foods with a bit of a kick. It's not a problem." I fork another bite in my mouth to prove it.

After a dessert of raspberry sorbet, William and Ruth give me a tour of the grounds, culminating with the tennis court. I assumed the court would be nice. I did not, however, expect to be stepping onto the most exquisite home court I've ever seen. It's a regulation-size hard court with a blue acrylic surface, a ball machine, a locker room stocked with racquets and balls, and even a few rows of padded stadium-type seats for spectators.

"What do you think?" Ruth asks, and I turn to find both my grandparents looking at me hopefully, as if they're praying this will meet my standards and I'll want to stay.

"I think I've never seen anything more beautiful in my life," I say, and they beam in satisfaction. "Would you mind if I practiced for a little while?"

"Please do!" William says. "We'll leave you to it. Do you remember how to get back to the house from here?"

"I think so. But I'll call you if I get lost."

I select a racquet from the locker room. I know I could run back to the house for my own stuff, but I've found my own slice of heaven and I don't want to leave it yet. I'll bring my tennis bag down here tomorrow.

I serve one ball, then two, three, over the net, warming up my shoulder. I bounce on my feet, testing the give of the court. I stretch. Run circles around the net.

And then, my racquet in one hand and a brand-new ball in the other, I position myself square in front of the ball machine.

The rest of the day passes in a blissful blur.

CHAPTER TWENTY-TWO

The heavy duvet weighs down on me pleasantly. Airy, translucent fabric drapes from the posts rising from the bed's four corners. The sound of lapping water drifts in through the open French doors.

My first morning at my grandparents'.

I sit up amidst the numerous pillows, feeling more rested and alert than I have in a long time. Yesterday's stint on the court was amazing, and dinner last night was delicious. I'd put on the lavender dress before meeting Ruth and William in the dining room at seven; they seemed pleased by that. And the steak was cooked so perfectly that it only took one tentative bite before any guilt I'd felt after spending the weekend at Catherine's farm sanctuary fled my thoughts.

There are no new email notifications on my phone. I choose to take that as a good sign, that Mellie spent the night actually sleeping. But there's a part of me that wonders if she's okay.

I get dressed in practice clothes and go downstairs. Ruth is at the kitchen table with a steaming mug of coffee, reading a book on her tablet.

"Good morning," I say, pouring myself a glass of water.

"Good morning, Dara. Did you sleep all right?"

"More than all right. That bed is really comfortable."

"I'm so glad to hear that!"

I open the fridge and take out two eggs, then put a pan on the stove to heat.

"You don't have to do that," Ruth says, standing. "Let Penelope fix breakfast for you. She can make anything you like. Penelope!" she calls loudly from the kitchen doorway.

Can she make a bottle of hot sauce appear out of thin air? I like my eggs spicy. "Oh no, that's all right. I'm used to cooking for myself. I don't mind at all."

Ruth's lips thin, and she watches disapprovingly as I crack and scramble the eggs, but she doesn't press. "Your grandfather took the boat out early this morning," she says, "but he asked me to let you know that he's arranged some meetings with the three tennis pros at the country club beginning at one o'clock this afternoon."

I blink. "He did?"

She picks up on my confusion. "You said you work with a trainer, correct? Or you need to? There are some very talented people who work at our club. I've taken a lesson here and there, and I'm always so impressed by what they can do. We thought maybe you'd like to choose one of them to train with."

"Wow. That's so nice. Thank you!"

Ruth steps closer as I push the eggs around the pan. "We meant what we said, Dara. Whatever you need. We want you to be happy here."

"In that case . . ." I say.

"Yes?"

"I need to sign up for those tournaments. The deadline for the Virginia one is tomorrow, I think."

"Let's do that right now, then!" She snaps into action, opening a new browser window on her tablet, propping up the device so the screen is facing out, and positioning two of the kitchen chairs around it.

I laugh as I plate my eggs and bring them over to the table.

Signing up for this summer's tournaments in Virginia, South Carolina, and North Carolina takes far less time than I feel like it should. I already have a player identification number from my time on the junior circuit, so with only a few clicks and a few entry forms, I'm registered. After all these years of struggling, striving, it's all disconcertingly simple. No choruses singing, no parades, no confetti poppers.

But there is a light ignited in my chest. A newfound feeling of rightness. Odds are I won't win any of these tournaments—you can't get to your destination without taking the journey first. But at least I've finally boarded the train. And Ruth is so excited to help me do this—it feels unspeakably good, having a parent figure get behind my dream.

Later, at the country club, a sprawling place where everyone seems to wear the same crisp white clothes and speak at the same low volume, I meet Keith, Debbie, and Monique, the local tennis pros. I get to do a mini-lesson with each. Ruth says it's entirely up to me who I go with, and to pick the one I like best.

I rule out Keith right away. He's an incredible player, and I do think he would be a good coach, but having another male coach in his fifties would remind me too much of Bob. Training with a woman who's actually played on the women's circuit would not only open up a whole new view of the game for me, it would be enough of a separation from my years with Bob that it would keep the guilt at bay. I hope, anyway.

Debbie is someone I think I'd like to be friends with. She's in her midtwenties, and the tight bun she wears her reddish hair in reminds me of Mary. We hit the ball back and forth, and she keeps calling out compliments like "Wow, I didn't learn to serve like that until I was twenty-three!" or "Great shot!" I get the sense that she's new at this, and while I'm glad I'm impressing her, I don't know if she'd challenge me enough.

Monique, on the other hand, is fierce, both in her ability and her instruction. She wears her hair in lots of little braids that she ties back into one thick braid while on the court, and the muscle definition in her arms is goal-worthy. She plays in about fifteen tournaments a year, and is both the highest-ranked player and most businesslike of the three.

"Show me what you've most recently been working on with your trainer in New York," she says when we get on the court.

I demonstrate my two-handed backhand. Bob was right—it's gotten really good, even after nearly a week of not practicing very much. I expect Monique to at least smile, but she just watches and nods. "Again," she says in a *What did you think? You'd hit one ball and I'd give you a gold star?* tone.

I hit the shot several more times, waiting for her next instruction.

Finally, she holds up a hand. "What else?"

"Um. We were actually just about to start focusing more on my backspin lob," I say.

"Show me."

I do, and she just nods again. Monique is the complete opposite of Debbie. I wonder if she even knows *how* to smile.

"Let's play a set," she says, taking up position across the net.

She is the toughest opponent I've ever faced. I manage a few points, but they're not easily won.

"Your defensive game needs work," she says matter-of-factly, echoing what Bob said at our last session.

"I know. And I'm ready to put the work in."

She assesses me a moment more and then says, "Very well," apparently pleased at my response.

We set up a schedule: two-hour training sessions, five mornings a week at my grandparents' home court. It's a far cry from the measly two shared sessions a week with Bob and Mary, and the commute's a lot better too.

Monique's style isn't exactly warm and fuzzy, but I trust her. She picked up on the same problems in my game that Bob did. That's worth more to me than any résumé or ranking. I know I'll be able to learn a lot from her.

When we get back from the club, Ruth and I take a walk along the shore. I give her a hug—the first one I've initiated on my own. "Thank you," I say.

She hugs me back, but far more gingerly than usual, and I realize my sweaty workout clothes are grossing her out. I don't think

I smell, but I end the hug and step back a bit just in case. "You're very welcome, dear," she says.

"I . . . need to make a phone call," I tell her. "Would you mind giving me a few minutes?"

Her demeanor closes off in a flash. "Who are you calling?" There's an edge in her voice I haven't heard before.

She thinks I'm calling Mellie. "I have to call Bob, my tennis coach back home."

And just like that, she relaxes. "Of course. I'll give you some privacy." She goes to dip her feet in the water, and I sit in the sand.

I know I have to make this call, but right now I'd give anything not to. There's a knot in my stomach again—not the before-a-match nerves, and not quite the anxiety I felt before I met my new family. More like the unsettled feeling I experienced every time I talked to Mellie about tennis, because I knew what I had to say was going to make her unhappy, and I was about to ruin the good thing we had going.

I take a deep breath and dial.

"Back at it tomorrow, yeah?" Bob says upon answering. "You know what they say about idle feet."

I thought the saying was about idle hands. "Hey, Bob. Actually, that's what I'm calling about. I know I said I'd be back to training tomorrow, but . . . I'm going to be staying with my grandparents in South Carolina for a while."

There's a pause. "For how long?" All jokiness has vanished.

I watch as Ruth waves to a woman wearing a floppy straw hat. They strike up a friendly conversation. Must be one of the neighbors. "I don't know," I tell Bob. "For the foreseeable future."

"What about tennis?"

"Nothing's changed," I assure him. "My grandparents have an incredible court on their property and I found a local pro who's going to train with me. And I signed up for three tournaments this morning. The first one's in Charlottesville in a couple weeks."

Another pause. A longer one this time.

"Bob? You there?"

"Sounds like you've got everything figured out." He sounds hurt. "Call me when you're back, I guess."

Guilt gnaws at me. I feel like I cheated on him and then dumped him and made him feel like it was all his fault. But what else am I supposed to do? "I will," I promise.

I'm going to miss him, but I vow to keep in touch.

Boats float by serenely, like leaves in a pond. One of them is probably William's, but I haven't learned how to distinguish his boat from the others yet. Two little kids and their dad dig for mussels, and a seagull swoops down and snatches one right out of the boy's hands. A dog kicks up sand as he runs in pursuit of a ball.

Sam would love it here. So many scenes perfect for capturing on film.

Ruth waves me over.

"Dara, meet JoBeth Montgomery." She indicates her hat-wearing friend, a petite, brunette woman a little younger than Ruth but just as put together. "She lives down the beach from us. JoBeth, this is my granddaughter, Dara."

JoBeth gasps, and gapes at Ruth in disbelief. "Not *the* Dara?"

Ruth puts her arm around me proudly. Possessively. "The very one."

"Nice to meet you," I say, and shake her hand.

She unabashedly surveys me from head to toe, like she's going to go paint my portrait later or something. "Well! What a pretty, polite young woman! You seem to have turned out just fine." She sounds surprised.

I tilt my head. "Sorry?"

She leans in, like we're best friends sharing a secret. "You have no idea how worried your grandparents have been, knowing you were out there being raised by . . . you know." She shakes her head sadly.

What is this woman getting at? I open my mouth to respond, but Ruth cuts in. "I'm sorry, JoBeth, but we do have to be going. We'll talk soon." She places a hand on my arm and guides me away.

"Wonderful to meet you, Dara," JoBeth calls after us.

"What was that all about?" I ask. Clearly, William and Ruth have told their friends about me. But it's what they may have been saying about Mellie that I'm more concerned about.

"Oh, she just knows how much we've missed you." She bends down to pick up a seashell but then tosses it when she sees it has a crack. "Now, we've got the court and trainer and tournaments sorted. I called our travel agent, and she's making all the airline and hotel arrangements. What's next?"

"Um . . ." I try to shift gears as we turn in the direction of the house. "I actually need to get a passport. Do you think you'd be able to help me with that?"

"You don't have a passport yet?" she says, almost angry. "Let's go do that right now, shall we?"

"It might be complicated, though. I know you need to show them your birth certificate, and mine says Dara Hogan, not Dara Baker."

She purses her lips, thinking. "I suppose you could apply for it under the name Dara Hogan, then?"

I shake my head. "I think my mom legally changed our names to Baker. But I don't have any of that paperwork. I guess I could ask her for it—"

"No, no, you don't want to do that," she says hurriedly. "What if . . . what if you changed your name legally again? Back to Hogan . . . or even to Pembroke, if you like." She looks up at me innocently, as if this idea has just occurred to her. But she says it so easily that I have to wonder. "And then you can apply for the passport with that name."

"Oh. That could work, maybe." But what name would I choose? "Let me think about it?"

"Take all the time you need." She pats my back. "I'll never forget the first stamp I got in my passport. My mother took me to Paris for a week when I was sixteen." She sighs wistfully.

"Wow, that sounds amazing."

"It was the trip of a lifetime." She smiles. "Perhaps you and I can go together sometime. Depending on your tournament schedule, of course."

"There are actually tournaments in France," I say. "Maybe we could do both at once."

"Well, there you go! Consider it done."

....

I have some downtime before dinner, so I take a shower, get dressed in jeans and a T-shirt since I can't keep wearing that same dress, and check my email. Some spam and information about the tournaments, but nothing else. I was hoping the next chapter of the Celeste story would be waiting for me. I wonder if Sam told Mellie where I am, and if she's upset.

Ruth lent me one of her books, so I bring it out to my terrace to try to read for a while, but Bob's disappointed voice, the fact that it's been over twenty-four hours since Mellie wrote to me, and the uncharacteristic radio silence from Sam keep tripping through my thoughts, distracting me. Why is it that I finally have everything I've ever wanted, and everyone's mad at me for it?

And if Mellie really is unhappy with me for coming to stay with the Pembrokes, is it a healthy, normal kind of unhappy, or is it the I-should-have-Niya-go-check-to-make-sure-she's-still-breathing kind of unhappy?

I end up just watching the river.

Ten minutes before dinner, the alarm I set on my phone goes off, and I fight my way out of my daze and head downstairs. I've learned that in this house, early is on time, and on time is actually late.

"Dara," William says as we eat, "your grandmother and I were talking, and we'd love it if you'd consider calling us Grandma and Grandpa."

I swallow my half-chewed bite of baked salmon with toasted almond and summer squash salad. Their faces are expectant, rosy, a little nervous.

It's a reasonable request, considering they *are* my grandparents and they've taken me under their wing like only two people who really care about you could. But it feels . . . forced. Names like "Mom," "Grandma," and "Grandpa" should only happen one of two ways—you think of the person as that from the very beginning, as if it's their actual name, or they earn it over a long period of time and trust and comfort. We're on our way to the latter, but haven't quite arrived yet.

I can't say that, though. "Okay," I say. "I'll try to remember to."

They beam. Then Ruth says, "Dara's thinking of changing her last name to Pembroke, William. Isn't that wonderful?"

My fork clatters against my plate.

"Really!" he exclaims. "Well, I believe this is cause for a celebration!" He leaves the table, and returns a moment later with a chilled bottle of champagne and three glasses. "To our family," he toasts after we've each taken a glass. "Finally complete once more. May Celeste be watching down on us and smiling."

I take the tiniest sip possible and try to maintain my smile. They're so happy; I can't ruin it.

But in my mind I'm rereading Mellie's email—the one about Kristen's sister changing her first name, and how that was such a revelation to Mellie. All the Marcus talk this week, the Grandma/ Grandpa stuff, the eagerness of my grandparents to turn me into a Pembroke . . . I never thought about it before, but names really do have meaning. So you should probably make sure the one you have is one you like.

Ruth and William continue eating their dinner. I push my food around.

I came here to meet my family, learn where I came from. And I've done that. I'm still doing that. But could it be possible that where I come from and who I *am* are two different things? I don't know if I want to be Dara Pembroke. I don't think I should have to be, to be part of their world.

And I definitely don't want to be Dara Hogan, after learning about the Hogans from Mellie's emails.

"Um," I begin timidly, and they look up.

"Yes, dear?"

"I'm so sorry, and I don't want you to think I'm not grateful for everything you've done for me . . ."

They wait.

I can't meet their eyes. "But I think I'm actually going to keep my name. Baker."

Ruth barely reacts, just rests her fork and knife on the edge of her plate and pats her mouth with her cloth napkin. William, however, doesn't hide his disappointment. "Oh, I . . . did we misunderstand something?" he asks, glancing at his wife.

"No," I say quickly. "Not at all. I did tell Ruth—Grandma— that I'd consider it. She wasn't wrong. I just decided right now."

"I see," he says.

"Dara Baker might not be who I was born as," I say, trying to find the right words, "but it's who I am now. I feel comfortable as Dara Baker. I know her." *I like her.*

"We understand," he says, nodding. "We just want you to be happy. Don't we, darling?"

Ruth nods. "Yes. Of course. That's the most important thing."

The atmosphere has changed, though, and I say the first thing I can think of to bring us all back together again: "I was wondering if you had any old videos of Celeste that I could watch." There are framed photos of her all over the house, but I'd love to be able to get a sense of her demeanor, her movements, the shape her mouth took when she spoke.

That gets Ruth to smile. "As a matter of fact, we had all our home movies transferred to digital files a few years ago. Is there anything in particular you'd like to see?"

"Everything," I say. "I want to learn as much about her as I can."

"Ask and you shall receive!" She finishes her champagne, folds her napkin, and places it on the table. "Are you finished with your supper?"

"Yes," I say, and it's true, though I didn't eat much. "It was delicious. Thank you."

"I'll have Penelope serve the coffee and dessert in the television room."

There are dozens of videos. William helps us get set up, then leaves Ruth and me to reminisce on our own, claiming this should be a time for grandmother/granddaughter bonding. I suspect he secretly fears the videos will make him too emotional.

Celeste was the baby of the family, and her parents clearly worshipped her. We start at the beginning, with the grainy recording of Ruth holding wrinkly, newborn Celeste as they're wheeled to the car outside the hospital. Little Catherine, only two years old, wearing a pale-blue dress, saggy tights, and a crown that says BIG SISTER, toddles beside the wheelchair, peering over the edge at the new baby.

A video from a few years later shows Celeste and Catherine under a pink sheet tent in Celeste's bedroom, Catherine reading to her sister from a storybook about farm animals. They appear to not know Ruth and her camera are watching them. "Do the piggy voice, Catherine!" Celeste begs in her tiny soprano, and Catherine obliges, puffing out her cheeks and putting on a silly accent.

Another video is of nine-year-old Celeste at a playground. "Mom, look!" she shouts, waving, and the camera zooms in as she zips her way across the monkey bars. Her blonde ponytail swings behind her in the breeze.

"She looks like me at that age," I murmur.

Ruth pulls her misty gaze from the image of her happy, very much alive daughter on the screen. "You look like her now too."

I smile sadly, and nod. Catherine had said the same thing. It's nice to hear from the people who knew and loved Celeste. "The dimple," I say, pointing under my eye.

She nods. "That's part of it, yes. And your voices are similar. You sound much more like her than Catherine or I ever did."

"I never even thought about what her voice sounded like," I whisper guiltily.

"Oh, my dear girl." Ruth tucks me in close to her side, so my head is resting in the crook between her shoulder and neck.

My phone, which is on the coffee table in front of us, beeps with a new text. I jump a little at the sound—I haven't gotten a text in a while. *Maybe it's Sam.* My heart beats harder. I sit up and click the screen on. Not Sam. Not Mom. It's from Mary, of all people.

Bob told me you're not coming back. Thanks for telling me. He's not the only one you're abandoning, you know.

Crap. I did forget all about Mary.

Another text comes in.

I'll see you in Charlottesville. Get ready to lose.

Mary's playing in the tournament. Which means Bob will be there too. My stomach squirms. I don't want to have to face them. She's right—I did abandon them. I wish I could give them an explanation, tell them what's been going on. Surely they'd understand then. But who knows who they'd tell. I can't put Mellie at risk.

Ruth pauses the TV. "Is everything all right?"

I make my phone screen go black without replying to Mary. "Yes. Everything's fine. Sorry."

The home movies continue. There are birthday parties and Christmas mornings, school plays and ballet recitals, visits to the zoo and Disney World, graduations. Celeste is happy and smiling in all of them, often hugging her sister or holding hands with her mother or teasing her father. It's clear she loved her family very much.

By the time we reach the end, I feel a bit closer to my birth mother. I'll never get the chance to truly know her, but at least now I have a sense of her. A more complete image to hold on to.

"I'm so glad you had these," I say to Ruth as she turns off the TV and we collect our empty coffee cups. "Thank you for showing them to me."

"Thank you for asking," she says. "It's been a while since I've watched them. I think I needed it as much as you did."

As I make my way to my room, a thought occurs to me: There must be video of Mellie and Celeste's *wedding* somewhere too. Now that I know I had two parents who loved each other, who married each other, I can't help wanting to see what that looked like. The dress, the kiss, the dancing, the cake.

But then I'd also have to hear people calling Mellie Marcus. I'd maybe even have to hear her call *herself* Marcus in the recitation of her vows.

As I get ready for bed, I decide to ask Ruth about the wedding album—and only the album—soon.

I slip under the expensive duvet and slide my phone off the nightstand so I can write to Mellie and ask her to send me the passport documentation. But just as I do so, it dings with a new email. Finally.

To: acelove6@email.com

From: Mellie.Baker@email.com

June 25 (9:49 PM)

Subject: Coming out

Dear Dara,

Celeste and I fell in love like Serena Williams serves: fast, hard, and with a little bit of magic.

We couldn't get enough of each other. During the days we were busy—me with training, her with school—but the nights were ours. She slept most nights at my new apartment; her dorm was basically just a storage unit for her stuff now. I cooked for us while she studied, and then after dinner, we'd talk and read to each other and watch movies and play games and do puzzles. We went on long runs together on Saturday and Sunday mornings.

I said "I love you" first. She said it back immediately.

Her friends became my friends. They were interesting, wonderful people. A couple of them were even openly gay.

I went with Celeste to her parents' house for Thanksgiving and Christmas. Believe it or not, the Pembrokes and I got along well back then. They welcomed me instantly.

She was at all my important matches, cheering me on.

But there were things I still hadn't told her.

She knew I was driven, and she knew I struggled with depression, and she knew I was estranged from my family. She just didn't know why. But she stuck by me, and said she knew I'd tell her when it felt right. Which allowed me to breathe easier temporarily, but put a lot more pressure on me long-term. Eventually, I would have to tell her. Either that, or leave her. Both felt impossible.

Celeste urged me to see a therapist, but I resisted. It was the obvious place to try to start to work through things; I knew that. But I knew if I spoke to a therapist I would have to tell them the whole truth—they wouldn't let me off the hook like Celeste had. And, honestly, it felt wrong to tell anyone without having first told her. She was the most important person in my life. She was part of me. I trusted her. She had to be the first person I told.

I was just so scared.

But the feelings weren't going away, and no matter how hard I fought, or how much I focused on other things, they were taking over an increasingly more prominent part of my thoughts. I was slipping too—I'd gone into a makeup store and bought a tube of mascara, without ever fully deciding to do so. I'd just been walking by the store and it suddenly felt imperative that I go inside and buy something, anything. And a few times, while Celeste was at class, I'd tried on some of her dresses. I told myself I would stop doing it, but I knew I wouldn't. It felt too good. And I desperately needed to feel good.

So one night at dinner, about a year and a half into our relationship, I forced the words out.

"Celeste, I have something to tell you."

"What's up, babe?" She took a bite of the grilled asparagus I'd made and gave me a thumbs-up.

I cleared my throat. "Can you put the food down for a sec?"

She laughed. "Sorry. I'm famished."

"This will only take a minute."

She seemed to realize how nervous I was then, and her expression sobered. "What's wrong?"

I shook my head. "Nothing's *wrong*. I don't think. Actually, I don't know. Uh . . . you'll have to tell me."

Her eyebrows pulled together, but she didn't say anything.

I took a deep breath. "I think—I mean, I know—I'm transgender." My voice cracked on the word, but *I did it*. I got it out.

She pursed her lips, pulled inside her own thoughts, and my entire body shut down while I waited—I couldn't breathe, move, think. The only thing still working was my heart, which was beating even faster now than it had been before I said the words. Finally, she asked, "What is that?"

I expelled the breath I'd been holding. *Of course.* She hadn't had the word dancing around her brain, taunting her, for years like I had. And this was before all the TV shows and movies and the celebrities coming out—trans issues weren't anything close to mainstream. Celeste honestly had no idea what I was talking about. The realization almost made me laugh. But now I had to do something I hadn't anticipated—I had to explain.

So I did, as best I could. I gave her the textbook stuff, the basic definition, and then I kept it specific to me, my own experience.

She remained perfectly quiet and still. One thing was clear—she definitely hadn't suspected. Her eyes grew glassy, and they flickered as if she were thinking hard. I imagined she was reworking our entire relationship, past and future, in her mind. I felt like the worst kind of garbage, tearing down her illusions of who I was, what our life together was. I only hoped there would still be a foundation standing when I was done.

I told her about the mascara, and I told her about her clothes. I told her how envious I was of her—of her body, her pronouns, the way she was perceived by the world.

"But . . . do you . . . ?" she started, then shook her head and pressed the heels of her hands against her eyes. Her dinner was pushed away now, forgotten.

"Do I what?"

"You want to be like me. I get it. I mean, I *don't*, but I'm hearing what you're saying. But . . . do you still want to be *with* me?"

My heart broke in half. "Oh my God. Of *course* I want to be with you." I grabbed her hands. "That's why I'm telling you all this.

You're the first person I've ever told. I love you, and I trust you, and I needed you to know me—all of me."

"And this is why you've been so down?"

"I think so. Maybe. Yes." I didn't tell her, though, about how sometimes I thought about slipping away, leaving the world behind for good. About how it had always felt like a solution, ever since I was a kid. She didn't need to know that. And the very fact that I was telling her about me now meant I was trying to *live*, right? I was trying to find a way to be okay.

"And it's why you don't talk to your parents?"

"They didn't *know* know, but they knew I was different—I think they thought I was gay—and they weren't okay with it."

"But you *are* gay. At least you think you are?"

I blinked. "No, I . . . what?"

"You said you think you're a woman . . . on the inside. And you said you still love me and want to be with me. So that means you think you're . . . a lesbian." She was speaking slowly, clearly trying to make sense of it all as she went.

I hadn't thought of it that way before. "Oh. Well, I guess so. Yes." I didn't like the idea of yet another label, yet another thing to make me *different*, but if it helped clarify things for Celeste, I was on board.

"But I'm not a lesbian," she said.

"I know."

"But . . . you want to . . . ?"

"Do I want to what?" I asked. I kept my voice soft, as if the room were filled with sleeping babies. "You can say whatever you're thinking."

She chewed on her lip. "I don't know. Become . . . a woman?"

"Yes," I said right away, and was sure my own expression was as shocked as Celeste's was. But now that the truth was out, I felt clearer. I'd opened up space in my mind for even more truth, more possibilities. I *did* want to present as a woman full-time. I wanted it more than anything. "But I can't," I said.

"Because . . . ?" Her tone was almost encouraging now. I could tell there was something she wanted me to say here, but I didn't know what it was.

"Because it's hard. And expensive. And because I need to keep playing tennis. I need to make it. I can't prove my parents right."

She looked down. "And because of me, right? Because you still want to be with me?"

I nodded profusely. "Yes." A little twinge of guilt prickled my stomach then, because I *hadn't* considered Celeste in my reasoning to keep living as the wrong gender. It had always been about my parents and tennis and not veering from that path. And of course the impossible logistics, and the fact that I didn't know if I was strong enough, emotionally, to handle what would inevitably come at me. But Celeste and I had always been so solid that I'd started to take her presence in my life for granted.

There was a stretch of silence. Celeste took her hands back and placed them in her lap. Then she got up, poured herself a glass of wine, and took a long sip. She came back to the table, but didn't sit down. "Listen, Marcus. I love you. I still want to be with you. And if putting on my clothes sometimes, when no one else is around, is going to make you happy, I can live with that. As long as you don't stretch them out." She raised an eyebrow.

I laughed at her joke, and felt warm all over. I couldn't believe it. She was saying it was okay. She was saying she understood.

"But it has to be in private," she continued. "You can't even do it around me. If that's not okay with you, we have to break up. I'm not a lesbian."

I nodded. "Absolutely." It made sense, though she didn't seem to grasp that whether I transitioned or not, I was still a woman.

"Nothing's going to change." She was telling me, not asking.

"Nothing's going to change," I agreed.

And to the rest of the world, nothing did. I remained a he, as far as Celeste and everyone else were concerned, and life went on.

But now that I had permission, I allowed myself to "go there" more than I ever had. I started buying some pretty things of my own to put on at home when she wasn't around. I started tweezing my eyebrows . . . just a bit. I grew my hair longer . . . also just a bit. Celeste saw the new clothes and new underwear in my dresser; she saw the makeup in the bathroom cabinet. She didn't say a thing about any of it.

It was new, exciting, and enough. For a little while.

Love,
Mom

A wet spot has developed on my pillow, and I realize it's tears. I wipe my eyes and flip the pillow over. Then I click "reply."

To: Mellie.Baker@email.com

From: acelove6@email.com

June 25 (10:20 PM)

Subject: Re: Coming out

Thank you for telling me this. Ruth, William, and Catherine have told me a lot about Celeste, but every new story helps bring her a little more into focus for me.

I'm in Hilton Head, at William and Ruth's house. I've signed up for a few tournaments, and Ruth said I could play in one in France, so I'm going to need to get my passport now.

Would you mind sending me copies of our name-change documentation?

Thanks.

I add "Love, Dara" but delete it before pressing send.

    Five minutes later, another email comes in.

To: acelove6@email.com

From: Mellie.Baker@email.com

June 25 (10:25 PM)

Subject: Re: re: Coming out

Dear Dara,

Everything you should need is attached. I love you.

Love,
Mom

CHAPTER TWENTY-THREE

The next day marks one week since I left Francis. Ruth takes me shopping after practice. They're hosting a fund-raiser tomorrow night for a friend of theirs who also happens to be the junior senator from South Carolina. They apologized profusely and said they sent out invitations months ago and that they never would have planned it if they'd known I would be here. They said if it makes me uncomfortable to have a bunch of strangers in the house when everything is already so new for me here, to just say the word and they'd cancel it. I appreciated that, but told them I don't mind. The fact that they're so generous with their time and home and wealth—not just with me, but apparently with all sorts of people and causes—is one of the things I admire most about them.

And so now I need something nice to wear. The lavender jersey dress isn't going to cut it this time.

"This shop is one of my absolute favorites," Ruth says, pulling into a parking spot in a cute little downtown area. "The owner is a little funny, and normally I wouldn't consider shopping here, but he has the best collection on the island, so what can you do?"

"Funny?" I ask. The way she says it, I don't think she means he's a comedian.

She gives me a look over the top of her designer sunglasses. "You know."

"I don't." I mean, I *do*. I'm just a little surprised she'd say that.

She presses her lips together as if considering whether to explain, but then just shakes her head and opens the car door.

As soon as we enter the shop, salespeople descend upon us. "Hello, Mrs. Pembroke," a young woman with her hair back in a perfect chignon and her feet crammed into stiletto heels says. She kisses Ruth on both cheeks. "Welcome back. May we bring you some sparkling water?"

"Yes, please, Nadia. With lemon. And one for my grand-daughter as well."

"Of course." Nadia gestures to one of the other salesgirls, who scurries away to get the drinks.

"Nadia, this is Dara."

Nadia takes both my hands and lifts my arms up to my sides, then steps back to study me. "She's exquisite."

"Isn't she?" Ruth gushes.

"Um. Thank you," I mumble. I'm not feeling particularly *exquisite* right now, with my post-shower wet hair and regular old clothes, next to the supermodels working in this store.

"Dara is going to need a cocktail dress for an event tomorrow evening. That's priority number one. But I'd also love to set her up with a few basics. Tops, skirts, pants that fit her properly. If I have to see her in another pair of skintight leggings and a ratty tank top, there's no telling what I might do!"

Ruth and Nadia share a laugh, and I feel my cheeks burning.

The other girl brings the water, and I sip it gratefully.

Nadia walks us through the store, pulling things off racks, holding them against me, asking my opinion. Sometimes I shake my head *no way*, but most of the time I just shrug. I don't know anything about fashion. The fitting-room rack slowly becomes laden with hangers.

I'm relieved when it's time to try everything on, because it means a few minutes alone behind a closed door.

When I'm modeling one of the dresses for them—a black-and-white, cinched-waist, knee-length thing that isn't something I would have chosen for myself but is definitely better than the light-blue poofy thing I tried on last—a man comes over.

"That is lovely on you," he says, and though it's clear he works here—he's in all black like the rest of the salespeople—he actually sounds genuine, not sales-y. He's tall and thin, with perfectly trimmed facial hair. His shoes are very shiny.

Ruth turns around; he's standing just behind her chair. "Hello, Derek," she says, and her voice holds none of the warmth she bestowed on Nadia or even the other girl who seems to have no name.

"Hello, Mrs. Pembroke," he says cordially. "So nice to see you again. And who is this fetching young lady?"

She doesn't rush to introduce me like she usually does, and that's when it clicks: This is the owner. The "funny" guy she doesn't want to give her business to.

"This is Mrs. Pembroke's granddaughter, Dara," Nadia supplies.

"I didn't know you had a granddaughter! Welcome, Dara!" He comes over to me and kisses me on both cheeks. Guess it's store policy or something.

"You really think it looks okay?" I ask him, lifting the fabric of the skirt out to the side and studying myself in the mirror.

"Absolutely. It wouldn't even need any alterations. What's the occasion?"

"My grandparents are having a fund-raising dinner for a senator. Vernon McDougal, I think?" I look to Ruth. "Is that right?"

She lifts her chin. "Yes, that is correct. He's a friend."

Derek's jaw tightens perceptibly, and his smile becomes just a bit more strained, but it doesn't leave his face. "I see. Well, you're sure to be the belle of the ball in this dress." Another customer enters the store then, and he excuses himself.

I'm pretty sure something just happened here. And I'm certain I have no idea what it was.

....

"That's your third miss," Monique calls out from the other side of the net without breaking her serving stride. It's the next morning, and I'm running up and down the baseline at top speed, hitting slice after slice. It's an extreme defense move, the main goal being to simply keep the ball in play.

Three misses out of several dozen hits doesn't seem that bad to me. Bob always said that it's okay to miss sometimes—no one is perfect, and errors are part of the game. The more important thing is to learn how to recover, to not let the misses mess with your head and throw your entire game off course.

Monique has a different philosophy. She points out the things I do wrong far more than she compliments the things I do right. "You're never going to be the best unless you act like the best," she says, disappointed, hitting another ball.

My focus zeroes in even tighter. Run, breathe, slice. Run, breathe, slice.

I don't miss again.

Ruth comes over as I'm packing up my gear. She's already dressed for the party, even though it doesn't begin for hours. "I just heard back from the travel agent," she says. "Everything has been arranged. We leave for Charlottesville two weeks from today. She booked us a lovely suite at a historic inn with a terrace overlooking the gardens."

"That sounds great! Thank you so much." I bounce a little on the balls of my feet, riding a new wave of excitement. My worn-out calves aren't happy about it, but I don't care. In a matter of weeks I'll be playing in my first professional tournament.

"What do you think, Monique?" Ruth says. "Is our girl ready?"

Monique looks at me appraisingly. "I think she'll do fine." After today's critique session, I'll take it.

On the walk back to the house, I ask Ruth if she would mind showing me Mellie and Celeste's wedding album. We've both been so busy over the past couple days that there wasn't really a good time to bring it up. But the catering vans in the driveway and the uniformed staff bustling around the property, bringing in glass-ware and hanging lights, make me think of what the Cherry Hill house must have been like on the day of the wedding.

"Is it important that you look at it today?" she asks, her tone clipped.

I shrug. "I guess not."

Our footsteps seem to get louder in the silence that follows. I'm beginning to think it was the absolute wrong question to ask, or the absolute wrong time to ask it, when she sighs. "Yes, all right. Come, I'll show you where it is."

The album is in one of the many guest rooms I hadn't yet stepped foot in, in a drawer at the base of a shelving unit. Not exactly prime real estate for such a valuable memento.

But when I go to take it from her, she holds it back.

"I want you to know," she says, "that the *only* reason we kept this is because they're some of the most recent pictures of Celeste that we have. She was happy and beautiful that day, and that's how we choose to remember her." I nod, but she keeps going. "Other-wise I would have burned this entire book long ago. I will never forgive him for convincing her that his . . . *affliction* was normal. He made a mockery of the affection she had for him. It makes me sick every time I think about it."

I stare at her, my heart pounding in my ears. I've never heard Ruth speak like this before. The last time she spoke about this book it was with fondness. At least I thought it was. I knew she hated Mellie for taking me from them, and I knew they weren't on board with Mellie being trans, but what she's saying now is different. Deeper. And after the way she treated Derek at the store yesterday . . .

"Oh, also," Ruth says, finally relinquishing the book. I hug it to my chest. "It's best if we keep our . . . *family history* quiet tonight. The people coming to the dinner wouldn't necessarily understand about Marcus's . . . situation."

Seems like you don't understand, either, I think.

Things tilt a little in that moment. The family portrait in my head becomes singed at the edges. Could this be how Ruth and William felt all along, but they're only starting to show it now that we're getting more comfortable with each other? Now that I'm finally under their roof?

I think back to Mellie's last email, the one where she came out to Celeste. The way she told it, it didn't seem like she'd had to "convince" Celeste of anything. Mellie told her the truth, knowing it meant she might lose her, and Celeste stayed of her own volition. They were two adults who loved each other and made an agreement with each other, imperfect as it may have been.

I thank Ruth for the book, dodge the event staff and their armloads of tablecloths, and escape to the gazebo out back.

The album is packed with photos from the wedding of two people clearly in love. Celeste in her flowy white dress, walking down the aisle on the arm of her father. Marcus—Mellie—in her crisp tux. The bridesmaids, Catherine included, in pale pink. Ruth in mauve, dabbing the corner of her eye with a handkerchief. The canopy of flowers under which they recited their vows. A wedding-cake topper of a couple playing tennis. And a candid, intimate shot of Mellie and Celeste stealing a quiet moment to themselves while their friends and family dance the night away under the tent. They're forehead-to-forehead, unaware of the camera, both of them cradling Celeste's pregnant belly.

....

I don't know if Mellie somehow sensed that I looked at that album today, or if she was just about to get to this part of the story anyway and it's nothing more than coincidence. But her next email, which comes in as I'm getting ready for the party, hits me hard, punching right through a place that had already been worn thin.

To: acelove6@email.com

From: Mellie.Baker@email.com

June 27 (5:40 PM)

Subject: You

Dear Dara,

What I'm about to write is important. Everything I've written so far has been important, but what's in this email is going to be crucial in answering some big questions for you. I'm scared to write it, though, because I don't want you to take any of it the wrong way. I want you to know that you are the best thing that ever happened to me, and you were from the start. Even while you were still baking in Celeste's belly. You have always been, and will always be, my everything. Please remember that as you read.

Okay, here goes.

Celeste getting pregnant was, like I said, the best thing that ever happened to me. But it was also the worst.

We hadn't planned on it—we were in our early twenties, and Celeste was still in school. I'd recently qualified for the French Open—my first Grand Slam tournament—and was training non-stop. We weren't even engaged yet. But despite it all, we were thrilled. I never knew you could want something so badly but not even know it until it happened.

I proposed to her, and we had a hurried but beautiful wedding at her parents' house. I was overjoyed to know that I was going to get to be with her forever.

It didn't take long, though, for darker feelings to work their way in. Celeste was getting to experience one of the most wonderful, miraculous parts of womanhood . . . and I never would, no matter what. I was consumed with sadness; it was like puberty all over again but times a thousand. I know it sounds selfish, but I was unable to look at it as simply being a "parent"—instead of "mother" or "father"—and all the wonderful things that come along with that, regardless of your gender. The pregnancy was a glaring reminder that even if I transitioned, I would never be part of this club. It was a reality I'd always known, but had been able to ignore. Now it was front and center, the pivot point around which our lives rotated.

As Celeste's middle grew, and we heard the heartbeat and saw the sonogram pictures and chose a name and bought little onesies and booties and dresses, the ground beneath my feet crumbled.

The arrangement with Celeste was no longer enough. I was not okay. I saw now that our agreement had been a Band-Aid, and a flimsy one at that, not a sustainable fix. I don't think the Band-Aid would have been ripped off quite so violently if not for the pregnancy, but it would have fallen off eventually.

Things got even worse when you were born. I was at once happy and indescribably sad. (Again, I beg of you, please do not read too much into this. It was *not* your fault, and I'd do it all again in a heartbeat.)

I couldn't go on like this, drowning and grasping for a raft but unable to clamp my slippery, wet fingers around it. I came to understand that I was going to end up one of two ways: living as a woman or dead.

The choice felt impossible.

Transitioning would mean giving up Celeste—like she said, she wasn't a lesbian. It would mean giving up tennis, because going through the process publicly wasn't an option for me. There was no way I'd be able to endure what Renée Richards had; I wasn't nearly that strong. It would mean admitting I hadn't proved my parents wrong after all. It would mean being poor again, because I had virtually no job experience apart from tennis. It would mean an even shakier relationship with the world—I'd finally be on the raft, but it would be filled with holes.

But if I didn't transition, and stayed living as I was, everything would fall apart anyway. Celeste was getting fed up with me—I was making things more difficult for her because now she had *two* of us to take care of—and I was distracted and unable to train. Either way, I was losing.

There was only one way out. After all these years, I was finally going to give in. I was convinced it would be so much easier for us all, you and Celeste included, if I ceased to exist anymore. I started to plan how I was going to do it, and began counting my remaining time in days, rather than months or years.

And then, six months after your birth, Celeste was hit by the drunk driver.

I thought I'd known pain before. I'd known nothing.

But suddenly I was a single parent. My parents had left me all alone, and I wasn't going to do that to my daughter. You were my priority now—nothing else mattered.

I finally booked an appointment with a therapist, and she helped me understand that the only way you were going to be happy was if *I* was happy. And the only way I was going to be happy was if I at least *tried* to transition.

So that's how I ended up on this road. I quickly realized that transitioning wasn't merely a necessity—it was an opportunity. To consider who I really was, and who I wanted to be.

The first thing I did was quit tennis. My trainer was stunned. And very unhappy. I told him it was because I had a baby to take care of now, and that my life was headed in a different direction. Walking away from tennis was even harder than walking away from my family. This time, I was leaving something *good* behind. The last good thing in my life, besides you. The thing that had saved me when I didn't know how to save myself. But every time regrets and doubt crept in, I reminded myself what I was getting in exchange.

My therapist referred me to a transgender support group, and I made friends who were on similar journeys—people who used feminine pronouns for me and didn't question for one second that I was who I said I was. Kelly Ann, the woman I mentioned to you the other day, had transitioned in the late 1950s, well before the term *transgender* even existed. She was beautiful and wise and funny and had the most loveable "I don't give a shit" attitude of anyone I'd ever met.

Equal parts excited, terrified, and absolutely clueless, I threw myself into cosmetic changes with the ferocity I'd previously reserved for tennis. If there was one thing I knew how to do, it was give something my all. It was nice to be able to transfer that instinct onto a new goal. It made this new journey feel just a little more comfortable—familiar, in a strange way—and made the absence of tennis in my life easier to swallow.

I grew the hair on my head out and shaved and plucked almost everything else—that part was pretty easy. I started wearing clothing designed for women—that part was not. I needed clothes that reflected my identity, but that didn't look ridiculous. Wearing an ill-fitting, borrowed dress around the house with no one except the mirror watching me wasn't going to cut it anymore. I didn't feel comfortable trying clothes on in fitting rooms or asking for salespeople's advice yet, so I ended up hastily breezing through stores, grabbing a few things off the racks, and buying them before anyone could ask me if I needed assistance. I'd try them on at home, only to be sorely disappointed each time I couldn't get a top past my shoulders or a pair of jeans to fit both my waist and inseam.

It wasn't only the sizes that were confusing. I'd spent years day-dreaming about women's fashion, only to find out it was a lot harder than I'd expected to settle into a style of my own. I couldn't seem to figure out what was pretty *and* age-appropriate *and* fit me correctly. You hear a lot about adult trans women going through the stages of adolescence all over again after they transition—suddenly, we're all that girl who desperately wants to fit in, but has no idea what to do with her body. We haven't had time to figure it out like cis women our age have; we haven't had a chance to make our mistakes yet. I leaped into the shiny lip gloss and sparkly, ruffly, teenybopper outfits blindly, because to me those things said "GIRL!" I ended up looking for all the world like Barbie's kid sister with a few extra years under her belt.

I returned so many clothes to stores those first few months that I had to find new neighborhoods to shop in because the sales-people started to remember me and would groan every time they saw me coming. Eventually, I asked my new friends for help, and they gave me tips on the best makeup to hide stubble, and how to dress my body. I finally found a few pieces that worked: a flowy blouse with delicate blue flowers and buttons near the cuffs. A knee-length denim skirt. A pair of ankle boots with a two-inch heel. This was the first outfit I left the house in.

Keeping my head up as much as possible, I pushed your stroller three blocks to the grocery store, bought a few things—though I couldn't have told you what they were, I was so in my own head—sat on a park bench for a little while watching the dogs play, and went home. We were only out for an hour, but the sense of accomplishment I felt would have been worthy of a climb to the peak of Mt. Everest.

It wasn't perfect. I did get looks. I did hear whispers. A couple of parents ushered their kids across the street so they wouldn't have to share a sidewalk with me. I'd thought transitioning would be easier if I wasn't in the public eye anymore. What I didn't antici-pate was that it was of course completely obvious to anyone who looked at me what was going on. I didn't have to be a tennis player to face ridicule.

But I didn't give up. That fact, in and of itself, was reassurance I was doing the right thing.

I put my phone down for a second. I remember one day a few years ago, when Mom and I went to the mall to get some new school clothes. A group of kids was hanging out at the fountain, and as we walked past, we heard several of them harassing three teen girls in headscarves. Words like *terrorist* and *deported*. Clearly, they were parroting sentiments they'd heard on TV or at home. The girls were doing a fine job of standing up for themselves, but Mom didn't keep walking.

She told me to hang on a minute, and went right up to the bullies and said, "Someday you're going to be the one in the vulnerable position. You might be misunderstood or mistreated or targeted for who *you* are. And you're going to look back on this moment or other moments when you treated your fellow human beings without compassion, and you're going to be sorry. But by then it will be too late—you won't have anyone left to help you. So, right now, why don't you make the choice to add kindness to the world instead of hatred?"

The kids just gaped at her.

She asked the Muslim girls if they were all right. They told her they were. And then she and I went to the Gap.

We never talked about that moment. I never thought about where it may have come from. But now I see. She was the one who was bullied, whispered about, feared. Simply because of who she was.

I go back to the email.

Gradually, I became more comfortable. I learned to pay attention to the display mannequins and mimic how the window dressers had put ensembles together. I started to take note of the brands that fit me well, and I developed a light, even hand for makeup. The hormones I'd been taking softened my face some, and I began to develop my curves. More and more often, strangers would refer to me as "she" or "ma'am." Each time it happened, a warm shot of adrenaline hit my heart.

I took a name. I'd been kicking a few possibilities around for a long time, but now it was time to decide. I sat you on my lap one morning after breakfast story time and asked, "What should Mama's name be?" The question was more rhetorical than anything else. You were hardly a year old. The only words you knew were "cup" and "juice," which was your universal name for all drinks. I just needed a sounding board, and you were my most captive listener.

But you looked up at me with those big blue eyes, the same as mine, giggled, and reached out to the picture book on the sofa next to us. It was open to a page that featured Mellie, the pink-haired wood fairy, your favorite character. Do you remember that book? I think we still have it, somewhere.

I knew you had no idea what I was talking about; you probably just wanted me to read the story for a third time. But the moment felt special, and the name felt right.

Mellie. It was the same beginning initial as my birth name, it was pretty and feminine but not too common, and it was a name *you* loved too.

I filed the paperwork quickly.

We had a party at the day care center for your first birthday. The parents and teachers had watched my evolution from the earliest stages, so they were less inclined to see me as a woman or call me by my chosen name. They were kind to my face, but I caught their stares and murmurs—I'm sure I provided them gossip fodder for a good two years. But I was feeling good now. Even with all the sadness in my life, I was happier than I'd ever been.

Shortly after your birthday, six months after walking away from tennis, I applied to nursing school. It was the only other thing I thought I could be happy doing. It reminded me of Joanna, and the doctor/nurse games we used to play with our dolls.

Hands shaking, I checked the box marked "female" on the application.

That's all I'll write for now. As always, call me if you want to talk. I love you.

Love,
Mom

She did it for me. The phrase is on a loop in my thoughts as I sit for the woman Ruth hired to do our makeup, as I request a cranberry juice and club soda from the bartender, as I stand by my grandparents' side and say my "hellos" and "Pleasure to meet yous." As I talk about tennis with guest after guest, because most of these people belong to clubs and have taken lessons.

She did it for me.

So she could be able to give me a good life.

The way she described making that choice, the choice that wasn't a choice at all, and how she started out terrified and not knowing what to do . . .

I'm beginning to think I might not know as much about this stuff as I thought I did.

I think back to Sam's and my beer-fueled conversation, when he asked me how much I really knew about transgender stuff, and I brushed him off. And then later, when he corrected my terminology and told me he'd been reading about it.

Something Mellie wrote comes back to me now too: *Google knows all.*

Ruth hurries to my side. The women I'm standing with are talking about which universities their children are hoping to attend—and some of these kids are still in elementary school. "Excuse us for a moment," Ruth says to the ladies. "I'd like to introduce Dara to the senator." The women smile approvingly. I'm just glad for an excuse to get away from this conversation.

I follow my grandmother across the room to where William is chatting with a man in a crisp blue suit and red tie. This close, his hair appears to be dyed black, but there's still a bit of gray at his temples. I wonder if he does that purposely to look distinguished.

"Vernon, this is our granddaughter, Dara," William tells the man. "She just graduated from high school and is about to play in her first professional tennis tournament. Dara, this is Senator Vernon McDougal, US senator from the great state of South Carolina."

They toast to that, and Vernon says something generic, at which I smile and nod equally as generically, but internally I'm rolling my eyes at William's sudden loyalty to a state he's only lived in for two years.

"You're very lucky to have such wonderful people as grandparents, Dara," Vernon says. "In the short time we've known one another, we've become great friends."

"Yes, they've been incredibly generous and welcoming," I say, thinking that's a pretty neutral response until I catch Ruth's glare and remember I'm not supposed to say anything that would tip off that we haven't actually always known each other. "How did you all meet?" I ask, redirecting.

"Oh, I believe it was at an event similar to this one, is that right, Ruth?"

"Yes, it was last year at the Cantons' dinner. We got to talking politics, as usually happens at these things, and hit it off immediately."

I smile and nod again. I'm beginning to feel like a robot. But I don't know what else to contribute. "Do you know if dinner will be starting soon?" I ask my grandmother.

She checks her watch. "Yes, I'll have the caterers begin transitioning everyone to the main dining room in about ten minutes. Why, are you very hungry?" She seems concerned.

"Oh, no, I'm fine. Just wondering." *Wondering if I have time to get away from the party and go online for a few minutes.*

Someone else comes over to introduce himself to the senator, so I use that as an excuse to slip away. I don't think I could get away with going all the way up to my room, so I decide on the bathroom at the other end of the first floor, by William's home office, the one Ruth told the caterers to use.

I lock the door behind me, flip the toilet lid down to create a seat, and take my phone from the clutch bag Ruth insisted I carry even though we're at home.

What do I search for?

I try *What it's like to be transgender.*

The screen fills with results—support groups, personal blogs, psychological studies, podcasts, medical journals, interviews in major publications—and I vow to never take modern technology for granted ever again. I can't imagine what it was like for Mom, having to navigate her way with only a few random library books, some old-school online forums, and her own thoughts to get her by.

I click on links randomly, trying to read as much as I can before having to sit through dinner with a bunch of strangers. I don't know why I suddenly feel like I have to learn everything right this second. I didn't give it much thought before now, and obviously, the information will still be there tonight, tomorrow, forever. There's time. But for some reason it feels important.

There are an estimated 1.4 million transgender people living in America today.

Gender dysphoria is not *considered a disorder.*

Not all transgender people have surgery.

Transgender=a term for those whose gender identity differs from that which they were assigned at birth.

Transsexual=a term for those who have changed, or intend to change, their bodies through surgery and/or hormones. This term is considered outdated and has largely fallen out of use.

Forty-one percent of transgender and gender nonconforming people have attempted suicide, compared with a 4.6 percent national average.

Most states do not have laws ensuring job protection or protection against discrimination in the workplace for transgender people, and as a result many turn to sex work as their only option.

White trans people often receive more support, representation, and benefits, and are at a lesser risk of violence, than trans people of color, especially black trans women.

The statistics and facts roll through my brain, and I try to grasp on to them. But it's when I read a quote from someone's blog that I stop reading, and just sit and think.

I think well-meaning cis people often have difficulty under-standing, the blogger wrote, *because they try to frame it from their own point of view. They think,* What would I, Jennifer, feel like if I wanted to be a man? *They don't think of it as fact—an "I am" statement instead of a "what if" statement. They don't take them-selves out of the equation long enough to consider how trans people are so often mistaken for something they're not. They're mistaken for Jennifer, a woman, when Jennifer is actually a man. But because everyone assumes Jennifer is a woman, he's told he has to pretend to be one.*

And I think, maybe, that's what it comes down to. Not trying to make sense of it in relation to my own life, but instead just really listening. Really trying to understand what Mom's telling me. I'm not sure I've done such a great job of that lately.

But even now that I'm starting to better understand her as a transgender person, and better understand her as a parent, and even better understand why she might not have felt comfortable around the Pembrokes, I can't quiet the part of me that still doesn't understand why she thought her only other option was a life of hiding. Why would she go to such an extreme?

Something is still missing.

I check my email again. We've got to almost be at the end of the story.

Zero new emails.

I stand up, smooth my dress, and splash cold water on the back of my neck. It's been a lot longer than ten minutes. Ruth is probably looking for me.

I wonder what Sam's doing. He's got to be home by now.

Quickly, before I lose my nerve, I send a new text message.

I'm sorry.

A few seconds later, he responds. *Me too. I shouldn't have left like that.*

Only after the words appear on the screen do I realize how scared I was that he wouldn't write back. That I messed things up forever.

No, you should have. I was being a jerk.

Only a little bit. ☺ And then: *I miss you.*

I miss you too. I think about asking if he went back to Sarah. For all I know they could be together right now. But if they are, I don't want to know.

On my way back to the dining room, I take a selfie. Expensive party dress, fancy makeup job, and behind it all, far more miserable than someone who has everything she's ever wanted has a right to be.

Wish you were here, I type, and send it.

You look like shit, he replies.

It's the only thing that could have gotten me to laugh right now.

As the weird, illogical smile warms my face beneath the makeup, it hits me that Sam has *always* been the one to make me feel better. No matter what's going on or where we are . . . or if we're at the tail end of the biggest fight of our lives. I'm not myself without him.

I take another photo, still laughing. I send it.

His response comes immediately. *Beautiful.*

You make me happy, I write back.

Right back at ya, he says.

When I walk into the dining room, I'm grinning from ear to ear.

CHAPTER TWENTY-FOUR

I slide into my seat next to Ruth. The salad course has already begun.

"Where were you?" she hisses into her shoulder.

"In the bathroom. Sorry, Grandma. Tummy ache."

She presses her lips together so hard they go white behind her lipstick. But she doesn't say anything else. Diarrhea probably isn't on her list of approved dinner party conversation topics, either.

William stands up and clinks his wineglass. The din of conversation cuts off. "I'd just like to say a quick thank-you to all of you for coming this evening and helping to support Senator McDougal's reelection campaign." Vernon does a half stand to the sound of applause, waves around the room in thanks, then sits down again. "Together, we will ensure another six years of traditional values and religious liberty in South Carolina." The guests all applaud and cheer.

My fake stomachache turns into a real one.

Traditional values and religious liberty. I know what that means; anyone who watches the news and reads political posts online does. It means everyone in this room, including my grandparents, actively puts their money and votes toward making sure LGBTQ people feel a little less like *people.* They want to repeal marriage equality and force trans people to use the wrong public bathrooms and take away gay couples' children and allow businesses and hospitals to refuse service to anyone they want. No wonder Derek got quiet at the mention of Vernon McDougal's name yesterday.

"And," William laughs, "if you haven't opened your checkbook yet, don't worry, we'll catch you on the way out." Everyone laughs like it's the funniest joke they've ever heard.

I stare at my salad.

Maybe it's because I'm hearing this right after reading all that stuff online, but I can't shake the sudden feeling of extreme claustrophobia, of being trapped between two very different worlds—one that I don't want anything to do with, and one that I dismissed before ever really seeing it.

William encourages McDougal to say a few words. While everyone's attention is occupied by whatever political pandering he's spewing, I Google his name under the table. It only takes seconds for the picture of the man to become much more complete. The discriminatory bills he's worked to pass. The petitions and protests against him from gay rights groups. My suspicion was right—this is a person who uses his position of power to make sure people like Mom aren't ever going to be viewed as equals under the law.

Guilt cascades over me. I should have done my research before putting on this stupid dress and eating this fancy food and being cordial to these people. I just never thought the Pembrokes would be like this.

You didn't think it or you didn't want to think it? the other half of me asks.

The signs were there. The way Ruth spoke about Mom earlier, the way she forbade me from mentioning "the situation" to anyone, the way they're nodding along with the senator now . . .

The private tennis court and the paid tournament tour aren't feeling quite as free as they once did. Not that I think the Pembrokes have been bribing me—I do believe they care about me and want to give me everything they never could. I just don't know if I feel comfortable taking it anymore, knowing where else their money has been going.

But the tickets have been booked. The plans have been made. It's my best chance to make something of myself on the pro circuit. I don't know what to do.

I keep my mouth shut throughout the rest of the evening. I smile and do my best to look pretty for all the people who keep telling Ruth and William I'm pretty, like it's really a compliment to them instead of me.

At the end of the night, I say good night, wash the makeup from my face, and get into bed. The last thing I do before falling asleep is email Mellie.

To: Mellie.Baker@email.com

From: acelove6@email.com

June 27 (11:43 PM)

Subject: (no subject)

Mom,

I'm so confused. Today was weird. Things here are not what I thought they would be.

You said if I had questions, I should ask. Well, I'm asking now. Tell me why you ran away. Tell me why no one could know who we used to be. Tell me why you lied. Straight talk, like the rest of your emails so far. Please.

I need to know the end of the story.

xo,
Dara

And the next morning, I have my answer.

To: acelove6@email.com

From: Mellie.Baker@email.com

June 28 (12:21 AM)

Subject: Re: (no subject)

Dear Dara,

Are you all right? What's going on? If something's wrong, please just get out of there. Come home.

I've tried so hard not to interfere, to give you the chance you asked for to get to know the Pembrokes for yourself. That's why I've been holding off on telling this part of the story. I didn't want you to think I was trying to influence you again. You deserved to be able to form your own conclusions about them. But now I'm wondering if maybe I should have taken the risk anyway. I don't know. If I did it wrong, yet again, I'm sorry.

I'm actually in the middle of writing the end of the story right now. Give me a few minutes, and you'll have your answers.

I love you. Come home.

Love,
Mom

I'm glad I was asleep when that email came in, because the waiting between when that one was sent and the next one was finished would have been torture. But they're both in my inbox now, sent hours ago.

To: acelove6@email.com

From: Mellie.Baker@email.com

June 28 (1:15 AM)

Subject: The end

Dear Dara,

I hope that by now I've at least managed to show that I never intended to live my life in the closet. I've dealt with fear and intimidation and depression and denial, but when it comes down to it I've never been ashamed of who I was. I like who I am.

Celeste was the only person I officially came out to, not because I was embarrassed, but because I haven't had many trustworthy people in my life. If my parents had been supportive, or if Kristen's and my friendship had lasted longer, I would have come out to them too. I didn't stick with tennis not because I felt I had to live in hiding, but because I was mentally fragile and unable to deal with public scrutiny, ridicule, and debate. And when I did eventually transition, I intended to live as openly as a cisgender person would.

I never wanted to lie. I never wanted to pretend I was something I wasn't. I had planned on telling you everything from day one. You *were* aware of it all back then; you just don't remember now.

So this is all to say that the only reason any of us are in this position today is because of what the Pembrokes did. I know you've probably told them our last name and where we live and what our lives have been like, and though it makes me ill to think about—this is the very thing I've been running from all these years, after all—I know that I don't own our story. It's yours too, and you can choose what to do with it. And if the Pembrokes have to be in our lives at all, I'm thankful it's happening now, after you've turned eighteen and we don't have to fear the law anymore.

You and I saw William and Ruth a lot after Celeste died. They wanted as much time with their granddaughter as possible, and I was in favor of that. Two weekends a month we got together in Philly or Cherry Hill and went to the children's museum and to lunch and the park, and they bought you everything you pointed at in the toy stores.

This was at the height of my transition, and I dreaded their reaction to my rapidly changing appearance. I never officially came out to them—I was finally showing the world who I was, and that was a big enough step; I didn't feel the need to *tell* them too. The only person in my life who'd deserved an explanation was gone. And I was working hard in therapy on not seeking the approval of others, especially more parent-like figures. My only goal was creating mental and environmental stability for myself and for you.

But Ruth and William weren't blind. I saw the way they looked at me—adding up the clues, mouths turned down in disapproval. I waited impatiently for the other shoe to drop, wondering each weekend we were scheduled to meet if this would be the time they said something. I think they had been hoping the "problem" would just go away without them having to address it. Conversations like this weren't considered polite in their circles.

Finally, one Saturday afternoon, eight months after I began hormone-replacement therapy, I announced my acceptance to nursing school, and was met with silence. No congratulations, no handshakes. They were caught up in some silent communication with each other, matching frowns on their faces.

"I know it's not *that* exciting," I continued, "but it's important to me. Classes start next month . . ."

Ruth turned toward me, studying me intensely while somehow never looking directly at my face. She took in my red-and-white skirt, the way I crossed my legs when I sat, the gentle curl of my hair. William stared into his cup of coffee.

I knew what they were thinking. They hadn't been listening to a word I was saying.

Ruth reached across the table to rest a hand lightly on mine. I steeled myself. "Marcus, sweetheart," she said softly. "I wonder if it's maybe a good idea for you to speak with a grief counselor."

It took a minute for me to understand what she was saying. They thought I was having an extreme reaction to losing Celeste. That was how they'd explained it to themselves.

I took my hand back and placed it in my lap.

"Why?" I asked calmly. "Are you working with one?" I knew they weren't.

Ruth's toffee-colored lips became pinched. "We're worried about you, is all. First you quit tennis, and now . . ." She trailed off, as if she didn't have words for whatever this was. She waved a hand, indicating my entire body. "We know Celeste's passing has been hard on you. We understand. We miss her too."

I straightened up. "I work with a therapist twice a week, actually," I said, cringing at the deep tenor of my voice. We all noticed it, I was sure—how I was trying so hard to be one thing, but my voice clearly said I was another. That one piece of evidence won the argument, with no option for an appeal. I vowed in that moment to begin taking voice lessons.

"Oh, really?" She seemed surprised.

"Yes."

"What sort of things do you talk about with him?"

"Her. And that's private." I knew I should just acknowledge the issue at hand: find clear, nonthreatening words to make all this easier for them. If they had been nicer, I probably would have. But there was a biting aggression in her voice that was decidedly unkind. I wanted to lift you out of your high chair and get the hell out of there. Wishful thinking.

Ruth sighed and pressed on. "You know what I mean, Marcus. What's with the cross-dressing?" She whispered the last part. She sounded like she was mad at me for forcing her to be the one to get to the point. Like I was purposely embarrassing her by expecting her to sit in a restaurant, in public, with me as I was now.

Well, I wanted to say, *I'm not particularly thrilled about discussing the very personal particulars of my biology and psychiatry with you people, either.* I didn't, because I knew that either way, it was time for this conversation to happen.

William remained silent. But his jaw was clenched, and his eyes kept darting at you, as if the more we talked about this, and the more real my situation became to them, the more danger you would be in.

I took a measured breath to both pad my emotional armor and ensure my voice remained steady, and said, "The term is trans-gender. Not cross-dresser."

They finally looked at my face. I worried they were going to lose the battle to keep their eyeballs snug in their sockets.

"This is who I am," I said, keeping the explanation as simple as possible. "For as long as I can remember, even when I was a very small child, I have known that I was a girl, regardless of the gender I was assigned at birth. I assure you this is not a reaction to grief, and it is not a recent development. Celeste knew. She supported me." I left out the fact that she'd had a caveat. It wasn't important right then.

"What do you mean, she *knew*?" Ruth's voice was markedly louder now. She'd lost the battle, or will, to remain civil, and a few people at neighboring tables turned our way. I remember you were startled by the sudden change in energy, and began to cry. I picked you up and settled you in my lap with a bottle. You were warm and still had that baby smell, and your nearness slowed my pulse.

"Celeste and I loved each other very much," I said. "We had no secrets."

"So, what? You're going to get a sex-change operation?" Ruth spit out, appalled.

"I don't know yet." I didn't bother correcting her on the terminology this time. It wasn't worth it. "But I don't see how it's any of your business."

"Of course it's our business! You're our granddaughter's father. It's not healthy for a child to grow up in this sort of environment! It's *perverse*."

I stood up, trembling, and placed you in your stroller. Dropping some money on the table to cover our portion of the bill, I said, "I disagree. It's healthiest for Dara—and me—that I live my most natural, happiest, most confident life." I left the restaurant before I said what I really wanted to.

I didn't hear from them again for over a month. They missed their next two visits. I knew that everyone was entitled to their opinions and I shouldn't expect the whole world to be fine with, or even understand, my transition, but there was a huge part of me that was relieved they'd disappeared from our lives.

The world kept spinning. My name change was approved, and I got a new driver's license to celebrate.

Nursing school began—I made a couple friends there too. I suspected *they* suspected, but they didn't bring it up, and neither did I. It was, somehow, a nonissue.

You were thriving in your day care program, and liked televised tennis matches more than cartoons. I watched your wide-eyed, baby-faced fascination, and made a silent promise to put you in lessons when you were older, if that was what you wanted.

I decided to move forward with gender-confirmation surgery—top surgery, trachea shave, and the facial feminization procedures—and started planning and budgeting for that. I considered bottom surgery too, but I wasn't absolutely certain if I wanted it. And, like I said, it was expensive and complicated, so I knew it would have to be down the line, if ever. We were doing all right, living on the tennis earnings I had left and the life-insurance money we had received as Celeste's beneficiaries, but there was no way I could justify paying out of pocket for such a major operation.

All in all, we were settled. We were doing well.

And then the police arrived at my door.

Two uniformed officers, a man and a woman, and a tired-looking young man in a baggy suit.

My first thought was that something had happened to one of my neighbors and the cops were looking for information.

"May I help you?" I asked.

"We'd like to speak with Marcus Hogan," the female officer said.

"It's actually Mellie now," I said. The name change was official, and I was going to use it, dammit. "But yes, that's me."

The two police officers appraised me, their furrowed brows giving way to recognition. They had clearly been told I was trans. But by whom? And why were they looking for me at all?

"I'm Officer Natch," she said. "This is Officer Cruz and Malcolm Jones, a social worker with Child Protective Services."

My stomach dropped and terror tightened my chest. You were still at day care—I'd had two classes that morning and was planning to pick you up after lunch.

"What's going on? Is my daughter all right?" I said in a rush.

"Don't worry; she's in good hands," Jones piped up from behind the officers.

Something about the way he said it told me that the "good hands" he was referring to weren't at the day care center. "What does that mean?" My fingers found the doorjamb and gripped it tightly. "Where is she?"

"She's safe at our office downtown."

"You took her out of day care?"

Jones nodded.

How could they do that? *Why* would they do that? I didn't know if you were okay. I didn't know if you were scared.

"What the *hell* is going on?" I shouted, taking a step forward.

Jones exchanged an uneasy look with the police officers, as if to say, *Want to help me out here?*

Officer Cruz stepped in front of the doorway so I couldn't get past. He was standing too close, and his bulky, bullet-proofed chest was intimidating. "Calm down, please. We need to speak with you, and it will be easier for everyone if you cooperate."

I stared at him, my breath stuttering wildly. Panicked, confused tears prickled my eyes. "I don't understand what's going on," I said weakly.

"Can we come in?" he said.

I stepped out of the way. The four of us sat down in the living room. I couldn't get my leg to stop shaking or my thoughts to focus. You were out there somewhere, and I had no idea where you were or if you were safe. Just because this random stranger said you were didn't make it so.

"Mr.—or is it Ms.?" Natch began.

I nodded dumbly. I couldn't even be happy about her obvious effort to use the correct title.

"Ms. Hogan, we have received a call accusing you of child abuse," she said.

"*What?*" I blurted. This had to be a mistake.

She continued. "The abuse, as told to us, is of the sexual nature. The alleged victim is your one-year-old daughter, Dara Hogan." It was almost as if she was reciting a memorized list—her tone was inflectionless, the words nothing more than bullet points. "As I'm sure you know, we take these reports very seriously. We'd like to ask you a few questions."

Anger seized my throat. "Who told you this?"

"I'm not at liberty to disclose that information."

But it didn't matter. There was only one possibility. "It was Ruth and William Pembroke, wasn't it?"

All three of them remained silent.

"You don't have to tell me," I said. "I know it was them. They think there's something wrong with me." I looked them each in the eye. "But it isn't true! You have to believe me. I would *never* . . ." I gripped my temples to try to block the headache that was blasting forth. "God, I can't even think about it. There's nothing more important to me than making sure Dara is safe and healthy and happy."

The police officers remained impassive. The social worker watched me carefully.

"Do you want to hook me up to a lie detector?" I held out my forearm. "Please, do it! I swear I'm telling the truth. *They're* the ones who are lying!"

"We understand these situations can be complicated," Natch said evenly, "but like I said, we still do need to ask you some questions."

For the next hour, the three of them grilled me, writing down my answers. Their questions spanned huge distances, from my own history (Was I abused as a child? Please explain the circumstances surrounding my sexuality and gender identity.) to what my parenting techniques were (What do I consider an appropriate way to discipline a child? Please describe Dara's typical bath time routine.).

A small part of my brain told me I shouldn't speak to them without a lawyer present. I wasn't under arrest—yet—but that could change at any moment. All it would take was one wrong answer. But I was scared and desperate to get you home safe, and I figured complete cooperation would be the quickest way to make that happen.

After the questions, they took a look through the apartment. I don't know what they were expecting to find, but they didn't find it.

"Thank you, Ms. Hogan," Jones said as they headed to the door. "I'll let CPS know your daughter is cleared for pickup."

"So I can get her back? It's over?"

He nodded. "We have what we need for now. We'll be following up with the day care center, and if you have any personal references you can direct us to, who can vouch for you as a parent, that would help as well."

I thought for a moment. My new friends hadn't yet spent much time with you and me together. And it probably wasn't the best idea to alert my professors and colleagues to the fact that I'd been accused of such a heinous crime.

"I'm sorry," I admitted. "I can't think of anyone. I hope that doesn't hurt my case."

He shook his head once. "Everything appears to be in order here, and the tip we got did not provide any specifics, so there is currently nothing to base a case on. You're free to retrieve your daughter at any time."

"That's a relief. Thank you."

Once they were gone, I leaped into my car, drove as fast as I could, and pulled you into my arms the second I laid eyes on you. Jones had been right—you were fine. The childcare room was nice, and you were clean-diapered and smiling. I was the one who'd been traumatized. Which was exactly what Celeste's parents had wanted. Their aim with this asinine stunt had been to hurt *me*, not you.

I thought about calling them, yelling at them, sending them a letter that said, *How dare you?*

But I was lucky that whatever I'd said and whatever the police officers saw at our home, they believed me. I just wanted to forget it had ever happened, so my plan remained the same: do nothing and hope we'd seen the last of them. I wasn't going to feel guilty about keeping you from your grandparents if your grandparents didn't want to be involved in our lives.

A few weeks went by, and I heard nothing from the Pembrokes. I hadn't managed to completely go back to the place of ease I'd been in before the police knocked on our door, but I was getting there. It was comforting to know that you'd never remember any of this.

I should have known that wouldn't be the end of it.

Three weeks after the police visit, I received a court summons. The process server stood in the exact spot outside the apartment door where the cops had torn down my illusion of safety, and with the handover of a simple envelope, finished the job.

Ruth and William Pembroke were suing for full custody. They were trying to take you away from me, completely and forever.

The lawsuit said I was a sexual deviant, that I shouldn't be allowed around children. They weren't going with the child *abuse* angle this time, but rather claiming that because I was trans I was perverted and screwed-up and not equipped to provide an adequate home for a minor.

Standing there at my front door, staring down the hallway from which the process server had long since disappeared, I felt like the floor of the apartment—no, the earth's very soil—had turned into fast-acting quicksand, and if I didn't do something drastic, I would get pulled under. I'd lose everything.

They were trying to take you from me. Do you understand how serious that is, Dara? They were not going to stop. And, this time, there was a very good chance they would win. They had money. They had influence. The transgender protection laws aren't great now, and back then they were even worse.

They were going to take you away. After I'd worked so hard to be okay, to provide a stable, loving home for us, you were going to grow up without parents. I'd tried to stop history from repeating itself, and yet here it was, laughing in my face.

I let the door swing shut. The force of it rattled my bones.

I stood in place, paper in hand, mind racing, for a while.

What am I going to do?

Slowly, at first, and then all at once, the answer came to me.

I still had time. I had to take you away before Celeste's parents could.

My feet sprang into action, not at all rusty from the year away from the court. I darted around the apartment, packing essentials, making arrangements.

We left town the next morning.

No wonder your first instinct was to run when you found out I'd been keeping the truth from you. You and I are alike in so many ways.

In the days that followed, we headed west, staying in a different motel every night until I found us a short-term, under-the-table lease on an apartment just over the New York State border. I changed our last name and my cell phone number and wiped away all the traceable details I could think of. I dropped out of school.

We stayed away from the city and any place where we may have known someone. We lived in a few different places in Pennsylvania and New York, all small towns where it would be hard to trace us to, but none too far away from Philly—my first surgeries were coming up, and had been scheduled far in advance, so I needed to be able to travel into the city for them. I felt confident knowing you wouldn't be coming with me, that Philly was a big city and the Pembrokes rarely left Cherry Hill. There was little to no chance I'd run into them while spending a day or two in the hospital.

I considered canceling the appointments, but then I realized that going through with the procedures could only help us. This was a long-term decision I was making. You were still a baby—you were going to grow and age and soon you'd be unrecognizable. It would only be beneficial for the same to be true for me. If these alterations, which I'd already planned and already wanted, would help leave the person they knew behind, at least on the surface, I needed to try. I told Kelly Ann what was going on—she was the only one I told—and she offered to help us. She knew what it was like to be treated unkindly, unfairly. She was a fighter, and approved of my becoming one too.

I feel like I should clarify something here. Up until this point, going stealth—that's when a trans person lives completely as their gender identity, not informing most people of the fact that they're trans—had never been my ultimate goal. I know I've said it before, but it's really true: I hadn't intended to live such a private life. When I dreamed of transitioning, and when I finally began the process, all I'd wanted was to feel like *me*. That's one of the wonderful things about being trans—you *know* yourself, because you have no choice but to confront your identity head on. What other people saw in me didn't matter as much. But now the stakes had changed. I'd taken you away from people who'd told the courts that I was a danger to you. I'd dodged a court summons. I didn't know what would happen if Celeste's parents or their lawyers found us, but it couldn't be good.

So I vowed to live under the radar, be as unassuming as possible, and never breathe a word of any of this to anyone. If there were people looking for us, all it would take was one slipup.

Every reason you're unhappy with me now can be traced back to the moment a single piece of paper was handed across my threshold. I know it's irrational to hate that process server—he was only doing his job—but I do. I *hate* him.

Over time, I took voice lessons over the phone with an expert in California, and did electrolysis on my facial hair. Turns out you can take all the hormones in the world, but once hair grows, it's pretty impossible to make it stop. I went back to school—a different one this time—and completed my qualifications.

By the time we moved to Francis, you were three, you had no memory of where we'd come from, and we'd left our old life—and everyone and everything in it—far behind. We'd said good-bye to Kelly Ann two moves prior; it was difficult, but she understood. No one knew our secrets now, and no one suspected a thing. I allowed myself to keep those few photographs and papers from before, but that was all. I suspect the Pembrokes called off the search eventually, though I don't know for sure.

I think the first true breath I'd taken in years was on the front porch of our house.

There was just one step left in my transition process, and it was arguably the most important and symbolic one: I wanted to have the gender and name changed on my birth certificate. I'd had such a fraught relationship with that thing for so long, the document that dictated to the world that because I was born with a certain physicality, I was expected to perform a role for the rest of my life. Though I didn't have a copy of the original certificate, I knew it was out there, and I wanted it gone.

It took a few more years for New York State to pass the law that would allow the update of gender markers on birth certificates without bottom surgery. But once that happened, I still didn't take the step. It didn't feel right to allow myself that final gift of peace and safety—not until I was certain *we'd* found peace and safety together, as a family. The house in Francis had brought us closer than we'd ever been, but there was still the smallest possibility of the Pembrokes finding us. So, I've waited.

I hope this helps you understand, Dara. You thought I was being selfish and took you away from your grandparents and that life with no concern for how it would affect you. I get why you thought that. But now that you have the whole story, I hope you can see that it was actually the complete opposite—I did it all *for* you. And I'd do it all again. I also hope you can understand that despite the lies, I never lied to you about who I was. I'm Mellie Baker. I'm a woman; I'm your mother; I'm your mom. And I love you—always.

Love,
Mom

CHAPTER TWENTY-FIVE

The picture in my head of my formerly perfect, then slightly tarnished extended family becomes nothing more than a stock photo family in a store-bought frame. All illusion, no substance.

I propel myself out of bed, down the hall, down the stairs. Everything's already been cleaned up from the party. The house is spotless.

"Ruth!" I shout, sliding in my socked feet on the polished wood floors. "William!"

They come hurrying into the foyer, Ruth from the kitchen and William from the muck room. He's in his boating gear.

"Dara? What on earth . . . ?" Ruth says, a hand to her heart. "What's wrong?"

I stare them down, my chest heaving. "Is it true?" I demand.

"Is what true?" William asks.

"Did you try to get Mellie arrested for *child abuse*? Did you try to take custody away from her?" I say the words clearly and distinctly, so there will be no need to repeat.

They exchange a glance. "We didn't realize you've been in contact with him," William says, effectively telling me everything I need to know.

"Did you drop the case? Or is it still open?"

Ruth sighs, resigned to the truth being out now. "We did drop

it, some time after the trail ran cold. That was about ten years ago."
The way she says it, so proud, it's like she thinks I'm going to thank
her for being such a reasonable, selfless human being.

"I can't believe you would do this to her," I whisper. "I . . ."
I can't believe I didn't know.

"Now, Dara," William says. "It's not as simple as all that. Please,
let's sit and discuss this." He holds a hand out toward the living
room.

I don't move. I just stand there at the bottom of the fancy stair-
case, in my old pajamas, which I'm sure Ruth disapproves of, looking
back and forth between them. Only now is it clear that all this time
I had that picture in my mind of who my family might be, they had
a similar picture of me. The perfect little girl who was ripped away
from them. But not only do they clearly not know me at all, they're
only interested in getting to know the parts of me that fit their
vision. My mother, one of the most important people in my life, is
not welcome in their family portrait. Well, fine. People who would
do something like they did are not welcome in mine.

"No," I say, trying to match William's faux calmness. "I don't
think that would be productive." *I've been lied to enough.* There's
no decision to be made here; I know what I need to do. "I . . . I
want to thank you for everything you've done for me. I appreciate
it more than you know. You were a gap in my history for so long—"
My voice breaks, betraying me. I clear my throat, raise my chin,
and forge on. "And I'm grateful for the opportunity to have gotten
to know you. But you have to know, *you* are the reason we didn't

know each other until now. You are the reason you didn't get to see me grow up. Not Mellie."

Ruth sucks in a breath. "That's not—"

"Also," I continue, "your politics suck. I don't understand how people like you, who have *everything*"—I gesture around at the impressive foyer with its expensive furniture, fresh flowers, and one-of-a-kind artwork—"could ever fight *so* hard to make sure others never achieve a fraction of what you have." I take a breath, feeling clearer than I have in ages. "Ruth, please cancel the travel arrangements. I hope it's all still refundable. I'll be withdrawing from the tournaments."

"But that's your dream!" she says, not understanding the weight of what I'm saying.

"It is," I admit. "But I'll find another way." By the time I finish speaking, I'm already halfway up the stairs.

The last time I ran away, I had no idea what I was doing or where I was going. This time, I know exactly where to go. Home.

When I come back downstairs minutes later, bags packed, Ruth and William are sitting in the white upholstered chairs in the foyer, shell-shocked.

"Good-bye," I say. "And thank you again." They stand up, but we make no move to hug each other.

Ruth begins to cry. "Dara, please, don't leave. You have to understand—the only thing we're guilty of is trying to make sure you had a good life. That's all."

By tossing my mother aside, she means.

William, to his credit, just says, "Drive safely."

I nod. And then I'm out the door.

....

The trip home is long. Thirteen hours due north, not including stops.

It's a lot lonelier doing the drive alone, without Sam taking pictures or tapping at his Viking game from the passenger seat. I wonder what his bus ride home was like: if he was missing me too, or if he made friends.

When the old factory with its *Believe* wall comes into sight, I pull into the turnoff and grab a racquet and ball. I laugh at the simplistic joy that comes with hitting the ball against the concrete with no fancy court, no demanding trainer. I hope this place never gets torn down and turned into a Target or an office park. It's special. I don't linger long, though. I have somewhere to be.

I'm just over the North Carolina border when I have to stop for gas. While the tank fills, I open Mellie's last email and hit "reply."

Thank you, I write. It's the entirety of my message. There will be more to say later.

Then I text Catherine. *Did you know?*

She responds while I'm at the register paying for a prepackaged mozzarella and tomato sandwich and a bottle of water. It's clear she's spoken to her parents, because when she does text back she doesn't bother acting confused. *Yes. I didn't agree with it, but I knew. I'm sorry.*

I go back to my car to eat before getting back on the road. The sandwich tastes like rubber and for a brief moment makes me miss the Pembrokes and their gourmet meals. But I'd rather live on gas station food for the rest of my life than make the kind of compromises they were asking me to. As I eat, I Google Marcus Hogan. There's not a ton of information available—this was before the days of documenting absolutely everything online—but I do manage to pull up some old ranking lists and a couple of images. Mom wasn't just a player—she was *good*. I'm surprised to find that I'm proud.

By the time I hit Virginia, I really have to pee. The bathroom at the next rest stop is filthy and has no soap, but the lady at the next sink over lets me borrow her hand sanitizer.

These thirteen-plus hours feel like forty. But I keep reminding myself that with each mile I drive, I'm closer to Mom. To Sam too. Even if he is with Sarah again, he's still my best friend. It keeps me going.

Somewhere in West Virginia, I get another email from Mellie. I pull over to read it.

To: acelove6@email.com

From: Mellie.Baker@email.com

June 28 (5:49 PM)

Subject: Niya

Dear Dara,

You're welcome. Thank you for listening.

Sam is home. He came home a few nights ago, but I didn't know because I've been avoiding Niya. She's been calling, wanting to know what's going on, and I did what I do best. I hid. I'm not proud of it.

But I sent you that email last night, and woke up today feeling different. Free. You know everything. Finally. The Pembrokes know where we are, but it's too late for them to cause us any more damage. My fears aren't quite so scary anymore.

So I called Niya today and asked her to come over. She brought Sam with her—that's how I learned he was back. He sat there beside his mother as I told her everything. About me, about my past.

She was surprised, to say the least. Sam hadn't told her anything. But she listened. She was hurt that I hadn't trusted her, but she understood why I'd felt like no one could know. She didn't understand much about gender-identity issues, but she asked questions. And when the visit came to an end, she gave me a hug and thanked me for telling her.

In a strange way, you finding that box and running away was the best thing that could have happened. It forced me to start living the life I'd always intended before the Pembrokes messed it all up.

So thank you for that.

I love you.

Love,
Mom

Okay, no more delays. I've never been more ready to be home.

....

It's dark when I finally make it back to the little yellow house. It looks a lot smaller than I remembered.

Mom's car is in the driveway. She must still be on a break from work.

At the sound of the rolling wheels of my suitcase on the front path, her silhouette appears in the doorway.

"Dara?" she gasps through the screen in the door.

"Hey, Mom," I say, shocked that my voice sounds so gravelly. I haven't done much talking today.

She runs outside and throws her arms around me. I drop my bags, and we stand like that, embracing each other, for a long time. This hug is familiar and comforting, like a perfectly worn-in sweater.

"I'm sorry," I whisper.

She shakes her head; I feel it rather than see it. "You have nothing to be sorry for. I'm the one who's sorry."

After everything we've been through, all the crap falls away with those few short sentences.

"I was just about to make some tea," she says, stepping back a bit and wiping her blotchy eyes. "Would you like some?"

I study her for a moment. She's the mom I've always known—long brown ponytail, tired eyes, enigmatic smile—but I understand those features in an entirely new way now. She wanted long hair for so long, and now that she has it, she no longer needs to hide behind it. The lines around her eyes are evidence of her pain, her perseverance. Her smile doesn't hold her secrets—it holds her *story*.

"Tea sounds great," I say at last. "Can we order a pizza too? I'm starving."

She smiles. "Extra spicy peppers?"

"Always."

We hug again.

"I missed you so much, Mom."

"Oh, honey. Me too." She takes my suitcase handle and we walk inside. Everything is just as neat and clean as always—except for the absurd amount of hot sauce bottles covering the kitchen counters. There must be close to a hundred here, all different heat levels and brands.

"What . . . ?" I look at her, bewildered.

She shrugs sheepishly. "It was how I coped. I know it's pretty manic, but it helped me to take action, looking forward to the day you came back and we could try all these together. I even found coupons for some of them."

A laugh bubbles up, expelling any lingering heaviness. Mom worked through her depression by buying the world's largest supply of hot sauce. I can't think of any better sign that she really is okay.

I call in the pizza order, then lug my suitcase down the hall and dump all the clothes into the washing machine—even the ones I washed at the Pembrokes'. It feels important to get a clean start.

I consider that as I shower and dress, and as I curl up on my little bed, a towel wrapped around my hair. There are more things I need to say to Mom before we can fully move forward.

A knock sounds at my door.

"Come in," I call.

Mom stands there, holding up two boxes of tea. I point to the green tea with ginger. She turns to go.

"Hey, Mom, can you come here for a minute?" I sit up and pat the bed beside me.

She hesitates as if she isn't sure she's going to like what I'm about to say. But then she comes and sits, setting the boxes of tea on my nightstand.

"I'm sorry it took me so long to understand why you don't like the Pembrokes," I tell her.

"They're complicated people," she says with a sigh. "But they're not evil. They really did think they were doing the right thing."

That reminds me of the political fund-raiser. I tell her about it, and she doesn't seem particularly surprised.

"I know this is the last thing you'd expect me to say," she says, "but I do hope that eventually you'll be able to have some sort of relationship with them."

I shake my head. "No way. Not unless they apologize."

"Even if they don't."

"Mom!"

She smiles sadly. "They're your family, for better or worse."

"Yeah, more like *worse*." But the second I say it, I remember what Mom wrote about the Hogans. The Pembrokes, for all their faults, did give Catherine the farm, even though they didn't understand why she'd want to be in that line of work. And they were willing to give me anything I wanted without explicitly asking for anything in return. Mom's parents never gave her anything—not even their love. "Mom?"

"Yes?"

"Do you ever think about trying to track down your family?"

She nods. "I looked them up this week."

"You *did*?"

"Yeah. All that reminiscing made me realize I'd shut them out of my thoughts for probably a little too long. Not that I have any interest in reconciling with them. But I realized I had no idea if they were even still alive."

"Are they?"

"All except my father. He died four years ago. Heart attack."

I don't know what to say to that. *I'm sorry* doesn't feel quite right. "Are you all right?" is what I end up going with.

"Yes. I am."

The teakettle begins to whistle in the kitchen. "What about the rest of them?" I ask. "Do you ever think of reaching out? You write pretty good emails . . ."

She smiles at that. "Maybe my sister, Joanna. Someday. I don't know if I'm ready yet."

"Maybe Kristen too? And Kelly Ann?" I ask.

"Maybe, yeah."

There's something else I want to say about Mom's emails, but the teakettle won't let us ignore its piercing wail any longer. Wordlessly and in tandem, we get up, go to the kitchen, and make our tea—hers with sugar, mine with lemon. We sit at the table with our mugs and sip slowly.

Then Mom remembers the hot sauce. She stands up and grabs one of the bottles—Devil's Nectar—and two spoons. She holds them up, eyebrows raised.

"Bring it," I say.

She pours a little in each and we clink spoons and down it. "Oh my God," I rasp, coughing. "That's *hot*."

Mom's eyes are watering, and she waves a hand in front of her face as if to cool it down. "That's an eleven."

"An *eleven*?!" It's hard to speak. My tongue is on fire. I take a gulp of tea. "We've never had an eleven."

"I think that's the hottest hot sauce I've ever had in my life," she says, getting up and sticking her face in the freezer.

I start to laugh, and before long we're both in hysterics. "Mom," I say, when the giggles die down and she's rejoined me at the table. "Do you ever think of publishing your story?"

Her eyes bulge. "What?"

"You love writing, and you're really good at it. And your story is . . . important. It helped me understand. It might help other people understand too."

She sits back in her chair. "I've never thought about it. My impulse is still to keep everything private, after all this time."

"But you said you'd wanted to live openly. Now you can."

"I guess you're right." She blinks away tears again, and this time they're not from the hot sauce. "So what's going on with tennis?" she asks.

I look up at her. It's an obvious attempt at a change of subject, but still. She's waiting for my answer, actually interested in what

I'm going to say. She's not closed off. There's no wall. "I'm going to withdraw from the tournaments. I don't want the Pembrokes' help with this. I want to make it on my own."

She nods. "And you will."

"I was thinking of looking into application deadlines for the spring term . . ."

Her hand flies to her mouth. "Really?"

"All right, don't get too excited. I figured I'd try it for a semester, see how it goes. If I could get a scholarship, it really would make the most sense, financially. I wouldn't have to depend on anyone." Mom's expression is so happy, I almost don't want to lay my ultimatum on her. "*But* I'll only do it if you practice with me sometimes."

"I will. I promise." She takes my hand again. "I admire you, Dara. This journey you've been on, your determination to find your own way. Even when you've been knocked down, you keep fighting. *That's* why you're going to be a champion someday."

For the first time since I've been home, I start to cry. "Thanks, Mom."

The doorbell rings.

She grins. "Pizza's here."

CHAPTER TWENTY-SIX

The next morning, I do four things.

First, I go for a long run.

Then I make some calls. The first is to Monique to let her know I've moved home. She sounds a little put off, but not too torn up about it; I suspect she's going to miss the paycheck more than she'll miss me. Then I call Bob and resume our training schedule. He actually *woots* when I tell him. I text Mary to fill her in, and she texts back a thumbs-up emoji. I think I'll bring them both dark chocolate on Tuesday.

I call the juice stand too, and get my job back. Arielle's making me start at the bottom of the seniority ladder again, but it's better than nothing.

When the calls are done, I withdraw from the tournaments. It hurts my heart a little to do so—I was *so* close—but it's the right thing. Mom did promise she'd take me to get a passport this week, though. And she's going to renew her own too—she told me last night she's never had a passport with the correct gender on it. But first she's going to take that long-awaited final step and update her birth certificate.

Finally, I put on a T-shirt, my favorite leggings, and my bravest face, and get ready to go next door.

Mom's in the kitchen, organizing the canned foods in the pantry. "Where are you off to?" she asks.

"I need to go see Sam."

"Why do you look so nervous?"

I sigh. So much for the brave face. "Things between Sam and me have gotten . . . complicated."

She tries to hide her smile. It doesn't work.

"What? Don't tell me you knew."

"I suspected."

I try not to blush. "Well, whatever you suspected, it's probably over before it began. I think he went back to his ex."

Mom tilts her head to the side. "I don't know if he did or didn't, but if you have feelings for him, you should let him know."

I chew on my lip. "Yeah." Wait. I don't have to be the only one on the spot here. I straighten up. "I think you should consider dating too."

She splutters.

"Seriously. Go online. Find people."

"Dara!" she says with a laugh in her voice. Before she can say anything else, I duck out the door and cross the lawn.

The little blue house is filled with the aroma of Ramesh's baking. He pokes his head around the corner of the kitchen. "Dara! Long time no see! Want a coconut cake? Fresh out of the oven!"

"No, thanks," I say. "Maybe later."

Niya comes down the hall and startles when she sees me.

"Hey," I say, a little awkwardly.

"You're back!" she says, surprised.

I nod. "I am."

"Your mother must be very happy." I wait, but it's the only thing she says about Mellie. I know in that moment that Niya and Mom are going to be just fine.

"She is." I smile, and head downstairs.

Sam is at his computer, as always. I lean against the doorframe and watch him, undetected, for a minute. How many times have I witnessed this exact scene? Sam so lost in his work that he doesn't notice me at the door, his fingers moving rapidly across the track pad, his other hand propping up his chin, his hair in his face. And how did I never feel these butterflies fluttering around my belly? Why did I have to drive halfway across the country to realize that I've been living right next door to the perfect person for me?

"Hi," I whisper.

He jumps so high I worry his chair is going to tip over. But he catches himself and stands up.

"What are you doing here?" he asks breathlessly.

"Oh, sorry, is now not a good time? Okay, see you later, bye." I spin around and jokingly begin to leave.

His hand shoots out and catches my arm. "Don't you dare."

I turn back around. We're much closer to each other now. He gazes down at me, his eyes searching. "So, does this mean you're back?"

I nod.

"For good?"

I nod again.

"Want to talk about it?" he asks.

"Not right now. But I will."

"Okay."

"So, um . . ." I step back just a little. I have to ask. "What happened with Sarah?"

He runs a hand through his hair. "Nothing."

Something small, hopeful, flickers in my chest. "Nothing?"

"I was going to go back to her. But I thought about it a lot on the ride home, and I realized that was just a reflex to things going south with you and me."

"Oh." The flickering goes flat, and I look away. I don't know what to say. *He was going to go back to her.*

"Dara," he says, taking a step forward and closing the distance I'd opened up. "My reasons for not being with her haven't changed."

I meet his eyes, and find there's something there. I can't name it, but it's promising. This is all so new; I don't know how to read him. I don't know how to take control of this situation. What if I take a risk, and it ruins everything? What if I say the wrong thing, and he turns me down? Or what if he doesn't turn me down, and our friendship is replaced with this far less familiar, far less confident thing? What will happen if things don't work out down the line? Would that mean the end of us?

All these questions have me feeling more tied in knots than ever. But despite all the reasons to stop, I can't. I'm on the court, and the ball's been served. I have to hit it.

Plus, not *all* change is bad, right?

"You should know something," I say.

"What?"

I take a step closer. "I didn't spend the night with Matt."

His breath catches. "You didn't?"

"No. I slept on the couch."

He searches me with his eyes. "Why?"

Another step. We're inches apart now. I run my hands up his chest and grab a fistful of the material. "Because he wasn't the guy."

Sam's chest rises as he takes a breath. I can feel his heart pounding. *He's nervous too.* "And who might—"

I don't let him finish. I use the shirt to pull him to me. Our mouths collide like they're asteroids on the same trajectory, and the resulting explosion is all light and stars and fire.

The butterflies go crazy.

Sam wraps his arms around me, and lifts me a few inches off the ground. "Glad to see you've finally come to your senses," he murmurs.

I laugh. "Me too."

He sets me down and we kiss some more. I never want to leave his arms. Well, except to go kick ass on the tennis court. And try that new Amazonian yellow hot sauce Mom ordered from Brazil. But then I immediately want to come right back here. Or to his dorm room. Or wherever he happens to be at the moment.

I pull back just a little. "Question."

"Yes?"

"How is this going to work? The long-distance thing, I mean."

"We'll figure out a way," he says, sounding so certain.

"Yeah, but that's the reason you broke up with Sarah. And you said all the reasons you ended things with her were still there."

"Dara," he whispers. "That wasn't the only reason I broke up with her."

"It wasn't?"

"No."

"What else is there? She's pretty and smart and—"

"She wasn't the girl."

My heart melts into a giant puddle. It's all he needs to say. I understand completely.

We start to kiss again. "Hey, Sam?"

"Hey, Dara."

"Thank you."

"For what?"

"For coming with me, for reading about transgender stuff, for having beers with me, for telling me when I was being stupid, for being right about so much . . ." I'm rambling now. "Basically, for all of it. I really think things are going to be okay between me and Mellie—maybe even better than before—and you played a big part in that."

He smiles. "I have something for you."

"What is it?"

"Well, it's not quite done, but . . ." He turns his computer screen to face me. It's the project he was working on when I came in. The picture is of us, at the bar in Virginia. My arm is around him and I'm kissing him on the cheek. It's the selfie I took with his camera.

But what I didn't notice at the time, all drunk and silly, was the way Sam was looking at me in that moment. Like a boy in love.

He's tweaked the photo a bit to illustrate this very fact. Where the light catches the darkness of his eyes, tiny twinkling stars have been added.

"You made this for me?" I whisper.

I look up. He nods nervously.

"I love you too," I say.

His whole face seems to be made of stars in that moment. He swoops down and kisses me again.

A couple weeks ago my entire life fell apart. Now I'm wondering how I could have possibly gotten so lucky.

"What do you think our moms are going to say about this?" Sam asks, laughing, his forehead to mine.

"About us?"

"Yeah."

I grin. "I think they're going to love it."

AUTHOR'S NOTE

Throughout the writing and editing process of *And She Was*, the importance of ensuring this story is as authentic and truthful as possible never left my mind. Though Mellie Baker is a fictional character, she is representative of millions of very real individuals—individuals who may have had experiences similar to hers, and individuals whose stories are vastly different. While I am part of the LGBTQ+ community, I am cisgender, which means I've had a responsibility to go above and beyond any typical level of research in order to do Mellie's story justice. From the very bottom of my heart, I want to thank the transgender community (including my brilliant sensitivity readers) for sharing your experiences—in your books and essays and on television and in your podcasts and in one-on-one conversations.

If you've read any of my previous work, you've probably noticed that I write a lot about family and identity and acceptance. I believe fiction has the capacity to change the world. Those of us who worry we may be alone in our feelings and realities often find comfort and strength in seeing ourselves reflected in the pages of a novel. And those of us who are seeking to understand other viewpoints are given the opportunity to connect with characters in novels and get a glimpse of the world through someone else's eyes. For these reasons, and many more, it was imperative to me that this book not be told strictly through Dara's point of view. Incorporating the perspective of an adult character into a young adult novel is a bit nontraditional, but, in this case, crucial. In the past, books tackling LGBTQ+ issues were primarily told solely through the points of view of straight and cis characters, thereby "othering" the very characters who the stories were about. I'm grateful I've had the opportunity to embrace Mellie's voice in this story.

Thank you for reading. I hope you enjoyed *And She Was*, and I also hope you'll consider reading books, both fiction and non-fiction, written by transgender authors. Here are just a few books on trans topics that I have read and enjoyed and recommend to readers. Happily, there are more being published every day.

George by Alex Gino

If I Was Your Girl by Meredith Russo

Beyond Magenta: Transgender Teens Speak Out by Susan Kuklin

Being Jazz: My Life as a (Transgender) Teen by Jazz Jennings

Redefining Realness: My Path to Womanhood, Identity, Love & So Much More by Janet Mock

She's Not There: A Life in Two Genders by Jennifer Finney Boylan

Stuck in the Middle with You: A Memoir of Parenting in Three Genders by Jennifer Finney Boylan

Trans Bodies, Trans Selves: A Resource for the Transgender Community, edited by Laura Erikson-Schroth

If you are a transgender or gender-nonconforming teen who is looking for someone to talk to, visit glaad.org/transgender/resources for an extensive list of resources and organizations.

ACKNOWLEDGMENTS

A very wise woman once wrote, "It takes a village," and never have I felt that truth more keenly than during the creation of this book. So, to start this long list of thank-yous, I'd like to acknowledge Hillary Rodham Clinton, a real-life superheroine who has inspired me in more ways than I can count. Thank you, Ms. Clinton, for proving that women—whether cis, trans, or otherwise—are unstoppable, despite a world that does its best every day to keep us down.

My eternal gratitude to my incredible editor, Aimee Friedman, for . . . well, literally everything. I'm a very lucky author to have found an editor who "gets me." And huge thanks to David Levithan as well, for championing this book from the start.

Kate McKean, Queen of Literary Agents, remember that email you sent me over four years ago with the teensiest, tiniest nugget of an idea for this story? Look what we did! We made a book!

Thank you to everyone at Scholastic who has worked on this project along the way: Ellie Berger, Alan Smagler, Mindy Stockfield, Rachel Feld, Tracy van Straaten, Lizette Serrano, Emily Heddleson, Olivia Valcarce, Melissa Schirmer, Lindsay Walter-Greaney, and Nina Goffi.

Mellie's story would not be what it is today without the insights of my phenomenal sensitivity readers. A gigantic thank-you to Mey Valdivia Rude, Annie Mok, Rachel Olivero, Parrish Turner, and Sharon Shattuck for your invaluable contributions.

Paul, thank you, as always, for being my cheerleader. With you by my side, I feel like I can achieve anything.

Susan Miller (aka Mom), Dara and Mellie's story might not be about us, but in a way it also is. I'm so grateful to have your support in everything I do.

There are a lot of pretty cool dudes in my family. Thank you to Cynthia, Rachel, Peter, the Araujos, Sam C., Adrienne, Emily, Adam, and Amanda, just to name a few. To my cousin K, you are amazing. I truly hope our country starts doing better for you. #ProtectTransKids

Thank you to my author friends and non-author friends alike: Mary G. Thompson, Alison Cherry, Lindsay Ribar, Mindy Raf, Amanda Maciel, Kevin Joinville, Steven Shaw, Caron Levis, Dahlia Adler, Brandy Colbert, Colleen Mathis, Michael Armstrong, Sarah Doudna, Renia Shukis, Casey Cipriani, and Carolyn Spagnoletti.

Some of my closest friends are also the most brilliant writers I know. Thank you, Corey Ann Haydu, Caela Carter, Alyson Gerber, and Laurie Boyle Crompton for reading my stuff and always being excited and bearing with me while I unload my troubles on you. Amy Ewing, without your friendship and support, I'd probably give up on all the projects I start. And I definitely wouldn't be a member of my hot sauce of the month club. Love you guys.

Some of my personal heroes happen to be trans women. Jazz Jennings, Marlo Mack and her daughter, Jenny Boylan, Janet Mock, Jen Richards, Laverne Cox, and Sarah McBride, I aspire to be half as cool and strong as you all are.

Finally, my dear friend Cristin Whitley was a bright light in the lives of all who knew her. This year, our world got a little dimmer. Cristin, this one's for you.

ABOUT THE AUTHOR

Jessica Verdi is the author of *My Life After Now*, *The Summer I Wasn't Me*, and *What You Left Behind*. She is a graduate of The New School's MFA in Writing for Children program, lives in New York, and firmly believes life is better with hot sauce. You can find her online at jessicaverdi.com.